FRACTURED

TOR BOOKS BY KATE WATTERSON

Frozen
Charred
Buried

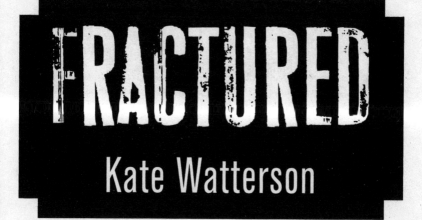

FRACTURED

Kate Watterson

A TOM DOHERTY ASSOCIATES BOOK · NEW YORK

FRACTURED

Copyright © 2015 by Katherine Smith

A Forge Book
Published by Tom Doherty Associates, LLC
175 Fifth Avenue
New York, NY 10010

www.tor-forge.com

Forge® is a registered trademark of Tom Doherty Associates, LLC.

The Library of Congress Cataloging-in-Publication Data
is available upon request.

ISBN 978-0-7653-7758-6 (hardcover)
ISBN 978-0-7653-7759-3 (trade paperback)
ISBN 978-1-4668-5676-9 (e-book)

Forge books may be purchased for educational, business, or promotional use. For information on bulk purchases, please contact the Macmillan Corporate and Premium Sales Department at 1-800-221-7945, extension 5442, or write to specialmarkets@macmillan.com.

First Edition: March 2015

Printed in the United States of America

0 9 8 7 6 5 4 3 2 1

For Carolyn Seale Muggenburg.
You are a very special person in my life.
Thank you for being a wonderful mother
and taking the leap without a net.

ACKNOWLEDGMENTS

I am always grateful for the terrific editorial insight I receive from Kristin Sevick and the wonderful support from my agent, Barbara Poelle. A nod also to my husband, who has evolved into a fabulous assistant (I wanted to say flunky, but for the sake of marital bliss, decided against it). Thanks for all you do to give me time to write.

FRACTURED

The killer woke in a pool of sticky blood.

It was a gradual process. First, fluttering eyelids and awareness of the unfamiliar surroundings, then rolling over with a shiver. Piercing light shone from above, clothes stuck like glue, and the oddest sensation, as if the panic that should be there just wasn't filtering through.

Was this dying? If it was, there wasn't any pain, though reports on the process were unreliable. No one beckoned and there was no heavenly music.

Drifting. The place was cold. The sickly sweet smell of decay was like another entity, hovering on the perimeter.

Where am I anyway?

Maybe it was hell.

It could be. There were some questions better left unasked.

Chapter 1

January in the north was bitter cold.

Homicide Detective Ellie MacIntosh stepped off the plane from Florida and walked with a queue of other passengers up a generic ramp and reminded herself that while she loved her mother, it was okay to be glad she was back in Wisconsin.

There was a four-below wind chill outside on the snow-dusted tarmac according to the announcement during their arrival. That was fine with her. She'd just spent ten days in paradise, and apparently, she didn't appreciate sunshine and white beaches as much as the frozen tundra of her natural environment.

To each his own.

It wasn't until she'd managed to grab her bag off the carousel and was rolling it through the airport toward the shuttle that would take her to long-term parking that she noticed all the people on their phones and remembered hers was still off.

Not that it was a big deal. She'd connected through Atlanta and checked it during the layover just two and a half hours ago.

Sixteen missed messages.

She stopped walking and stared at the display. Four of them were from Chief Metzger, her boss. People streamed by, talking and laughing, as she rapidly checked the other numbers and decided in what hierarchy to answer the flood.

At the end of it all, she called her partner first.

"Where the hell are you?" he asked instead of offering an actual greeting. Since that was typical of Jason Santiago's style, she didn't even blink.

"My trip was nice, thank you for asking," she replied. "Mind telling me what's up? I'm still at the airport right now." The wheels of her bag clattered across the floor and a speaker somewhere announced the arrival of another flight, making it almost impossible to hear.

"We have a second murder a lot like the one that happened a month ago. Male victim, multiple stab wounds, vicious lacerations to the face in particular."

"Our case?"

"Metzger says yes, since it looks so similar and we still have the first one open. Happy birthday."

"You pick out the nicest gifts. My birthday, for the record, is in June." A blast of cold air hit her as the automatic doors swooshed open, the breeze laced with a drift of snow and a hint of jet fuel. The sky was the color of burnished steel.

"I'm still at the crime scene. I'll text you the address."

He hung up at that point without saying anything else, and that didn't surprise her either. In resignation she slipped her phone back into her pocket, thought longingly of the glass of Merlot she'd planned on having in front of a warm fire, and boarded the shuttle. Hopefully Santiago would take the time to call Metzger and tell the chief of the Milwaukee Police Department she was on her way, but her partner was about as predictable as a pop-up thunderstorm. How he managed to be even semi-likable was a mystery, but there was no doubt he was an excellent cop.

In their first big case together, he'd saved her life. The second big case, she'd saved his, or he might right now be resting on the bottom of Lake Michigan. They were even, at least in her mind, in the deadly peril department, but it did prove they worked fairly well together.

Her car turned over very slowly after sitting in frigid temps for ten days, but at least it finally stirred to life. While it warmed up she made a call, watching the crystals on the windshield dissolve, her breath gradually no longer sending puffs into the air.

Bryce answered on the third ring. "Hi. Your plane must have been on time. How was the flight?"

He was one of the few who hadn't left her a message. "Fine. Listen, I know you were going to fix a special dinner, but I'm going to be late tonight. We have another murder that is apparently similar in some ways to the one Santiago and I worked last month. I'm heading straight to the scene."

There was the briefest of silences, and then he said dryly, "And to think I lingered in the produce aisle for a good fifteen minutes trying to decide on which heirloom tomatoes to buy for the salad. Call me when you are actually on your way home, okay?"

"I will," she promised, but didn't apologize. No one knew better than Bryce Grantham what her job entailed, especially as they'd met when she had investigated him in a serial murder case. "See you later."

Quickly checking the text that had already beeped in, she programmed it into her GPS and twenty-five minutes later pulled up to a row of faded houses that sat like tired old men on a bench, most of them showing the slump of neglect. Not precisely tenements, Ellie thought, pulling on her gloves, but built in the thirties or forties probably, identical, with sagging front porches, and neglected fall leaves scattered over postage stamp-sized front yards. It was a bleak image, not helped by the growing dusk and the light dusting of snow.

The house was easy enough to spot because it was the only one with the crime scene van in front of it, not to mention the bevy of police cars. Jason Santiago, hatless—he had to be freezing—stood talking to one of the techs, his hands thrust into the pockets of his coat, his curly blond hair catching the occasional flakes of snow. He didn't even acknowledge her presence as she walked up until the tech nodded and said, "Detective."

Her partner turned. "How come I always make it to a crime scene before you do?"

She shot back, "Because you don't have a life?"

"Ouch," the tech said with a grin, his nose a bright red from the cold. "She just got you. I'd better get back at it. We're wrapping it up."

Ellie stared at the house. She shivered and not just because of the frigid air. "This is a completely different kind of scene."

Santiago followed her gaze, his expression neutral. "True enough if you're talking about the setting. This is hardly the elite faculty parking lot of the University of Wisconsin's Milwaukee campus. It could still be the killer we've failed to catch so far because it is so similar. The body is on the front porch and only the medical examiner can say, but it looks like it has been there for a few days. In these temps, there's no real way to tell about decomposition, plus people aren't really enjoying the great outdoors, but a neighbor walks her dog and it seemed interested in that porch the past few days. Finally she went and took a look."

They walked up the cracked sidewalk together. It was almost too cold to snow, but not quite, since little white wisps floated by like tiny ghosts. Ellie asked, "We have a name?"

"Nope. No wallet, no other ID to pin down our victim. I think you'll see why using a picture isn't going to help identify him much."

There was a partial bloody footprint on the second-to-top step and she stopped to study it, and then glanced at the sad facade. The footprint was too compromised to tell much, but hopefully forensics would come through. "I can't imagine the person who lived here was also a college professor."

"Me either. The neighbor that called the body in said she wasn't sure just what he did. He just moved in a few weeks ago and she didn't even know the house had been rented. She's a bit older and all shaken up. Can't blame her. I'm no piker when it comes to dead bodies, and this is pretty gruesome. Just fair warning from me to you."

So much for what hadn't been all that much of a relaxing day anyway. She disliked flying and had been looking forward to a quiet evening. The emotional drain of the past week had left her hollow, like a fall leaf buffeted by a cold winter breeze. This really was *not* what she needed at the moment.

The screen door to the porch creaked on rusted hinges as Santiago opened it for her. "After you."

As much as she hated ever admitting he was right about anything, this time her often abrasive partner was absolutely correct. First of all, Ellie had never seen this much blood at any crime scene. The victim wasn't just white because of the temperature outside. The body was sprawled in a wide congealed pool of it, his coat and jeans were soaked, and his hair matted in a dark coating. The splatter was all over the front door and the wooden wall of the house.

Definitely the crime scene. Whatever had happened, it had been violent and occurred right on this spot.

First clue.

She was immobile for a full minute as she took it in, and to his credit, Santiago said nothing. His wisecracks often got on her nerves, but then again, she now understood it was his way of dealing with a very stressful job. That he was quiet now, spoke volumes.

"I'm not the medical examiner but I can say with some certainty he bled out, which meant his heart was still pumping." Ellie took in a steadying breath. One of her fears when she was promoted to homicide was that she might become immune to the horror of what human beings could inflict upon one another. It hadn't happened yet apparently.

The victim's face was a disaster, slashed to pieces, nothing intact, his nose half missing, the eyes covered in blood. She wasn't even sure they were still there . . .

Good God.

"This is worse than the university murder," she observed, glad her voice sounded even and professional because her skin was suddenly clammy and she had to consciously swallow. If there was one thing a homicide detective did not do, it was get sick at the sight of a dead body.

But this . . . this was the manifestation of a violence she found hard to comprehend.

"Look at his chest." Santiago, careful to not step in the blood pool, not easy considering the size of it, knelt and pointed. "This is what makes me sure we have a repeat offender. See the pattern?"

The victim's coat and shirt were ripped open. Unfortunately, she'd seen it before. Santiago was right. Same killer.

A cross. A series of stab wounds in the form of a perfect cross.

Ellie crouched down next to him, stripping off her winter gloves and shoving them into her pocket. She'd put on latex ones underneath in the car. "All the crime scene photos done?"

"Yep."

"Then let's take a little closer look."

Jason Santiago had to admire his partner's cool composure, but he'd seen the stunned expression on her face when she first realized the sheer viciousness of the attack. Ellie MacIntosh was an excellent detective, but part of that was because she processed a case on both an intellectual level and an emotional one. Truthfully, he'd been on the job longer than she had by a few years and he'd had a moment himself when he'd first seen the body.

This was a bad one.

The poor eighty-year-old lady next door was probably going to have nightmares for the rest of her natural life. While he waited for Ellie to arrive, he'd urged the woman to call her daughter and maybe spend the night somewhere else just until they caught the person who had done this to her neighbor.

Kind of a big promise.

More like *if* they caught him. They still had nothing on the other case.

Together they eased open the victim's open coat a little more, which wasn't all that easy to do since it was stiff with frozen blood. Underneath, his shirt had been unbuttoned and he'd been stabbed six times vertically, and four horizontally.

An exact match to the university murder.

Ellie stood. "Had to be postmortem. It's a signature of some kind."

His thoughts exactly. "Just like the last one." He rose too and inclined his head to the left. "I don't think there's much of a chance for a witness."

There was an abandoned school on the other side of the street. The windows were boarded up and the broken sign out front had once said: FRANKLIN ELEMENTARY. The city maintained the lawn obviously, since it had been neatly clipped at the end of the season, but it still held an unmistakable aura of disuse and desolation. That left the scenario of someone watching from across the street out of the picture.

He added, "Let's go check it out inside and see if we can get a handle on who and what this guy might be. Crime scene said they didn't really find much, but maybe we'll pick up on something. The door was unlocked and partially ajar when the first officer arrived."

Ellie said crisply, "If there were a witness someone isn't doing their civic duty because he's been here for a few days at least from the neighbor's timeline. By all means, let's go in."

She had blond hair that brushed her shoulders, with vivid hazel eyes that were disturbingly direct at times, delicate features, and a slender but athletic figure. When they'd first been assigned together he'd rejected the idea, knowing she didn't have his experience in homicide, but he'd eventually grudgingly accepted it because he hadn't been given a choice. Already he'd been skating on thin ice with the department, while she'd just solved a sensational serial murder case in northern Wisconsin.

So he'd taken the high road and not said much about it.

He was aware that she'd been assigned as his partner because not everyone wanted to work with him and she had been the new kid on the block. His smartass mouth frequently got him into trouble. On the other hand, they'd solved some pretty high-profile cases together already in less than a year.

There was no foyer, but that wasn't surprising considering the age of the house. The front door opened into the living room, and it was about as impressive as the outside.

Dreary curtains on dreary windows that looked like they'd just been left behind when the last tenant moved out. No couch, nothing but a single plastic outdoor chair facing a small television in the corner.

MacIntosh looked around, her expression thoughtful. "Not a single picture on the walls to give us an idea of his personality."

He didn't have any either in his apartment, so Jason muttered, "Doesn't mean a thing besides that he didn't have much of an emotional investment in this place."

Ellie's red hat stuck out in the center of the room, a bright spot in a sea of ambiguity. As she swept the room with an assessing gaze, he recognized the analytical look on her face. "Three weeks and he really hadn't moved, that I can tell. Why?"

She was right, but she was frequently right. The house smelled like mildew and maybe old socks, and Jason thought gratefully of his apartment in a complex that might be generic, but was hardly anything like this place. Jason pointed out, "The television is new."

It was, sitting on what looked like an upended milk carton by the wall. They went to check the kitchen. The refrigerator held a quart of orange juice, three cans of Budweiser, and absolutely nothing else. Ellie mused, "He was staying here, not living here. Treading water, giving himself time."

It wasn't like he disagreed, so he didn't comment. "Upstairs?"

"Let's go."

Gloom, more cold . . . even he was starting to feel depressed, and Jason could have sworn he'd conquered that monster, but these cold, empty walls were a little hard to take as they went up the narrow staircase to the first bed-room.

Square room, unmade bed, small dresser. No curtains even though the house faced east. The occupant would also have to look at that damned abandoned school and for some reason that bothered Jason more than anything.

The thought of those echoing halls . . . his ex-girlfriend had once told him he had too much imagination for this job, and while he scoffed at it—most of the department thought he was insensitive and irreverent—maybe Kate was right. He took one look out the window and turned his back. "Cozy, huh?"

Ellie prowled around and opened a few drawers—all empty—and didn't comment at once. The closet was small, and also empty. She frowned, looking perplexed. "Not hardly. What is going on here?"

Chapter 2

Home.

She wished it felt a little more that way. It wasn't that Bryce hadn't been his usual easygoing self, letting her gradually settle in, and his personality made that simple enough. That didn't negate her nagging feelings of displacement since moving in with him, but then again, living with another human being always involved some compromise.

Bryce must have heard her open the door. It was already after ten o'clock, pitch dark with a rising wind outside whispering along the eaves. And after that murder scene, she would be shivering anyway. Bryce was in his office, frowning at his computer screen, the house utterly quiet. He turned around in his chair, his gaze inquiring, when she came into the room.

She'd missed him. Ten days was a long time. The real question was, had he missed her?

Their relationship always left her guessing, and it was

probably her fault. It wasn't so much a lack of understanding as that they were navigating the treacherous waters of a relationship built on initial mutual distrust. At one time she had almost arrested him.

Always an interesting way to start a romance.

They'd gotten past it or there would not be a romance at all, but despite what she felt was the first true love affair of her life, Ellie was a very different challenge than his ex-wife. Suzanne Grantham had been selfish and complicated, and Ellie was probably also complicated but instead of selfish, he assured her he thought of her as just very focused.

Diplomatic if nothing else. Tall, dark-haired, good-looking, *and* diplomatic. What more could a girl ask for?

In an ordinary voice, he said, "Are you hungry? I made you a plate. Just let me save this and I'll be right there."

"No, but I could use a glass of water." The trip had taken its toll, and not just the traveling part, and then to arrive to such a horrific welcome hadn't improved her inner sense of desolation. She was aware she looked strained, and Bryce caught on quickly because he made no move to kiss her hello or even offer her a hug.

If he had, there was every chance she might splinter into a thousand pieces and cry on his shoulder, and that was not what she needed right now. Points to him for realizing it. Keeping it together was better. She wasn't as tough as nails just because she carried a gun and had a badge. She was probably quite the opposite because her empathy for the victims and their families drove her, but she didn't need to weep, she needed to regroup. Ellie went down the hall, took out a tumbler from the cupboard, filled it from the faucet, and drank half of it down. When was the last time she'd eaten? About twelve hours ago she'd managed to grab a bagel between connecting flights.

They had yet to discuss why she hadn't invited Bryce to go to Florida with her. She'd merely announced one day she was going, declined his offer to drive her to the airport, and had left. He still didn't ask why when he came into the kitchen, but merely said, "Can I take your coat and hang it up for you?"

"I don't know." She set down her glass on the granite countertop. "I feel like I'll never be warm again."

"Let me turn on the fireplace. Are you sure you don't want some food? I kept it warm."

She unzipped her coat. "Thanks. Yes to the coat, yes to the fireplace, but I can't eat right now. Hi, by the way." She handed him her jacket, briefly pressing her lips to his. Not much of a kiss, but an effort.

"There's an open bottle of Merlot still breathing on the table."

"Bryce, tell me you ate without me." There was reproach in her voice.

"I did. I live with a homicide detective, remember? They tend to have some interesting hours." Finally he asked, "Want to tell me what's going on?"

She decisively shook her head. "I can't right now. Don't ask why."

He wouldn't. If there was one thing she'd learned since she'd moved in with him several months ago, it was that he didn't push her for what she wasn't ready to give. It didn't help open communications that he was much the same way, but it did make for mutual understanding. She was also willing to give him space when he needed it, so that dynamic of their relationship worked very well.

He went into the living room, hit the remote for the gas fireplace, and accepted the glass of wine she'd poured for him before she settled on the leather couch, kicking off her shoes and curling her legs under her. She took a sip and stared at the flames. "Hmm. This I need. I missed it. Don't be surprised if I'm asleep in about two minutes."

"Missed Milwaukee in the dead of winter? Bare trees, snow, frozen lakes and ponds. Yeah, I can see the attraction." He sat next to her but didn't touch her. "Much better than sunny Florida. Why?"

It was time to talk about it. Ellie stared at the leaping flames. "Much better. My mother has breast cancer. That's why I went." There. She'd said the words.

He exhaled quietly. "Oh, I see. I think I understand now why you didn't invite me along for your tropical vacation."

"I should have explained." Ellie shifted a little closer and leaned her head on his shoulder, lowering her lashes. He felt warm and solid. "I needed to deal with facts before I could figure out how I feel about it all." She still hadn't figured it out. Well, maybe she had. She was terrified.

He slipped his arm around her waist. "I've picked up on that, believe it or not."

"Jody came too," she went on, referring to her sister. "We talked to the doctors and it looks pretty good, actually. They removed the tumor and Mom's going to start chemo, and since she's healthy and active, the prognosis is very positive. We went to the beach and relaxed . . . it was a decent trip all in all but you would *not* have wanted to be there."

He gave her a gentle squeeze. "That's good news overall and now I feel like a jerk for wondering why you didn't want me to come along."

She glanced up at him. "You didn't ask."

"I somehow got the impression you didn't want me to ask."

True enough. He had a point. "Her news is much better than the prognosis for the victim tonight. I predict he will enjoy a very prolonged experience on the table of the medical examiner tomorrow being taken to pieces." Ellie's voice was subdued. "If she matches the stab wounds to the university murder last month, I think this city might have a big problem."

The flames flickered convincingly like a real fire and Bryce took a moment before he asked, "How so?"

"It seems like there is a signature to both the murders. I have no idea at this point what it could possibly mean, which translates to not being able to predict what might happen next. We need to connect the two cases in some way other than the pattern of the knife wounds. The first victim was a college professor, and the second one we haven't identified, which is key in any crime. Maybe it isn't the same killer . . . I don't know."

"But?"

"I think there is a connection we haven't grasped yet. So does Santiago. There are different kinds of killers. Some are impulsive, some are methodical, some are opportunists, and some are . . . just insane. This seems like the latter, but to be trite, there's a method to the madness. We just don't see it."

"It seems to me they are all insane."

Ellie knew he meant it. Gaining satisfaction from the death

of another human being was beyond his comprehension—almost. Bryce hadn't shed a tear when she fatally shot a serial killer in northern Wisconsin and saved *his* life.

"I don't know." She relaxed against him more. "I'm not a psychologist, but I think there are degrees to everything. The victim tonight . . . it was *savage*. Over the top. I'm not sure just what we are dealing with."

She shivered and the room was warm, not cold. Bryce tightened his arm. "That bad?"

She confirmed with another shiver. "That bad. If I scream in my sleep, don't be surprised."

Jason slid onto a bar stool and ordered a beer.

He needed it.

While he handled crime scenes as well as anyone, and better than most if he had to call it, this evening hadn't been stellar.

The imprint of that man's hacked-up face would haunt him. There was no doubt he didn't like it, but his ghosts were what they were, and Jason couldn't banish them at will. Most of his life, he'd done his best, but they lingered like shadows in the corners.

Besides that, something had happened with Ellie. He sensed it and maybe it was the detective in him, but if he had to call it, she had not just gone off on a relaxing vacation. While she'd handled herself as professionally as usual, she'd been a little wired, and not just by the murder.

He picked up his beer and took a long drink. Right now she was probably in Grantham's bed. After all, that's the first place *he'd* take her if it was an option.

Then again, that had been one ballistic murder scene. Maybe not. He doubted she was in the mood for anything but a long, deep sleep.

The piped-in music started playing Van Halen's "Runnin' with the Devil." Seemed appropriate somehow.

Jason propped his booted foot on the bar stool and sang along in his head. The place smelled like stale beer and there were two biker guys in the back playing pool, but it was close to his apartment and he could walk over and grab a drink and not have to worry about crashing his career for a DUI. Besides, he might be sitting alone, musing over his half-empty glass, but at least he wasn't staring at empty walls, thinking about what he didn't have.

It was an enlightening discovery to realize he really hated being jealous. A counterproductive emotion and a waste of time.

He finished his beer, put several bills on the counter, and walked out just in time to see the accident.

Crosswalk. Impatient man with a cell phone to his ear ignoring the image of a pedestrian with a line through him, angrily arguing with whoever he was talking to and stepping out into traffic . . . it was a blur and happened very fast. The squeal of tires was like a human scream. The driver of the car coming south swerved, clipped another vehicle coming from the opposite direction, and both careened to a stop as the pedestrian, unscathed, hastily put away his phone and started to rapidly walk away.

No way.

Jason sprinted forward and caught sight of the driver of the southbound car climbing out. She seemed okay as she struggled to escape the airbag. Jason knew the other driver was fine because he had the door open to his vehicle and was cursing loudly.

Jason gained the opposite side of the street, ran around the escaping culprit with one hand on his shoulder, and flashed his badge. "Police officer, bud. You are so busted."

"Hey." The guy jerked back. He was well-dressed and well-groomed, his perfect hair just a little disheveled because it was a breezy evening.

"You aren't going anywhere," Jason informed him through his teeth, yanking him closer. "It's called leaving the scene of an accident, and I can tell you, judges really frown on that sort of thing. You'd better hope no one was hurt."

Expensive wool dress coat and a resentful face, though the guilty party didn't have much of a right to have that expression. Jason was hard-pressed to keep from throwing a punch, but he'd already identified himself as a police of-ficer. The man sputtered, "I didn't . . . didn't . . ."

"Think about anyone else?" Jason supplied, his voice icy. "I noticed. Then you tried to just walk away. Nice of you. Let's go."

The shove he gave was probably a little harsh, but he was pissed off. Apparently people had been reporting the acci-dent because he already saw a cruiser pulling up. He dragged the offender off the curb and onto the street, where traffic had started to back up because of the crash.

"Good response time, Officer."

"We do our best." The cop eyed the way he was hanging onto the other man. There was already another officer talk-ing to the young woman.

It was his pleasure to explain. "I'm Detective Santiago,

homicide, and this asshole walked into traffic on his cell phone and caused the accident. I am a witness, and I *will* testify in court."

The beat cop nodded and smiled broadly. "That's *sweet*. Makes my job easy, that's for sure. What are the odds . . . I'll call it in, Detective, and get someone to direct traffic." He pointed at the offending pedestrian. "You, come with me."

The young woman stood by the shattered remains of a headlight, looking just as broken as the plastic on the pavement. She wore a short coat in a soft blue color and heavy mittens but no hat, long chestnut hair loose around her shoulders.

Her shell-shocked expression was something Jason had seen before when he'd been on the street. The other driver was a beefy man in a parka, currently out inspecting the damage to his pickup truck. He gestured angrily as he talked to the cop who evidently was done taking the woman's initial statement. Jason walked over to her side. It hadn't been her fault. If he wasn't there, he imagined there might be a confrontation with the big guy, which she was not at the moment ready to handle. Jason asked her, "You hurt?"

"No . . . no, I don't think so. I almost hit him. I could have *killed* him." Her voice was barely a whisper, her lips trembling. She was pretty, and probably would be very pretty except she was pale as a ghost.

Damn, the wind was cold enough to slice right through a person. Jason hunched his shoulders and put his ungloved hands in his pockets. "Yeah, well, it would have served him right. Why don't you go get back in your car and get out your registration and driver's license. You'll freeze half to death out here in this wind and they are going to want to see both of those things." He eyed the vehicle. The hood was buckled pretty badly and there was an ever-growing pool of liquid that looked like antifreeze on the street. "Anyone you can call to come pick you up after all the questions are answered? I think they are going to have to tow your car."

She shrugged helplessly, looking distraught. "My roommate, I guess, but it's kind of late. Sometimes she takes something so she can sleep . . . God, this is awful."

"I'll get you a cab," he assured her. "Public servants. That's our job description."

"You don't look like a police officer."

He'd heard that one before. He probably would be more convincing with a surfboard under his arm and beach sand between his toes. Maybe it was the curly blond hair that somehow managed to look sun-streaked even in the dead of winter in fucking Milwaukee, Wisconsin. Jason's smile was thin as he thought about the horrific murder scene earlier. "This particular night, I kind of wish I wasn't. If you think your accident was awful, let me tell you, things could be worse."

"You'd better have insurance." The big guy came over, his expression holding the ugly fury of someone who'd had something unpleasant happen they didn't expect, his eyes fixed on the young woman. "Whatever happened, *you* hit *me*."

"Yeah, that avoiding killing someone, that's a real crime. Lay off." Jason shook his head and the look he gave the other driver was lethal. "I mean it, lay off. She's driving a BMW, sir. A pretty new one. Do you really think she doesn't have insurance? Feel free to be unhappy about your damaged vehicle, but don't be unhappy with her, get it?"

Considering the man outweighed him by about seventy pounds at a guess, it was a gamble, but he was kind of in the mood for a good fight. It had been an interesting—and frustrating—day.

Maybe it was something in his eyes, but the other driver raised his gloved hands, palms upward. "Look, I don't want trouble, but I was just driving down the street when she swerved into my lane. I need to know who is going to pay for this."

"I think you're going to have to let your insurance companies decide this question. I assume they'll sue the pedestrian. He'll get a ticket for crossing against the light and probably charged with contributory negligence."

"You a cop?"

"Homicide detective."

The man eyed him. "You don't look like a cop."

Jason replied sardonically, "Yeah, I know. Jesus, it's cold out here."

Chapter 3

Lieutenant Grasso was at his desk.

Of course.

Everyone had personal issues but Carl was legendary for spending a lot of time at work. He even got there earlier than Ellie did. It wasn't like she knew much about his personal life even though they'd worked together on a high-profile case a few months ago; he was a pretty private person in her opinion, except when it came to the job. He had a reputation for being astute and tireless, not to mention having a decade more experience than she did.

Why not take advantage of it?

So Ellie propped a hip on Grasso's desk and said without preamble, "I've got two mutilated victims without a connection except the way they were killed. If you have any thoughts, I'd love to hear them."

Grasso, as well-dressed as ever in an expensive dark blue suit and gray silk tie, nodded. "Hmm. Heard about that.

Rough case. It's all over the department now that we have a second victim."

She agreed with his assessment. It was actually an understatement. "The first guy . . . as far as we can tell was happily married, a successful professor at a big university, and we now have the second vic, who has no identity really, living in an essentially empty house in a downtrodden neighborhood. Not at all alike, but they were killed in the exact same way."

Carl was in his early forties, tough but without Santiago's outward bravado, and he leaned back and looked at her with true consideration. "The face-slashing thing again?"

"Worse this time." She didn't want to think about it. Any of it. Her dynamic with Bryce, the murder scenes, her mother's illness . . .

"Hmm." Grasso was nice-looking in a sort of understated way, but his eyes were certainly his best asset. Keen, riveting, and a compelling silver color. Even thoughtful, as he was at this moment, he just looked savvy and maybe a little too intense.

"Like an *empty* house," she told him with emphasis, a phone ringing in the background. "No furniture except a mattress, really, and a new television, and in the bedroom we found a backpack with a couple of shirts and a dirty pair of jeans. The trash had fast-food wrappers and aluminum beer cans. I'm wondering if he could have been a squatter. We're trying to track down the current owner. A neighbor told us that an older man lived there for years but he died and it passed into his estate, such as it was. If you saw the neighborhood, you'd know what I mean. Not the worst I've seen, but not the best either. The neighbors have a vague recollection of a grandson or a nephew but didn't have a name. Someone must be paying taxes on it but it has never been up for sale, at least not with a realty sign out front. The electricity is on though, so as soon as the offices open, I imagine we'll have a better hold on who our owner might be at least."

Maybe, she thought with well-earned cynicism. People did some damn strange things.

Grasso rubbed his cleanly shaven chin. "But the first victim was married?"

Ellie took a drink from her cup of coffee. It needed more cream because whoever had made it apparently went for industrial strength. "Married to a woman with an airtight alibi, and that's where I got the happily so, once she got past the hysteria of hearing her husband was dead. Mrs. Peterson was at a charity dinner for the university. Her husband missed it. She wondered why and eventually called in a missing person report, worried he'd been in an accident. Some accident that was. By then, his body had been found behind a row of bushes by the parking lot. He was a well-respected biology professor, widely published, and by all accounts that we heard, had a nice life. He drove a Mercedes, lived by the lake, and had been married for twenty years. Like this new victim, he had no ID on him when he was found."

Grasso adjusted the sleeve of his suit coat, his brow furrowed. "Robbery? There's got to be a link."

"Well, there can't be too many people wandering around this fair city willing to do that kind of damage to another human being over their wallet." Ellie recalled the haunting crime scene again and immediately tried to block the image. "At least I hope not. It's pretty brutal. If robbery is the motive, I can tell you that it *could* be robbery with the professor because he might have had money on him, but I highly doubt it with last night's victim. The dicey neighborhood aside, he had holes in his gloves and his coat wasn't heavy enough for a Wisconsin winter. He didn't have anything to steal besides that new television and it was still there. The door was partially open, so they could have taken it."

"All right." Grasso punched a key on his computer. "We have a national database for this sort of thing, and yes, I know you've already accessed it, but let me type in some keywords like 'university.' Your younger guy from last night could be a student. You might ask the president of the university, who I assume is very unhappy to have a vicious murder happen on campus. Give him a call and ask him to send the faculty a message to watch for a young male student who stops showing up for class. It's a long shot, I know. Half the students do a lot of work online and some of the classes are so large they couldn't possibly know who is there or not, but worth a try."

"I thought of that too. Good idea."

He shot her a glance. "What else—anything at all—did they have in common?"

"The professor and our potential squatter? Nothing I know of, but again, the second victim is unidentified."

"If he is truly indigent, that could take a long time."

"Unless he's committed a crime, yes. His fingerprints are being run."

"You aren't giving me much to go on, Detective." His tone was sarcastic.

"That's because we don't *have* much." She was well-aware of the challenges.

From behind her a familiar drawling voice said, "We have this."

She swiveled to see Santiago, pretty much his usual self, with a leather coat over a blue shirt, a knit tie, and worn jeans to complete the ensemble. But his blue eyes were compelling as always. It was pretty early for him to be in. He handed her a piece of paper that had a handwritten note to Chief Metzger.

All pathology reports not in so the autopsy isn't final, but I can say with certainty the knife used in the murders was not what the killer used to make the cross wounds in the chest of each victim.

It was signed by the chief medical examiner, which meant she'd done the autopsy herself probably due to the heinous nature of the attacks, and Ellie was glad because she thoroughly trusted her competence. If there was a detail that might help them, Dr. Hammet would find it.

"Kind of strange, eh?" Santiago perpetually seemed to need a haircut and when he ran his fingers through the curly strands in a habitual mannerism, it made him either fashionably disheveled or looking like maybe he forgot to even comb it.

What he needed was a girlfriend to point him at the nearest barbershop, but they had much bigger problems than his unruly hair. Ellie said slowly, "I can't imagine stopping in the middle of a brutal crime and switching weapons. One knife to kill the victim and make them unrecognizable, and another to leave some sort of symbolic message?"

Grasso speculated, "Something to do with the clergy?

Maybe you have a religious fanatic on the loose. Maybe your professor of biology taught Darwinism and the perp doesn't want to hear we crawled out of a slimy sea millions of years ago."

"Yeah, well, I'd rather picture two people getting it on in a garden myself, but I wouldn't kill anyone over it. Dammit, I'm starving and I need coffee. This is a police station. Surely someone around here has a donut or something." Santiago walked off, leaving Ellie still studying the piece of paper like it held the answer to their problem.

Maybe it did.

"There does seem to be a clear message, but the latest victim . . . I don't know. Whoever he is, I doubt he's a biology professor."

"If he was a student maybe he witnessed the university crime?"

"Possible I suppose, but it would have been nice of him to come forward. Peterson was killed a month ago."

"The question I would ask is, did he have something to hide?"

That was a *very* good question. Ellie said moodily, "If only we knew who *he* is."

"If he had information, you know law enforcement would ask him his address. That could be his motivation to keep quiet. If our speculation is right and he was trespassing, then he *did* have something to hide."

A good point. Ellie thought about it on the way back to her desk. However, if that was all true, how did the killer find him?

Too many questions, she thought with an inner resignation, and too few facts.

. . .

Jason was never happy to be called into Metzger's office. Usually it involved a raised voice—not his—and a scathing reminder that while he was one of the department's best detectives, he was also a pain in the ass.

This time the nuance was slightly different and he didn't like that either.

Not one bit.

The chief was an ex-marine, a big buff man with cropped hair and a perpetually serious expression, and there were premature furrows on his forehead and by his mouth. Jason had no actual idea how old Metzger was, and he sure as hell was never going to ask.

"Sit down." Metzger pointed at a chair in front of his cluttered desk with a pen and his voice was curt.

"Am I in trouble?" Jason stood there, feeling a flicker of dismay.

"Sit down, Detective."

"Fuck me," Jason muttered under his breath, obeying by sinking onto an uncomfortable wooden chair. Out loud he said, "I can't even guess how I could have done anything wrong lately, Chief. I'm casting back and coming up with nothing."

Metzger wore a suit that made him look fat when he wasn't at all since every inch of him was solid muscle. "What happened last night?"

"There was a murder. I called MacIntosh and we responded. We had no ready witness or real evidence, but we are digging deeper. Goes without saying."

"Not good enough."

"I just said—"

"Santiago, shut up. Just tell me what happened after that body was found."

He knew better than to say it, but he did it anyway. Being argumentative was one of his greater faults and he had quite a few. "That's kind of a contradiction. I can't shut up and still tell you what happened, and besides, what are we talking about? The murder? I haven't even had time to turn in a report and we don't have all the ME stuff and—"

"The governor's niece."

It was hard to come up with an answer because he was taken so off guard. Jason stared at the chief. "Excuse me? I could swear you just said something about the governor. I didn't touch his niece." He lifted his hands. "Got a bible? I'll swear on it."

Metzger barked out a laugh, and he didn't do that often. "Santiago, if you touched a bible, it would burst into flames."

A possibility about the instant combustion, but still, he was pretty much in the dark. "Then what is the actual question?" He added cautiously, just in case he *was* in real trouble, "Sir."

"I understand you witnessed an accident last night, apprehended the pedestrian who was trying to flee the scene, and in general are somewhat of a hero in all the right high places. I can't quite believe I am saying this, but in short, you made us look good for once."

The pretty brunette was the governor's niece? That explained her expensive car and cashmere coat. She came from a pretty prominent family. Jason shrugged. "She didn't mention it, so until you just told me, I didn't know who she was."

"She sure as hell mentioned you to her father, who told his brother-in-law, and in case you haven't noticed, the governor is on a campaign against reckless cell phone usage causing traffic accidents."

He'd seen the billboards and commercials. "Well, before you pat me on the back, it was more that the whole thing really pissed me off. The guy caused two cars to crash into each other and wasn't even going to check and see if anyone was hurt. He knew it too. He's lucky I am a police officer, because otherwise, I might have—"

"I get what you might have done. He says you manhandled him."

He'd known that shove had been a mistake. "Look"—he pinched the bridge of his nose for a second—"the sleazebag was just going to walk away. For the record, I was just guiding him back to the scene. Not a bruise on him, and I swear on my badge I kept my language clean and fairly respectful."

"You referred to him as an asshole."

"He *is* one."

Metzger crossed his arms and sighed. "All right, he does sound like one. By the way, the man you caught is an executive at a software company, and he's claiming you threatened him and wants to sue, but luckily, the governor is way on our side on this one and his niece is a witness. I just got off the phone with the mayor. Our ass is covered."

"That's good news. With all due respect, I've never had much of a yearning to see your bare ass, sir."

"Very funny. You just dodged a bullet. Keep it in mind."

It actually *was* good news, which Jason could use. It was nice to catch a break for once. He'd spent quite a bit of time last year recovering from being shot in the line of duty. He'd sunk so low as to watching women's golf on ESPN, bored out of his mind as he waited to be released by his doctor for active duty again. "I'm humbly grateful it turned out well."

"Yeah, well, that feeling is mutual, Detective." It was impossible, but Metzger looked amused for the second time. In one day. A first. "I hope you have a good suit, Santiago."

What the hell does that mean? "Why?"

"The governor would like to meet you." Metzger spread his hands. "Look, you and MacIntosh have solved some pretty high-profile cases, you've been shot on two different instances in the line of duty, and you apparently made an impression on the man's niece. I understand you took her home in a cab, paid for it yourself, and made sure she got inside safely, and you even called her mother for her."

"That cab cost me twenty-five bucks. I don't suppose the department will reimburse me, will it?" he said flippantly, joking. The young woman had been so shaken that when he offered to go with her, she'd looked pathetically grateful.

"You are going to dinner at the governor's mansion. Expect an invitation, and since I already know the answer to my question, go out and buy a nice suit. For God's sake have MacIntosh help you pick it out. She's going to be your date. He wants to meet her too."

No. No way. If there was more than a single knife and fork on the table, he was not socially up to it. His father's idea of a gourmet dinner had included cans and a rusted pan, and he wasn't much better. "Shit. Chief, come on, I don't want—"

"And don't forget a nice tie." Metzger reached for his

phone. "That's all, Detective. Our little discussion is over. Dismissed."

To say he was unhappy when he left the chief's office was an understatement. Jason passed two uniformed officers in the hall with only an absent nod and found that MacIntosh was at her desk, a frown on her face as she typed something on her computer. Her blond hair fell in a smooth curtain by her cheek and she swept it back and tucked it behind her ear.

Jason watched the feminine movement with involuntary fascination, standing by the side of her desk, which was much more organized than his. Then mildly, he said, "You want the bad news, or the bad news?"

She glanced up, her expression resigned. "I've been waiting for it. What have you done now?"

"What? Does the entire station know I was called into Metzger's office?"

"Of course. High school hallways don't have a thing on this place. What did you do?"

He couldn't resist playing with her a little. "The governor's niece."

Ellie's eyes widened in consternation. "You slept with the governor's niece?"

"Slept? Well, no. Sleeping implies something pretty friggin' different than what happened when I took her home last night." He lifted his shoulders in a negligent shrug. "Besides, she didn't tell me who she was."

Misleading, however not one lie so far. He'd taken the person in question home, politely left her at the door once she'd unlocked it, and gone home in the cab he'd called for them at the scene. All the perfect truth.

His partner misinterpreted that, which had been his intention, but to his surprise, totally stood by him. "That's not against the law if she is a consenting adult," she said stoutly.

"She consented."

"Then Metzger is out of line. He should know you better than that."

Jason grinned but it turned to a grimace and he told her the truth. "Sorry, I was just trying to be funny. Nice to know you'd have my back, but I really didn't sleep with anyone."

"What on earth are you talking about then?"

He told her as quickly as possible, glossing it all over, including his discussion with the chief. "I just thought I'd warn you that it might be possible that you'll get dragged into the situation."

She looked perplexed. "Me? How so?"

"Yeah, well, the governor remembers the past year and he found out you're my partner. I'm told we're both invited for tea and crumpets or whatever the hell it is they eat." Jason wasn't any more enthusiastic about it than she looked, so he changed the subject. "Hey, do we have the ME's full report yet on the latest victim?"

Chapter 4

Dr. Georgia Lukens liked her office. Soothing colors on the walls, some nice artwork hung here and there, an outrageously expensive carpet on the polished floor, and two doors, one to let the people come in from the waiting area and another one to allow them to exit discreetly. There was no couch, but instead two upholstered chairs because she did do some counseling that involved more than one patient at once, and a Tiffany lamp she'd inherited from her aunt on her desk.

Since she spent eight hours a day at least in the space, she was glad she found it soothing, because quite often, the problems of her patients were not.

Not that all of them were disturbing. She dealt with a lot of neuroses that were simple enough—a lack of confidence, a tendency to hold onto possessions for security, irrational jealousy, buried memories that might or might not be real, but every once in a while it got interesting.

Like at this moment.

"I have a case. I'm sure you watch the news." Ellie MacIntosh settled into one of the chairs. Georgia had found her intriguing as a person from the beginning because the somewhat delicate exterior of this particular police officer concealed a steely resolve that she suspected Detective MacIntosh took advantage of in her profession. It was reminiscent of how some of the most colorful insects were the most deadly. The inviting appearance concealed the potential danger.

They'd met when one of Georgia's patients was involved in a double homicide and to her surprise, once the case was resolved, Detective MacIntosh had decided to start seeing her for personal counseling. Not that there wasn't a double side to that either. Ellie frequently asked her for free consultations on psychological aspects in her cases.

Fair was fair. Georgia owed her.

"Sometimes," she responded neutrally. "I did hear about a mutilated victim found in an empty house. Yours?"

"My case, yes, not my victim." Ellie was in her early thirties, pretty and blond, with a sharp intellect and a surprising lack of the cynicism Georgia expected from someone in her profession. Their introduction to each other might have been under unusual circumstances, but there was an instant affinity, and Georgia found their relationship thought-provoking. There was no question this particular patient had some issues with commitment she was trying to work through and understand.

Georgia liked that she was being challenged as a therapist. When Ellie MacIntosh walked through the door, she was never sure what to expect.

"Tell me about it?"

Detective MacIntosh wore a simple navy sweater with slacks, and a pink blouse of some silky material to finish the ensemble. She looked, as usual, put together and competent and her eyes were direct. "It's bad." Detective MacIntosh said it succinctly. "Whatever they are saying on the news doesn't do the murder justice. 'Horrific' works but I don't think it's quite enough."

"It bothers you."

"I wouldn't be a human being if it didn't bother me."

Then it would be bad. Georgia was getting a sense of what it was like on the darker side, and here she thought she'd been exposed to it for years.

"But a human being did it."

"That's the problem. Excuse me if I disagree. Once a person crosses a line like this, they are no longer one of us. They've forfeited the right to be included in humanity."

Georgia carefully considered her answer. "I can see where taking the hard line appeals to your sense of justice."

Ellie MacIntosh interlocked her fingers and rested them on the desktop. "This doesn't have all that much to do with me and my sense of anything. The crime was really brutal."

"And you want to know what I think about the personality and motivation of the person who did it?"

Of course she did. Ellie tended to not talk about her problems directly and Georgia had already figured out as her therapist that letting this patient define the boundaries was probably for the best. If Ellie wanted to discuss something, she'd eventually bring it up.

In the meantime Georgia would happily consult with the Milwaukee Police Department on their dime.

. . .

"**I brought a** few pictures." Ellie reached into a briefcase and extracted the photos. "I'd *really* like to know what you think about this crime. All insights welcome."

Georgia Lukens was a valuable tool in the sense that not only was she trained in deciphering the psyche of all different kinds of people, but she had a quick mind that combined intelligence with compassion. Ellie considered their sessions to be more a chance to talk to a friend than actual therapy. While she loved her sister, Jody, she would certainly never discuss the details of a murder with her. Nor would she try to sort out her conflicting emotions about her relationship with Bryce.

Dr. Lukens, on the other hand, was a perfect sounding board.

When the pictures were handed over she could tell Georgia wasn't quite braced for the graphic images and had to fight to not recoil. She studied them for several minutes before setting them on the edge of the desk. "Brutal is right. I'd say you have someone on your hands that has a lot of rage inside them. I'd also say that the difference between the first murder and the second one is a sense of power. Your killer didn't get caught the first time. The second one is worse because there's more confidence."

"My thoughts too." And Grasso had said much the same thing. Ellie accepted the pictures back and brooded over them for a moment before tucking them into her leather briefcase. It was an understatement to say that solving the crime was much more satisfying than dealing with the fact a person had been murdered. "We have two very different victims, I'm afraid. We're still trying to make a connection."

"I hope you do soon."

"Me too. Santiago and I are going to talk to the professor's widow again. I hate to drag her into this second murder because I can say with reasonable conviction that she wasn't helpful to us in any way, maybe because she took her husband's death very hard, but now that some time has passed I hope she will be more cooperative and can link this second victim."

Georgia said neutrally, "I'd recommend not showing her that photograph then. My reaction was pretty visceral. I can't imagine hers. I assume it will bring back the vivid memory of identifying his body. That could not have been pleasant."

True enough, but luckily, Ellie hadn't been there for that moment.

"I wasn't planning on it." She slightly lifted her brows. "I know as police officers we develop a tough skin, but we are still capable of empathy. Probably more than most people actually."

Then she abruptly changed the subject because she needed to talk to someone about it. "Something is going on with Bryce."

"Oh? How so?" Georgia looked truly interested and maybe a little relieved they weren't discussing the murders any longer.

Ellie smiled ruefully. "On an effusive day he's pretty laid back and quiet. But I just have a feeling there is something I don't know about going on. I could be imagining it, of course."

"What has changed?"

"I can't put my finger on it precisely." She shifted in her chair, the slight movement restive. "I'm pretty good at sensing when someone isn't anxious to tell me something. It is a vital part of my job."

"Any idea what it could be?"

She had. That was part of the problem.

"I know he wants to get married and have children." Ellie exhaled and briefly closed her eyes. "I'm not ready and I don't quite understand why. As you know, that's why I'm here. I'm thirty-three. I can't wait forever. I'm afraid *he* won't wait much longer."

"Has he said that? Or are you just making that assumption because if you were in his shoes you wouldn't wait?"

Good question. Ellie thought it over. "He and I are not much alike."

Georgia said dryly, "My impression is that is an understatement, Detective, but it can be a positive balance in a relationship. You pay me for advice, so I am going to give some. He isn't a murder suspect, he is the man you currently share your life with on a daily basis. Ask him about it."

"Does it make sense I'm afraid to do that?"

"Does it make sense to worry over something when perhaps it could be resolved with a simple inquiry?"

"I'm not worried exactly."

"Ellie, I think you are."

Well hell, she thought in a very Santiago-like way, she probably was. She went ahead and said haltingly, "He sold his book. His agent called him last week."

Georgia seemed to consider her response carefully. "That's

wonderful news for him, of course. How do you feel about it?"

What an excellent question, except she couldn't answer it. Ellie smoothed her hands over her knees and thought over her answer. "I'm happy for him, since he's put a lot into it. This is his dream."

"But?"

"It's a two-book deal. He's thinking of going to New York for a while to get a feel for the sequel. Apparently it is going to be set there. The main character is an aspiring actor who is hoping for a shot at Broadway. He'd thought about writing it anyway, but now he has to."

"Interesting. Did Bryce ask you to go with him?"

It wasn't interesting, Ellie thought with a frisson of dismay, it was like a line being drawn in the sand. The comfort with their current relationship had been tipped suddenly sideways and it was the last thing she needed at the moment with her mother's diagnosis and this new investigation.

But that was a selfish view and she didn't think she was normally self-centered. There was just a small sense she needed to make a decision she was not ready to make.

He *hadn't* asked her.

She looked up at the clock and stood, not answering the question. "I think our time is up and then some. Thanks for the insights."

Chapter 5

Oh yeah, something was definitely up.

Jason had no illusions he was the most sensitive man on God's green earth—he wasn't—but he knew how to read people. There was no doubt it had kept him alive both when he lived on the street and during his years in the military.

Ellie was conflicted in some way and one look at her set face told him questions were not welcome. Fine, he understood working it out for yourself so he'd let her do just that.

Maybe she'd eventually tell him.

The Peterson house was a brick ranch in a nice neighborhood, with mature trees in the yard and a paved driveway. The dead professor's Mercedes sat like a neglected aristocrat off to the side of the garage, a dusting of snow giving it a venerable dignity.

Mrs. Peterson was about as chilly as the weather. The attitude was reminiscent of his last contact with the woman.

Ellie, dressed in a pale gray wool coat and a cap, took out her credentials and smiled apologetically, but her eyes held no warmth. The initial interview with the woman hadn't gone very well. "I'm sure you remember us. We are sorry to bother you again, but could we just ask a few more questions?"

The red carpet was not exactly rolled out. "Why?" Slightly overweight but still attractive with dark hair and pale skin, Mrs. Peterson wasn't friendly. The house smelled like cinnamon and cloves, and she was still in her robe and pajamas at ten in the morning.

Ellie said, "I'm sure you know there's been another murder."

He kept his mouth shut. Jason had learned some time ago that diplomacy was not his forte, so he just followed his partner inside when they were grudgingly shown in. It was one of those houses he hated, not because it wasn't beautiful, it was, *if* you admired pretension. Big windows, polished floors, artfully arranged chairs in what were no doubt supposed to be cozy conversational groupings for artsy cocktail parties. Black-and-white still shots were framed and hung on the walls. It came off as cold and impersonal to him, but then again, he had mirrors with beer logos and half-naked women on the walls of his apartment, plastic chairs on the tiny balcony overlooking the community pool, and a fifty-six-inch television mounted on the wall of the living room, so what did he know about good taste? Still, this house felt unlived in and sterile and he liked his place a lot better.

"What do you possibly think I can tell you that I haven't already?" Mrs. Peterson asked, gesturing at them to sit down but there was some reluctance in the act.

They both accepted and settled next to each other. "We don't know. It could be a bit of information you don't think is significant, but might mean a lot to the investigation."

Ellie looked like she always did during an interview like this one. Collected and empathetic, but not too much so. There was a businesslike edge to her when she talked to the family of a victim that they usually found reassuring.

Usually.

About two minutes into the conversation, sitting on a white couch—who had a *white* couch?—and listening to the vitriol, he got it that the woman blamed them for not immediately apprehending whoever was responsible for her husband's death. "I don't think the police are even trying," Pam Peterson said bitterly. "I sit here day after day and no one has told me anything."

His partner seemed unfazed by the rudeness, though he had to admit it bothered *him*. Being a police officer was a calling, not a career. They got paid very little really compared to what they had to do, the hours they worked, and when it came down to it, what they had to see that ruined any rosy glow a person might have about humanity. It was only with restraint he didn't shoot back a comment. If Ellie hadn't shifted a subtle distance so her knee touched his, he really might have gone over the edge.

"That's why we're here a second time. If we had anything to tell you," Ellie said as if she wasn't insulted, "we would, so please help us out. This second murder appears to be very similar to what happened to your husband. If both victims were chosen at random that makes it difficult to understand the motivation. If they were not and we can link them to each other, it could lead us in the right direction." Ellie handed Mrs. Peterson a slip of paper. "Does this address mean anything to you? It's where we found the second body."

The woman at least had the courtesy to look at it. "No."

Not helpful, but information was information.

"Can you think of anything that might link a young man, possibly homeless, to your husband? Did he do charity work? Volunteer at a shelter?"

If it was possible, Jason liked the woman even less when she looked slightly affronted. "Charity work? No, of course not." Then she at least seemed to hear how that response sounded for she amended coolly, "We have always been very active in raising money for the arts. The symphony, the local theater groups, that sort of thing."

"The arts, I get it. All those hungry people," Jason said sardonically. "Yeah, they are kind of a pain in the—"

"We're wondering if maybe this victim could have been a student." Ellie interjected the interruption smoothly, but she did level a swift warning glance his way. "The university has been very helpful, but can you think of anyone your husband mentioned specifically? A student that stood out to him maybe?"

That was one hell of a shot in the dark. They hadn't found any books in that musty house, but then again, his identification had been taken, so maybe the killer was meticulous about details.

"Not that I can think of." The words were ice cold.

Mrs. Peterson was just as unhelpful as the first time they interviewed her and seemed relieved—even after she complained about them not instantly solving the crime—when they rose to leave.

Once they were back in the car, Jason started it and pulled away, before he muttered, "What a bitch."

"I got the impression you feel that way, and maybe she did too. Keep in mind, she's still grieving." Ellie said it evenly. "Whether she is pleasant or not—and I agree with you, she isn't—do you think she knows anything?"

He wished he could say he did. "No."

"I don't either."

Jason guided the car down the street, consciously loosening the muscles in his jaw. "She is just ticked off that life isn't going her way. I'm hardly an expert on relationships but when you say grieving, I disagree. She's grieving losing the status of being a tenured professor's wife. Grieving *for* him? I'm not that sure that is part of the equation."

"God, you're jaded," Ellie said, her profile illuminated with a hesitant winter sun.

"God, I'm realistic," he countered, braking for a traffic light. "What next?"

"I hate to say this, but maybe a visit to the morgue. We'll get a report, but I think I'd like to talk to the ME face-to-face."

"I hate to agree to the suggestion, but maybe we'd better." He was actually pretty squeamish about the morgue. Crime scenes weren't a problem, blood didn't bother him, but stainless steel tables and the smell of antiseptic did.

"I want to get her impressions, not just what notes she makes on a piece of paper."

She was right. A face-to-face worked better always. Professionals tended to not draw conclusions—they weren't supposed to anyway, but it was enlightening sometimes to hear their abstract thoughts.

Law enforcement was not an exact science.

But he really had no desire to see that faceless corpse again.

Luckily, when they arrived, they were told Dr. Hammet was in her office, not down in the part of the building Jason disliked so much. She greeted them with her usual cordial reserve, a dark-haired woman who had replaced the previous medical examiner under very unusual circumstances. Jason liked her professionalism because he always dealt much better with straightforward people. She wasn't into sugarcoating anything, and that made his job easier, if not less disturbing at times. He could never decide if it was worse to be the one to arrive first at the crime scene, or if what she did for a living was more macabre.

"Detectives," she said, glancing up from the screen of her computer. "I was just finishing up the autopsy report on the victim from the other day. Good timing. I feel confident that is why you are here."

"You have that right." Jason was used to seeing her in scrubs or a white jacket, so her silk blouse and dark skirt were a little different, and there was an impressive array of diplomas on the walls, and even a lush banana plant by a window in the corner. Why he was surprised someone who dealt with death had a green thumb he had no idea, but he was.

Ellie said in her succinct way, "Is the report going to help us?"

Dr. Hammet shook her head. "I have no idea, but I did find something interesting."

. . .

Ellie listened as the doctor outlined the stomach contents of both victims.

"Some kind of cake with apples in it for Peterson and your second victim had eaten something like it." Dr. Hammet shuffled through several pages of papers. "Here it is. I broke down all the compounds but you'd find that boring and probably not really all that pertinent, and I am not speculating the cake was laced with Rohypnol, the drug more commonly known as rufilin. So much more likely it was put into a drink, but I found the similarity interesting."

She had to agree.

So did Santiago. He took the piece of paper from her hand, scowled at it, and then handed it back. "You're telling us they were given an effing date-rape drug by a cake-baking grandmother?"

The medical examiner was used to Ellie's partner by now and she merely lifted her brows. "It isn't a date-rape drug in a clinical sense. It is used to treat severe insomnia and sometimes anxiety. However, considering the amount both victims had ingested, I doubt they took it voluntarily. Had they been found in bed instead of in a parking lot or on a porch, maybe. As for the grandmother theory, Detective Santiago, it is unlikely an older woman had the strength to inflict those wounds even with a drugged victim. I was more thinking they might have eaten at the same restaurant or had the cake brought to them by someone, which would give you some connection besides the wounds. Both of them were first stabbed in the back. It looks to me like they staggered forward and turned around to defend themselves, like we all would, and at that point it got very ugly. Impaired and taken by surprise by the sheer volume of the attack, once they went down, they were assaulted by multiple wounds, the worst of it being to the face and neck. The chest wounds are postmortem. Those were not slashes. They were deep and careful, made with a different instrument."

Santiago was hardly someone who was shaken easily, but he took a moment and then questioned, "Instrument? Doc, what the hell does that mean?"

Dr. Hammet smiled thinly. "It isn't an ordinary weapon. I think it might be filed down to the shape of a deadly point, but it doesn't exactly cut like a knife, it just punctures, which is probably why the postmortem incisions are done . . . it's silver. I found traces in the wounds." She spread her hands. "The attacker doesn't trust he can kill with the instrument, and so he stabs the victims first and waits until they are dead before using the second source of the cross-like wounds."

"That's a damned scary image," her partner murmured, and Ellie had to agree. She asked, "So though I assume all of that is in the report, is there anything else that made you uneasy? Something that maybe didn't tick a box on your forms but still struck you?"

Dr. Hammet exhaled. "Look, I am not a detective. I only deal with the crimes in terms of the bodies they put on my table. But I'd say you have two killers working in tandem. One is a planner, and the other one is more than willing to do that kind of vicious damage to a human being. The planner is the brains, and the other one does the physical work of the actual attack. This is absolutely just my opinion, but alone I'd guess the attacker might be caught easily. They have to be covered in blood once they are finished. And the

planner would never go through with it. It's like a bank robbery. One goes in with a gun to get the money, and the other
one drives the getaway car. They have different skills."

Ellie went to the window. Down below cars crawled
along the avenue since it had really started to snow. White
flakes floated past the glass. She didn't like that idea at all.
"Two of them?"

"Different stab mark signatures. Bodies don't lie to you."

"Just as long as they don't start talking." Santiago walked
over and grabbed Ellie's wrist. "Come on, let's go. I have an
idea. Thanks, Doc."

"Detective, please don't call me that," Hammet requested,
going back to her computer.

"I can try to remember, but don't expect much," he said
as he dragged Ellie out into the hall. He turned urgently,
"Bear with me."

She looked pointedly at where he had ahold of her arm.
It was out of character since he almost never touched her.
"I assume you'll let me come of my own free will."

"Sorry." He let go. "But the person we are going to see
is probably still at home in bed. He kind of works the night
shift. Once he's up and headed off to work, he's hard to
catch."

"Mind telling me who *he* is?"

As they left the building, her partner held the door for
her, a particular courtesy he'd mentioned once was drilled
into his head when he was in the military, not by the father
that had kicked him out of the house on his eighteenth birthday. In a noncommittal tone he'd added that life on the
streets had been sending him into a downward spiral, so
he cleaned up and enlisted. Becoming an MP had helped

him get a law enforcement job when he got out of the service.

That was the sum total she knew about his past.

Just in the short time they'd been in Hammet's office the car had accumulated an inch of snow and the leaden skies threatened more. It was the kind of wet heavy snow that promised great snowballs when she was a kid. The temperature had been rising all day as a new front blew in, but it was supposed to plummet again tomorrow.

A far cry from the sunny beach she'd left behind in Florida just a few days ago, but that had hardly been a joyous trip.

When Santiago slid into the car and started it, he informed her, "He is a dealer I busted a few times that has a specialty in drugs like Ecstasy and other substances, all of which are against the law in the state of Wisconsin and pretty much everywhere else. How the hell he's still alive is beyond my comprehension, but he is one fucking connected asshole. I doubt he ever takes names, but whoever is killing these guys is getting the drug somewhere. He's gotten promoted . . . he deals to the dealers now, but maybe he can tell us who to talk to."

That was iffy, she thought as they pulled out of the parking lot onto a street full of slushy snow. "What makes you think he'll talk to us?"

"We went to high school together." Santiago lifted his shoulders in a negligent shrug. "When I say I busted him a few times, I meant I could have busted him a *lot* of times. To narcotics he's a problem; to me he's a source."

"Interesting way to look at it," she muttered. Big fat flakes were falling on the windshield now so fast the wipers weren't quite doing the job. The gutters were filled with slush. When the temperature dropped, it was going to be treacherous.

Paulo Astin proved to live in a very nice part of town, which offended Ellie in every way possible considering what he did to be able to afford a high-rise condo with security, but undoubtedly he needed the protection.

She waited curiously to see if he would really go ahead and buzz them up, but Santiago seemed confident enough, and in the end, he was right, though it wasn't very reassuring when he commented in the elevator, "Make sure the safety is released on your weapon. Paulo will be polite, but his friends are not as predictable. I'm hoping he'll be alone."

Now she was too. She glanced at her companion. "Sounds like this is a great idea."

Santiago's eyes were a particular shade of vivid blue she'd never seen before. Something between sapphire and a summer sky on a clear day. They reflected casual amusement, as if they weren't about to visit a drug dealer, who just happened to be an old friend. He checked his weapon as if to emphasize he wasn't kidding. "I just said it was an idea. I never said great. Don't worry. Paulo will like you. He's partial to blondes."

"Perfect." She did the same thing with her Glock. "Remind me to get specifics next time you have a suggestion."

"Will do." His grin was cheeky, but faded quickly. "If we're careful, we should be fine. He likes to dance under the law and not draw attention. Smart guy."

The hallway was polished and lit by sconces, lined by discreet doorways with embossed numbers. Jason obviously knew just where he was going, which she might question later, but for now, they were there and if there was a chance he could help with the case, then maybe it was worth it.

The moment Santiago rapped his knuckles on the door, it opened.

A man in a robe stood in the doorway, supporting the claim he might still be sleeping even though it was past noon, but Ellie was getting used to talking to people in their sleepwear on this particular day. He was dark-haired, with a fox-like face full of angles around a pointed nose, and eyes that reminded her of a doll, inexpressive and unblinking. His voice sounded like he'd swallowed a pail of gravel. "Jace, buddy. I'm kinda hopin' this is a social call, you know what I mean? Especially now." He looked Ellie up and down. "Nice. Who's the friend?"

To say she and her partner were friends was stretching it. Ellie took out her badge. "I'm Detective MacIntosh, Mr. Astin. We were hoping maybe you could help us out on an investigation as an expert, if you will. Can we come in?"

"Expert? I like that. Pretty diplomatic. Never been called that before." He stepped back. "Come on in. Babes are always welcome here even if they are cops. You should have called first. I would have picked up the place and put on some pants."

Santiago walked into the condo in front of her, and she didn't mind that at all. His warning was exactly what was on her mind when she realized who and what might be behind that door. Luckily, it was clear and it appeared they were alone with Mr. Astin.

The main living area was all about chrome and glass and Astin had what she suspected was a pretty great view at night, but otherwise there was no personality at all. No pictures, no art, nothing but a place he could probably walk away from without any regret.

Good idea. In his line of work it was best to have an exit plan handy.

Jason said, after a swift pointed survey of the main room, "We alone?"

Astin moved over to a couch and sat down. "We need to be? I was just having coffee. You want some?"

The last question was directed at her and the double entendre not subtle at all. Ellie had dealt with more than a few like him, so it didn't faze her. "No, thanks. We're here to ask if on a theoretical basis you might know where someone might purchase the drug that is known on the street as rufilin."

Those flat black eyes stared back at her. "Now why would I know that, sweetheart?"

"Because you're a drug dealer." Santiago sounded exasperated. "Jesus, Paulo, if this is your version of flirting, give it up. We work homicide. We aren't interested in your particular activities unless you kill someone, and then we will bust your dishonest ass. If you help us, it might win points toward your next arrest, which I have no doubt is coming if we find any evidence you contributed to a crime."

"Like what?" Astin looked defensive. "What crime?"

Time for shock therapy. Ellie took out a crime scene photo and handed it over. "This one."

"Holy mother of God." Astin crossed himself after looking at it for a minute, and let it drift to the floor. "People are just sick. No one on ruf would do that."

"We aren't saying they would." Santiago leaned up against

one of the columns. "Someone gave it to the victim. Where could the killer buy it?"

"Fuck, you think I know all the dealers in a city this large? I'm good but not *that* good."

"I think you are an excellent place to start. Do you supply it?"

"Ah, man, seriously? I'm not answering that. You might keep in mind it is possible to get a prescription for that shit."

"Let me rephrase." Ellie picked up the picture and tucked it away. "Let's say, Mr. Astin, I want to purchase some of that drug illegally. Can you point me in the right direction? Just as a helpful gesture to law enforcement. Have you ever heard of someone who sells it?"

He considered for a moment, and then inclined his head. "Maybe."

Chapter 6

Her eleven o'clock patient was a good half-hour early and Georgia suspected that was habitual.

"I kind of wonder if this is just a waste of my time." Rachel Summers softened that declaration with an apologetic smile.

Georgia wasn't surprised at the comment, but needed to really think about how she went about addressing it. In her experience almost everyone had a certain point when they wondered if therapy was just tossing money and time into the wind. After all, a patient was just asking another—very fallible—human being to look at their problems and give them solid, life-improving advice.

She decided on, "It depends what you hope to gain from this experience."

The young woman looked around and pointed. "I do like the pictures on the walls. Especially that one." She pointed. "It reminds me of the farm my grandmother owned."

An interesting avoidance of the issue.

The picture was of a solemn little girl sitting on the front porch of an old farmhouse, a chicken pecking in the dirt nearby, the rough frame handmade. Georgia had actually inherited it from her own grandmother.

Good memories were hard to come by sometimes, so she'd hung it in her office, just as she had her aunt's lamp on her desk.

This was their second session. Rachel was hesitant and had some nervous mannerisms that Georgia recognized. She constantly adjusted her skirt, crossed and uncrossed her legs, and while she was visibly still unsure, she was more comfortable than at their session last week.

"Your grandmother had chickens?"

"No."

"The house then?"

"Maybe that's it."

This was not going to be an easy patient to get to open up. "The last time we talked, you had a date. How was it?"

"I didn't go," Rachel confessed. "I didn't feel well."

"You do realize people often use that as an excuse, right? It is not at all uncommon to do so, but don't you think you would have felt better if you had gone?" Georgia had at first thought this patient merely introverted, but for such a pretty woman, she was certainly insecure. It was very, very early in their patient/doctor relationship to push for guarded confidences as to why, but Rachel had sought out therapy for a reason.

She wrapped a strand of long hair around her finger. "The thought of *going* made me feel sick. It's happened to me before. I wish I was more like my roommate. She's very confident."

"What is it that makes you anxious about a simple date?"

"I'm not sure."

"Think about it."

Rachel finally shook her head. "I found it hard to walk through the door at the last minute in the clothes Lea had insisted I wear, so I chickened out and instead went to a restaurant down the street and had a grilled chicken salad and an iced tea, lingered for an hour, and then went back to the apartment and lied about it. He only asked me out because of Lea anyway."

There would be some interesting notes later, but Georgia never did that in front of a patient. In her mind it was like talking behind their back. "Why do you think that?"

Rachel smiled faintly. "We were out and he saw her, bought us a drink, but he wasn't her type at all, so he asked me out instead. Story of my life."

It was starting to seem like that might be a very interesting story indeed. Georgia asked neutrally, "How does that make you feel?"

Jason drifted in a world of music and flickering lights. Movie, he realized coming awake, something action-packed. He had the volume louder than usual on the television, which would probably annoy his neighbors because a glance at the clock on the wall told him it was after midnight.

It could be why his phone was ringing.

Not the problem, as it turned out.

Astin didn't even clarify who he was, but Jason knew his voice. He said, "Try Ernie Gurst."

The loud music in the background made it hard to hear and Jason sat up, shutting off the television with the push of a button. "Where?"

"He sells out of a bar called Lenny's downtown."

"I know Lenny's . . . what makes you think Gurst can help us? Who the hell is he?"

"Hey. You wanted a tip, I gave you one. I asked around and he seemed to be the one with some information. Take it and run."

The line went dead.

Jason rolled to his back on the couch and propped his wrist on his forehead, trying to come fully awake. Outside the windows there were stars studding the sky, which probably meant the cold front had rolled in and the snow had stopped.

The roads would be like a skating rink but maybe this was the perfect time to go. These guys did business at odd hours, and it was just after midnight. Cold streets and nothing else to do so the hunters would be out.

So would the prey.

Jason was infinitely more interested in the people who bought from the dealers at this time. Getting to his feet, he went into the bathroom, washed his hands, and put on his coat and gloves. It was going to be well below freezing— he'd seen the forecast.

One splurge he'd gotten with his new vehicle—his old one had been blown up in the fall, which still pained him— was a remote starter. He pressed the button and watched out the window that faced the parking lot until he saw exhaust creeping out of the tailpipe. He wondered if he should call Ellie, decided against it because it was late, and then went down the stairs.

After a fairly harrowing drive downtown that took twice as long as it might usually, he parked next to Lenny's beside a rusting pickup truck and took a minute to send her a text. *"Maybe found ruffie guy. Let you know."* He added at the last second, *"At a bar called Lenny's."*

Just in case. If he got into trouble, at least Ellie would have a record on her phone of his last known destination. It was a little inconvenient to not have someone asking where you might be going at this time of night and expecting you back home. He'd lived alone since his ex-girlfriend Kate had moved out last summer. Sure, he'd eventually be missed at work, but it might take just a little too long for his liking. Not a bad idea to hedge his bets.

Lenny's was on a side street, a low-built building that looked like a pole barn, and the place was filled with bikers and hookers, but Jason never begrudged anyone getting out from the chill of the Wisconsin winter. He'd flipped up his collar in the parking lot and came in kicking the snow off his boots. The place smelled of cigarette smoke and stale beer, pretty much like any other dive bar. When he wandered over to the bar and ordered a coffee, the bartender looked at him in some surprise at his beverage of choice, but went ahead and poured it, handing it over without comment.

He would personally never want to be a bartender at a place like this because he was probably also the bouncer and he'd take odds there was a fight pretty much every single night. He asked, "Know anyone named Gurst?"

"I don't know anyone named anything." The bartender was built like a junior-high basketball player, whippy and thin, with a pockmarked face and a surly voice.

"Just need a word."

The guy drew a draft for another customer and delivered it down the bar. When he came back by he said, "You're a cop."

Perched on his stool, Jason laughed derisively. "Why is it legitimate people don't think I'm one, but certain others make me immediately?"

"You calling me a bastard?"

Jason rested his elbows on the worn counter. "I think this bar is owned by organized crime and no one wants me to look too deeply into that, and no, that's not why I'm here, so neither one of us should sweat it. Is Gurst here? I'm not going to bust him. I need his advice on a delicate matter."

That did it. The kid lost his bluster and polished the bar a minute before he jerked his head toward the corner. "He might be over there. He comes and goes."

Good enough. He didn't need it written in blood. "I won't mention my source. I never do. Maybe you should remember if bad shit really starts to go down here, the police are the first people you'd call."

It always amazed him how often criminals forgot that one crucial fact.

"I *don't* call the cops."

Jason met that challenging gaze. "But you would if you needed us. Like real trouble. Like you thought you might die trouble. Excuse me, but please put my coffee on Mr. Gurst's tab. I promise he won't argue the charge."

Gurst proved to be a little older than expected and had

a face like polished wood, with deep creases and a well-worn countenance. He could be thirty, but maybe even sixty. He fished, Jason guessed, and it wasn't on a lake in northern Minnesota. Off the shore of Mexico would be more likely because of the tan. He wore a heavy flannel coat and his hands were chapped. It looked like bourbon was his drink of choice, and he was on his tablet device checking e-mail. Jason slid in opposite and set down his cup. "Thanks for the coffee."

Gurst logged out and said aggressively, "Who the fuck are you?"

"Detective Santiago, Milwaukee homicide. A friend of yours told me you might be able to help me."

"Some friend. Fuckin' Astin. Help the police? That's a new one." Gurst took a drink and slapped the glass down and started to stand. "I don't think so. If I'd of known why he was asking me those questions, I wouldn't have said shit."

Jason guessed that was true, but if this was a real lead . . .

"Bear with me and sit the fuck down. I could take you in for questioning if you'd prefer that. Now, tell me, if I wanted to buy rufilin, where would I shop?"

Gurst looked defiant, but he did sink back into his seat. "That's a legal substance. Get a prescription and go to a pharmacy."

"But what if I didn't have a prescription?" Jason refused to back down. "I'm looking for a killer, not a dealer. I want the customer, not the seller, get it?"

"I'm not a snitch."

Jason lifted his brows. "I think you're looking at this the wrong way, pal. You help me out and you are helping out whoever sold to a killer. I'm pretty sure none of them want to be an accessory to murder, do they? This gives them a chance to get off the hook when we catch the guy I'm looking for. You're doing them a favor."

It had worked pretty well for Ellie, so he pulled out a crime photo, one of the most graphic, and slid it across the scratched table. "Maybe you can see why we are interested in taking whoever did this off the street."

Gurst wiped his hand across his mouth, his skin burnished in the artificial light and muttered, "Ah, Jesus Christ, man. Why'd you show me that?"

Two in the morning.

Bryce must have rolled over and found the other side of the bed was empty and cold. He shouldn't be all that surprised because it happened now and then. Once he'd tactfully suggested maybe Ellie should mention to her doctor the trouble she often had sleeping, but that idea wasn't met with any enthusiasm at all.

It was this new case. She was doing him a favor by not talking much about it. It would probably give him nightmares.

He came down the hall to the kitchen, wearing his robe. She was at the oak table reading, several books scattered around her, most of them open. She glanced up when he came in and offered an apologetic smile. "I was actually trying to *not* wake you."

"Just wondered what you were doing."

"Research."

"On?" She was drinking tea and he moved to the one-cup maker to make himself some decaf.

"A not particularly soothing subject."

"Why does that not surprise me? Like what?" He sat down and lifted his brows in inquiry.

She tucked her fuzzy robe—it was a light pink—more closely around her. "Killers who mutilate. Jack the Ripper is a pretty good example. I'm trying to get a handle on the profile. There are a lot of aspects of these two cases that bother me. I don't like it when I know it all means something but just have no idea what."

"Call your friend Montoya at the FBI."

Not a bad suggestion. Montoya was a profiler she'd met when she worked the case of the Northwoods killer, which had not been the finest time of *his* life, but Bryce knew Ellie respected the man's insights and they had been pretty accurate. He'd consulted with her on other cases as well.

"I might. Now that there is a pattern, maybe we can come up with something, but we just don't have any physical evidence at all. Not a hair, or a fiber, or even a weapon."

"Just the bodies." Bryce wrapped his hands around his cup.

They still hadn't really talked about his trip to New York. That was also keeping her awake.

Maybe it was time to say something.

Middle of the night? She wasn't sure it was a good idea, but then again, she'd put it off during dinner—she'd put it off for several days, in fact—and it was not going to get any easier. She liked to think he was intelligent enough to know that.

Ellie took in a breath, let it out slowly, and just said it.

"How long will you be in New York? You've not been very specific."

"It might be a few weeks or maybe even longer."

"I see. That makes sense considering the purpose of your visit."

"I wasn't sure what kind of reaction I might get."

Running a finger around the rim of her cup, she gazed at him. "What exactly did you expect?"

"For you to say I should go for as long as I needed."

"Is it disappointing I'd be supportive?"

"I don't know."

"Bryce, I can hardly ask you to put your dream second to me, when my job impacts our lives almost every single day. I'd like to think I'm more reasonable than that, and more realistic. This is your vision of your life and you should follow it."

He didn't look thrilled with her response.

"Your self-reliance leaves me off balance," he said, turning his head to look out the window at the chill black of a January night.

"My self-reliance is what you like about me," she contradicted. "If I needed you, I think you'd turn and run."

The hell of it was she could be right. That seemed to be exactly what he was doing anyway.

Chapter 7

Georgia was in an ethical dispute with her own psyche, but was just too fascinated to step in and end it.

No true physician allowed this situation, and yet here she was still stretching boundaries. She pursed her lips and then asked a mundane question. "How did you feel?"

Jason Santiago was a bit different than her usual patient. He dealt with personal issues so directly he probably didn't even need her, but there was no argument he was carrying a lot of baggage around, so talking to someone was not a bad idea.

He looked perplexed. "About what?"

"When you discovered so long after the fact that your father had passed away."

He thought it over for a moment, but then just lifted his shoulders. "I don't think I felt much of anything. It was no big secret he was going to drink himself to death. If anything, I was kind of surprised it didn't happen earlier. I was pretty happy it didn't happen in a drunk driving accident where he took out someone else too so I'd have to feel guilty about that."

"You'd feel more compassion toward a stranger?"

"He wasn't a man who inspired a lot of deep feeling." The detective lounged back in his chair, his long legs extended. As usual he was dressed a little carelessly, this afternoon in worn jeans and a denim shirt, his hair curling over his collar. He was attractive, but in a bad boy sort of way—never mind he was a police officer. She knew he'd been in trouble with his job a time or two because he'd freely admitted it. It didn't surprise her at all. If anyone would bend the rules if it needed to done, her impression was he would. For her part, she'd much rather be on his side than pitted against him.

"I sense you aren't all that interested in talking about your father."

"What you sense is that there isn't much else to say. He and I existed in a state of mutual indifference until I was old enough for him to tell me to get out. I didn't know he'd died for months because I hadn't seen him in so long no one knew where I was or if I was even alive. I was stationed in California at the time. As far as I'm concerned, he died anyway the day my mother walked out when I was five years old."

"You're angry with her."

"I'm pretty pissed she left me with him, but otherwise, I don't remember her all that well. Give me a break, after all, like I said, I was five."

"Do you think that is why you don't trust women?"

He looked at her with those very vivid blue eyes.

"Dr. Lukens, I don't trust anyone, man or woman, and if you did my job, neither would you. I've seen examples of man's inhumanity to man that make me want to wake up screaming at night."

It wasn't at all unusual for police officers to suffer from depression, and he also carried the burden of his less than idyllic childhood, plus active military service, but he wasn't clinically depressed as far as she could tell. That didn't mean he didn't have issues, but she didn't think that was one of them.

Georgia asked carefully, "An interesting statement. Do you?"

"Literally wake up screaming? No."

He wouldn't, she already knew that about him. She'd first seen him for mandatory counseling by order of the police department after he'd been shot in the line of duty and he'd been pretty unfazed by the event as far as she could tell. This particular patient was suffering from an entirely different sort of problem.

"Speaking of that topic, I understand you and Detective MacIntosh have a new case."

"She told you about it?"

"You know I don't directly discuss anything a patient and I say during a session. That policy is why you can freely say anything you want to me, and have the confidence I will never tell her or anyone else either."

His grin was irreverent. "You are a hardass about that, true."

"I assume you want me to be."

He sobered. "I don't even know why the hell I come here half the time."

That sounded familiar, but she'd heard it more than usual lately.

Georgia said noncommittally, "Most people find it helpful to discuss their problems. I doubt my input is a miracle cure, I've never thought so even from when I first went into active practice. It's more saying the words out loud instead of ignoring what is troubling you."

"This case would trouble anyone."

She'd seen that horrific picture and didn't disagree but had to choose her words carefully. "I am not a detective but it is an easy assumption the two of you are working on the recent similar murders that have been very brutal according to the news."

"For a refreshing change of pace, the media is telling the truth."

"It sounds like you are dealing with someone who might be acting out their anger at the world in an interesting way."

"Do you think?" Jason Santiago shook his head. "A sick one, that's for sure. Tell me, Doc, who wants to destroy someone's face? Not to mention punch holes in their chest in a religious symbol."

"I don't know." It was the truth. She'd been thinking about it quite a lot.

"Neither do we unfortunately." He shifted in his chair and changed the subject to why she suspected he came to see her in the first place. "I have a feeling Ellie and Grantham are having some kind of problem."

Now they were getting to it. It was no secret Ellie had only recently moved in with her lover, so Georgia responded neutrally, "When two people decide to live in the same house it is often a difficult transition."

"Yeah." He ran his fingers through his hair, which he often did. "Kate and I . . . we just expected it to be different when we decided to live together. All sunshine and happiness and not just sex and the occasional night out. There was toothpaste in the sink and mutual laundry and all that sort of crap. We just weren't good on an all-the-time basis."

"Are you hoping they aren't either?"

"Who? MacIntosh and Grantham?" He tried to look disassociated and failed.

He'd just called her Ellie, but it was MacIntosh now. "Detective, you know exactly who I mean."

"I don't know if I'm hoping for anything."

He was, though. Police officers might be used to people lying to them, but so was she. Half of what she did was sift through the falsehoods to try and find a truth.

"Maybe you should tell her about your feelings." Georgia had wondered about it all along. As far as she could tell, Ellie MacIntosh was completely unaware of her partner's attraction to her, and they dealt with each other on a professional level pretty well. Personally, Georgia was like a voyeur, looking in and waiting to see what might happen next.

That ended the session. He got restlessly to his feet and said in an unemotional voice, "I've a bit of a problem with that advice, Doc. I've never really loved anyone my entire life. It's like trying to teach a cripple to walk. I need to get the hang of it first, don't you agree?"

Unfortunately for him, she did.

. . .

The screen door banged repetitively in a thin January wind as they pulled up.

It was an interesting lead, and Ellie glanced at her partner as he parked the car in front of an old house that had a buckled sidewalk with snow-encrusted dead weeds growing out of the fissures. "Now this place I can see our second victim visiting, but not our first."

"Busted-down crack house." Santiago unsnapped his seat belt. "Besides, the professor didn't come here, but the killer might have. I'll be about two seconds. This guy isn't going to talk to me according to my source, but what the hell. It's worth a shot."

"*You'll* be about two seconds?" She opened her door. "Last I checked this was my job too. I'm going with you."

"The fuck you are." Santiago looked at her over the top of the car, his eyes unrelenting. "No. This is a gang neighborhood and they don't like cops. At all. Take the keys and be ready to drive if we have to leave in a hurry. That will be much more helpful than you walking with me to the door. You are, at this moment, a liability."

It was true that their arrival did seem to draw quite a bit of interest from the locals. Two Hispanic men had come onto the porch of the house next door, one of them smoking a cigarette—hand-rolled, so maybe it wasn't a legal substance, hard to tell—and neither one of them had a coat on despite the temperature, their muscular arms covered in tattoos.

Santiago tossed her the keys, giving her little choice but to catch them. "No flirting while I'm gone. You have some admirers."

She could deal with his attitude 90 percent of the time

since she'd gotten used to it, but not right now. "I see them. I'm going to stand right here and watch you walk up to that door. If there is any hint of trouble, I'll call for backup and be right behind you."

"Sounds good to me."

The scenario did make her slightly nervous, but she'd be an idiot if it didn't. Still, Santiago had done the legwork on this and she'd back him up. Knowing the contact would probably not talk to him, he must have a reason for coming to this questionable neighborhood.

At least she hoped he did. He had his faults, but usually stupidity wasn't one of them.

Someone answered the door and he leaned on the jamb, casual and conversational, but his right hand hovered near his coat and Ellie could see Jason was not as relaxed as he appeared. After a brief conversation through the screen, he turned and came down the broken steps.

"Okay, drive," he ordered as he got into the car and slammed the door. "Do it."

She did, pulling away from the curb quickly and gunning the motor. The shabby houses flashed past. "Did he tell you anything?"

"Nope." Santiago looked unfazed. "Unless you count the advice that I should take my questions and stick them up my ass."

"So what precisely did that visit accomplish?"

"I want the dealers to know we're looking for someone. So Ramon, who has no teeth due to meth and smelled like a wet ashtray by the way, won't help me, fine. But someone might if he talks about it. He has friends in all the wrong places."

Detective Jason Santiago had worked homicide a lot longer than she had, so Ellie weighed her response. "You don't think anyone will come forward voluntarily, do you?"

"Drug dealers? Hell no."

"Not even Gurst?"

"He's our best bet, but I doubt it."

She stopped at a corner and waited for the light. "Then?"

"They might hesitate to sell to whoever is buying if they seem unusual. At that point, our killer has to find a new source so he starts asking around a little. It's like tossing a stone in a pond. The ripple effect could pay off. Even those two gang members might help us out. You know they are going to ask what we wanted and if Ramon wants to keep good relations with his dangerous neighbors he might tell them, and they might mention it to someone else, and so on. I doubt the person doing this is one of the usual bad guys. If they aren't, then the idea of loyalty of any kind goes out the window. The drug culture is a unique entity."

Maybe it *would* work. She wasn't at all positive it was worth risking their lives to go visit some pretty sketchy people on such a long shot, but she'd done worse than pay a call or two in a bad neighborhood, and maybe he was right.

"So now? What's next?"

"Yeah, well, we need to go shopping." Santiago didn't look pleased at all, his expression surly. "That damn governor thing. For God's sake, I'm completely uninterested."

Metzger had stopped by her desk briefly and informed her that he'd told her partner she was going to be the fashion consultant. She found it paradoxically funny and annoying. At the moment, considering Santiago's expression, it was amusing.

The leaden sky was spitting snow again and the wind was picking up. Maybe she should have stayed in Florida. "You need to stop rescuing damsels in distress. Just a thought."

"I didn't." He sounded sincere and irritated. "Not in the least. I just stopped some jerk from walking away from the scene of an accident. It was nothing. No rescue was involved."

"I don't precisely agree with that, but I do imagine you didn't expect all the attention."

There had even been a clip on the news, mostly because of the governor's campaign against public cell phone use in situations where people really needed to be paying attention to what they were doing. That his niece had been involved had been emphasized.

Right place, wrong time apparently for Detective Jason Santiago.

"Look at it this way," she said, turning left on Lincoln. "You will get a unique life experience. From those come the memories we tell our children about eventually."

Her companion was his usual caustic self. "I didn't know we were planning on having children. Don't we need to do something about nine months before that event? Count me in, by the way. I'm free tonight."

Ellie always ignored his sexual comments since he seemed to go for irreverent shock value above all else. "We could go to the mall, but Bryce told me about a place in West Allis that he really likes. Try that?"

"You already knew about this little trip then?"

"Metzger has no faith in your taste." She couldn't insult him with what he already knew.

"And here he hasn't even been to my apartment. I've been

watching decorating shows on television but just haven't done anything about it yet."

That made her laugh. She had been to his place once or twice when he was recovering from his wounds after their last two big cases. "It's not that bad."

"I have it on good authority it is adolescent."

"Kate?"

"Yep."

The snow was now like they were in a globe, frosting the ugly piles on the street corners with a coating of fresh white powder. The psychologist ex-girlfriend, the one he only mentioned now and then, seemed like an odd choice for Santiago. Ellie had to ask, "So why didn't she change it when she moved in?"

"I kind of thought she would," he said in an offhand way. "Crap, it's snowing pretty hard. Is it really only January?"

Chapter 8

The house was in foreclosure when Frank Madison died."
Jason tossed the report he'd just printed on Ellie's desk.
"I'm not a lawyer, but my understanding from about the
fifth person I was transferred to at the bank, was that it
threw a real monkey wrench into the process. Not only does
foreclosure take a while, the estate went into probate with
no will. Apparently the owner wasn't paying his mortgage
but records showed he owned some shares in a mining op-
eration up north."

She picked up her cup of coffee and took a sip before
she set it down with a grimace. "Wow, that's cold and dis-
gusting. So I guess now we know why the house wasn't up
for sale."

He nodded, sitting down in the chair by her desk. It was
a nice view. Today she wore a scarlet sweater over some sort
of silky white blouse and the vivid color suited her, setting
off her blond hair. *Back to business, dude.* "It gets better.

Frank was a grumpy asshole according to everyone, but the neighbors were right, there is a nephew. He's the one who came and took all the furniture, but the bank has been paying the taxes and electric bill so the pipes won't freeze and their soon-to-be property won't be ruined or put up for auction by the county. At the moment everyone is haggling over those mine shares and we've two lawsuits pending. Until a probate judge decides how it all is going to go, the house is just going to sit there."

Her brows lifted over her hazel eyes. "Can I ask the million-dollar question? Does the nephew have any idea who our victim might be?"

"Not a clue."

She sighed. "I was afraid you were going to say that. I wonder how the guy got keys."

He'd thought about that too. "If he couldn't pick one of the locks, he called a locksmith, I'd guess. Claimed he got locked out, and once he was in, he went and bought new locks and installed them himself. Instant keys and it isn't hard to do."

"We can work that angle, I suppose. His identity would be really helpful. I assume locksmiths keep records of addresses."

"I think our best bet is to find out how our victim discovered the house was empty."

"Could be as simple as accessing public records on legal proceedings."

Jason didn't agree. "I think he'd have to have known the old man had died and the bank couldn't finish the foreclosure until the estate was settled. That probably means he knew someone who knew Frank Madison."

"He was retired and reclusive according to every single one of our interviews. Worked for the railroad for forty years and he'd been retired for fifteen. His phone records show nothing unusual; he didn't even call the nephew, just a couple of old buddies, and it was disconnected months before he died, so we are going back quite a ways."

Jason idly picked up a pen and read the side. *Marriott Hotels*. Could be from her trip to Florida. "I would ask why a man who had resources had just stopped paying his bills, but maybe it was dementia. He was reclusive and didn't talk about himself, and a few years ago, sold his car."

With his own father it had been the booze, but his old man actually also had the money until he got fired for being drunk on the job, and just hadn't paid the mortgage. All Jason had inherited was the bill for the funeral. Why hadn't Madison cashed in those mining shares and solved his problems?

He could tell Ellie was thinking about it. She had a certain way of narrowing her eyes and tightening her mouth just a fraction. "I suppose," she said after a long moment, "our victim could be connected to the bank. I mean, if he was someone who was handling part of the protocol to foreclose, and found out Frank Madison died, he would know both. He'd also know that the house was going to be empty, but that the heat and lights would be on, not to mention the taxes were going to be paid so no one else would be sniffing around."

He argued, "But it breaks down when you ask yourself why someone who works at a bank has to commandeer an empty house."

Ellie didn't blink an eye. "It does, doesn't it? Let's go find out who might fit his profile."

Action was always more his thing than paperwork so she wasn't going to get an argument from him. However, just as he stood up with alacrity, her cell phone rang and it was easy to see her expression was immediately smoothed to neutrality.

He wasn't perfect, but he would normally at least give her the courtesy of walking away for the sake of her privacy. Because of the look on her face when she answered, he found it impossible.

"Bryce. Hi. How was the flight?"

A cool greeting, but maybe that was just his perception. Flight where?

It is none of your business.

He did move toward his desk then, because when it came down to it, he liked to think he was a decent human being. There were times in his past when that mattered so much it kept him off the streets, even when he'd been pretty low. Decent. If he could call himself nothing else, that had meant something.

By the time he'd grabbed his wallet and shoved it in his pocket and checked the battery on his cell, Ellie walked by and said pointedly, "Ready?"

"At all times," he answered smoothly and followed her out the door. At least it wasn't snowing this particular afternoon but the brightly shining sun was indicative of a high pressure system that held the Midwest in a vise grip of frigid temperatures. His breath went out in clouds as they crossed the parking lot and luckily she'd already pressed the automatic starter, so when they got into her car, it was warming up. He said, "This is kind of funny, but when a friend of mine moved down to Virginia from here, he had a plug to keep his battery warm because he came from Duluth, and one day his new neighbor asked him if he had an electric car. The guy was serious. I about died laughing when he told me that story."

Her smile was reluctant, but at least it happened. "It snows there too." She started the vehicle.

"Sure, it snows." He squinted at the brilliant sky. "But butt-cold is something entirely different."

"Can you not utter a single sentence without something crude in it?"

"Occasionally, but it takes some effort." He warily sensed she wanted an argument and wasn't sure if he wanted to be the man to have it with her at the moment. Ellie was usually pretty even and controlled, and he'd seen her manage under duress before. Right now she didn't seem to be managing.

He might be basically decent but he wasn't subtle. "Hey, something wrong in Shangri-la?"

She took a right turn a little too fast and the car skidded on the slick street. "I don't know. I don't live there."

Bryce hadn't told her exactly when he was leaving.

It was all semantics at the end of it. He'd *said* he was leaving, he'd been packing in bits and pieces, but she resented the freedom he had to get up and go, even if she was happy for him about the book deal.

Still . . .

He was gone.

And there was no way to ignore the brutal truth that it was, when it came down to it, her fault. Maybe part of it was payback for not telling him before her abrupt departure to Florida about her mother's diagnosis, but she hadn't been ready to talk about it. For that matter, she still really wasn't. It was frightening, especially with her father gone from a heart attack several years ago, and Bryce had two healthy whole parents, whom she liked very much, but that wasn't the point. Could he even begin to understand?

The main bank branch was a white building with a faux colonial front facing a busy street and there was a queue of customers when Ellie produced her badge and asked if she might speak to the branch manager.

"We're on a fishing trip," she said when she and Santiago were shown with alacrity to the man's office. "I guess what we really need is an idea if this type of inquiry could even help us. I assume you can answer that question."

Josh Hansen was surprisingly young, energetic, and immediately punched up the computer on his desk. "I can try and see who had access to the foreclosure. I'm sure you realize, Detective, it could be a broad base of people. There are those that process the paperwork on various levels and it is also filed in court on a civil litigation basis. Let me try to see who handled the paperwork on our end."

Efficient. She liked that. No wonder he'd been promoted so young.

"Can you get names of anyone who has accessed the files?"

"That might take some digging." He was busy, pushing keys. "I can get anyone who might be *able* to look through it though. Not the same thing."

"If it is one of your employees, he won't be showing up for work." Santiago remarked, "If an address near that neighborhood pops, I'd love to hear it."

"What happened?"

"Bad things." Santiago looked bland. "Really bad things. Can we just leave it there? We're homicide detectives. Doesn't that say it all?"

Josh—he looked like a Josh with his ingenuous face—nodded. "Sure. Okay. Do you need a court order for this? Am I breaking some sort of rule?"

Ellie shook her head. "We have to have a court order for specific records, but we're just looking for a lead. Point us in the right direction. If we need a judge's signature after that, we'll get one, of course. This is just one branch, and we get that, but can you let us know if we are even remotely looking in the right place? Could one person working for your company access the foreclosure and also know about the owner's death because he lived close by? That's what we want from you."

"A to B. Gotcha." He typed in a few more words and hit some keys. "I'm not positive what I'll come up with but I'll cross-reference the addresses and see if anything shows in our records."

Despite how cooperative he was, nothing did, and Ellie had thought it wasn't likely to pan out anyway. When he rose apologetically, she shook his hand. "Thanks for your efforts. Here's my card if you think of anything."

Back to square one.

Santiago didn't seem thrilled either as they walked out of the building. "Well, that was a bust."

"It would have been too easy," she commented. "And we both know nothing about what we do is easy."

"You'd think we'd catch a break now and then."

It wasn't like she disagreed. "We do, it's just disproportionate to how hard we have to work for it. So, all brilliant ideas welcome right now."

He was a distinct pain, but he was also fairly canny. He said concisely, "I want to look at that house again."

Ellie was totally on board. They needed to reconstruct that scene.

"I think we should."

He hunched his shoulders. "Why is it so fucking cold here, dammit?"

"Would you stop griping about it? It's Wisconsin in winter. You should have paid attention in school. The latitude is a dead giveaway it might get chilly in January."

"I wonder if Miami is hiring right now?"

"Then you'd be complaining about the heat."

"Nah, I'd just walk around in my Speedo."

"Oh lord," she said in amused disgust.

But at least he'd made her laugh, and she really, really needed it at the moment.

Two very dead men, no motive or suspect, and Bryce was gone. She wasn't having a good day. "What are we looking for we might have missed the first time?"

Santiago glanced across the snow-crusted street, his expression remote. "I sensed there was something *there,* you know? Maybe it was nothing, but on the other hand, it might have *been* something. I don't like it when I get these gut feelings."

She got them too, didn't like them any better, and declined to comment. "It can't hurt to look again."

"Our bank guy was right. We need to connect the dots somewhere and so far it's a no-go."

"Let's take a second look."

It wasn't too far, and she parked in the lot of the desolate abandoned school, figuring that if her tax dollars were at work keeping it plowed, then maybe they could reasonably use it as civil servants. The house across the street had that same abandoned aura, and when they gained the front porch, the bloodstains had turned black and did not improve the ambience.

Santiago walked around the perimeter, looking out the screens. "You can see this place only from a few houses. That's it. The answer isn't here, not in the front. The killer was safe and knew it."

It *was* damn cold. Ellie looked at the splatter pattern on the floor and tried to reconstruct it in her mind. "He turned his back. Does that mean he'd brought the killer here, or had he answered the door, stepped out, and then invited the person in?"

Her partner looked thoughtful. "He knew his killer. We haven't doubted that from the first minute. He knew his killer, and the killer understood this house would be a perfect place for a bloody murder."

"The parking lot at the university was not a perfect place at all," she argued, walking around, the floorboards creaking with cold and age under her measured steps. "This place might be relatively private, but the first murder was really taking a chance."

"This could be a deflection." Santiago adjusted his scarf around his neck, pulling it up over his chin, his blue eyes reflective. "Trying to throw us off. Maybe it goes back to our dead professor. That frickin' weird cross on the chest of each victim though . . . he *wants* us to notice him."

At that moment she caught it. A flicker of a movement across the street, so brief it was possible that she imagined it. Ellie went entirely still. It happened again then, a movement behind one of the windows.

She said, "I think you might be right about the neighbors. Let's go talk to whoever is in that abandoned building instead."

Chapter 9

The call for the extra appointment had been somewhat of a surprise. Georgia had thought Rachel might be one of those patients who tried therapy but then decided it was too difficult to open up. The sessions caused so much anxiety for some people, and they were relieved when they decided to never come back.

Apparently not in this case.

"I stood on the pier and thought about it," she said with a visible shiver. "The water was black and cold and a boat floated by like a ghost, dark and silent except for the low hum of the engine." She repeated, "But I thought about it."

"Jumping in?"

"Yes. The water, even the boat propeller. That would be fast, wouldn't it?"

This was at least an explanation of why she'd come in

the first place. All of Georgia's patients had a story, but not all of them understood it. "How often have you considered suicide?"

Rachel looked reflective. On this gray afternoon she wore a long dark skirt, short boots, and a beige sweater. Her hair was tied back with a simple band and there was not a trace of makeup on her face. "Maybe more than I know. It's there in the back of my mind all of the time. I'm not sure I understood that."

Not an unusual answer. Georgia reflected that now maybe she had an answer as to why Rachel had decided to see a therapist. She asked, "Why *didn't* you jump in?"

"Remember that date I canceled? He asked me again and this time I said yes. We went to dinner and then took a walk by the lake." Her smile was thin and humorless. "If I had jumped, he might have been stupid enough to try and rescue me."

"Tell me more about him. Did you enjoy yourself?"

Her patient obviously had anticipated the question as she didn't react in any way. "I was unprepared for the outcome of our evening." Then unexpectedly, she blurted out, "My roommate threw out my shoes. I found them in the trash."

The afternoon sun faced the evergreen hedge outside the window and the blinds were lowered for privacy but opened enough to allow some light in. There was nothing really to see out there but the parking lot, so Rachel's sudden preoccupation with the view was unwarranted. Her averted profile spoke volumes.

What outcome? Georgia almost asked but decided the change in subject was a not-so-subtle signal the question would be unwelcome, so she said instead, "Why would she throw out your shoes?"

"I don't know. I'm afraid to ask her."

There had been two choices.

Jason could have refused, expressing his personal preference of not going anywhere near that forsaken old school, but his childhood problems were not conducive to the investigation. He'd had to stay in detention fairly often—he'd never claimed to be an angel—but he could swear those cold empty hallways echoed with the pain of every lonely child that had sat at a desk when all the other students had gone home.

It had happened to him often enough.

His father, when he noticed at all that he was home late from school, had told him it served his sorry ass right, and maybe that was true.

He really didn't believe in ghosts—not at all. But there could be an essence, he thought as he tried the side door to find it chained from the inside, the slight give enough to provide an eddy of stale air through the crack. It smelled dead to him, like despair and frustration and emptiness . . .

Hold it, get a handle.

He wasn't ten years old any longer.

"You sure you saw something? There are no service vehicles in the lot." He followed her around the corner of the building. Sidearm or not, he wasn't enthusiastic about prowling deserted halls and empty classrooms in the gloom. Actually, he wasn't enthusiastic about it at all.

Unfortunately, her answer was full of conviction, the chill

breeze blowing a strand of hair across her cheek. "I'm sure. Someone was watching us. They probably heard or saw us pull in and park."

And it followed that if they were watching them, *maybe* they had seen something the night of the murder.

"There are steps down to a service entrance on each side." Ellie gestured toward steps leading down into a hole that was dark and no doubt cold and led to a lower level of the building. "Let's try that. All I want is an open door. Whoever is there got in somehow. It could be a caretaker of some sort moving around."

Jason had made a brief call to the chief with the address, but he hadn't heard back yet if someone was scheduled to be there. The lack of a vehicle besides Ellie's car didn't give him much hope they were going to get a positive response.

"They could be long gone." Jason shone the flashlight from his phone down the steps. At the bottom a metal door with peeling paint presented an unappetizing barrier. "There are a dozen exits to this place."

"But this one is swept clean. Where's the drifted snow?"

She was right. He saw the steps were clear. "Could be the angle of the wind," he argued even as he went down first, seeing several discarded cigarette butts in the corner. He crouched down. "But the wind doesn't smoke. Motherfuck. It could be innocent like you said, just the maintenance staff, but I can smell tobacco."

Ellie's face was somber, her hair pale in the darkness. "If I'd broken into this building, I'd have used this door. It is on the opposite side from the street and pretty hidden."

"It's covered. Maybe they are camping out here to get a break from the cold."

"In this weather?" Ellie was halfway down the steps and turned to him.

He jiggled the handle. "You think Milwaukee doesn't have homeless people?"

To his dismay, the door opened.

His lucky day. The only thing worse than those silent halls and rooms upstairs, he discovered, was the basement of an old empty school. Ellie pulled a pencil flashlight from the pocket of her coat and flicked her light over piles of old desks, folded cafeteria tables and chairs in stacks, broken ceilings tiles—no doubt asbestos from the age of the building, he thought darkly—broken shelving, and just about anything that obviously had no value any longer.

Something rustled in the corner. He did not want to know in the least what it was. He muttered, "This is some creepy shit."

"You're a homicide detective."

"So it must be *really* creepy shit," he said defensively.

"Stairs over here." Ellie headed toward the right corner of the room, unbuttoning her coat as she went, not because it wasn't cold, because it was, but so she had easy access to her weapon. Good call. He'd already unzipped his jacket and taken off his right glove.

The door at the top wasn't locked either and the hallway was almost as dark as it was below. The only illumination came through the doors on each end, and those had each been partially boarded up.

Jason felt his phone vibrate and he slipped it out of his pocket "Text."

Ellie echoed his low tone. "Metzger?"

He read it. "Yeah, no one is supposed to be in the building. Last check was scheduled two weeks ago. The city is still trying to sell it."

"Good luck to them. In this neighborhood . . . And what is up with that? Everyone just moves in, no rent required?"

Jason surveyed a row of rusting lockers. "I think I might sleep on a park bench instead. Let's go look, but my prediction is, whoever might be here has so many options to move around, it would take us hours to even search this place and all he'd have to do is slip past us, which would be dead easy in a building this size."

"I'm hoping for a witness to give us a clue as to the identity of the victim." She swung the beam in an arc across sagging ceilings. In one spot electrical wiring hung free about three feet above them. "Doesn't look like turning on the lights is an option. Maybe we should ask if a couple of uniforms could come help us search."

He could swear the place smelled of a million-plus cafeteria meals, most of which had apparently involved stewed tomatoes, coupled with the scent of mildew and disuse. "We can ask, but I've got to tell you, I'm not all that anxious to hang around a long time to wait for them to show up. I'll send the chief a message but let's get started. The sooner we are out of here, the better."

Ellie threw a curious glance over her shoulder. "You and I waded through waist-high grass full of snakes and who knows what else last summer, in the dark, after a ritualistic killer who burned his victims, and you weren't even fazed."

True enough, but he preferred a known quarry.

"Yeah, what a great idea that was. It seems to me I was shot twice that particular night." He pointed at the doorway to their left. "Let's start there."

. . .

The search was probably as fruitless as Santiago had pointed out it might be.

Every room had a closet for coats and supplies, the walk-in coolers in the kitchen had the massive doors off their hinges and were set aside, and the custodial closets were still locked.

He was right. This needed to be continued when they had more help. Ellie's slim flashlight was not going to be enough once it started to get truly dark and she could tell her partner was really jumpy.

Or maybe he *should* be more edgy than usual.

The place was a bit atmospheric with the gloom and the deserted air than she disliked as well, but if there was one thing she'd learned about Jason Santiago it was that he had a way to sense danger that seemed ingrained; she was still trying to figure that one out since he didn't talk about it much.

"Hold it."

"What?" she asked sharply, as his hand came out to block her forward movement.

He stopped and went still. "I hear something."

She caught it too, the sound of someone running at the back of the building and then the clear slam of a door. Santiago took off toward the reverberation, and from past experience she knew he could outdistance her, but Ellie followed, the shrouded hallways not helping, their footsteps ringing on the old tile.

Most of the doors would only open from a bar on the

inside unless a key was used from the outside. It was difficult to tell exactly where the person they were looking for might have left, or even if their quarry ducked into a classroom somewhere, and after a left turn by an auditorium, Santiago stopped, breathing audibly through his nose, and shook his head. "We can't do this. The acoustics in a building like this are all over the place. I think we need to get permission from the city to bring in some investigators, even if our guy is long gone, and really look it over. Either way you slice it, it's a gamble with our time and theirs."

He was right.

"Someone *is* trespassing."

"They are," he agreed, his face tight. "Surely the neighbors have noticed something."

They left the way they'd come in, and the dingy basement seemed even more sinister on the way out. It was impossible not to contemplate how easily a person could hide among the piles of furniture and various debris. If they could have skipped using the flashlight, that would have been better since it made them visible as a target, but one of them probably would break a leg tripping over some bit of debris in the dark. As it was, Santiago took it away from her at the bottom of the stairs in one of his masculine gestures that she supposed was his notion of gallantry. She found it annoying when it happened. Ellie would have argued when he jerked it from her hand, but had learned it was usually a futile exercise.

"I'll go first," he announced tersely.

"If you want to be the one to get shot at—again, I might add—be my guest."

His face was all planes and hollows by the meager illu-mination. "Maybe I just want the hell out of here more than you."

She actually thought that might be true, which was say-ing something because she wasn't enjoying herself much ei-ther. When they emerged, the sky was starting to go from azure to indigo, and as they went up the cement steps, the first thing they saw was a patrol car in the parking lot next to Ellie's vehicle. One of the officers, in earflaps and a heavy jacket, was writing down the license number.

Santiago flicked off the flashlight and handed it back. "Someone was paying attention. If they called in our car being here, maybe they saw whoever left. This could be just what we need."

She fully understood the flicker of excitement in his voice. The best part of any investigation was the possibility of that first break. Santiago said loudly as their shoes crunched the crisp snow in the parking lot and they approached the cruiser, "I'm just reaching in my coat for my badge. We're Milwaukee homicide."

The second officer had gotten out of the car when he caught sight of them. He nodded but his hand rested on his hip near his sidearm, and in this neighborhood she didn't really blame him.

"Detectives," said the one with the earflaps, after taking care of examining their credentials. "I've heard of you. Northwoods killer case. You mind telling us why you're here?" He was thick-shouldered and had the accent of a true Wisconsin native, his cheeks ruddy from the cold.

"Murdered man in that house right there a few days ago."

Ellie pointed across the street. "Mind telling us why you were checking out my car?"

The second cop was younger and slimmer, a red-head with an angular nose and sharp chin. "There's a gang of local kids that keep breaking into the school. We drive by now and then, just in case we can catch them at it. We had to wonder what someone might be doing parked here. This car doesn't exactly match the neighborhood."

"I think we may have crossed paths with those kids." Santiago briefly outlined what had happened.

"Sounds like them. They just hang out as far as we can tell, though there's some interesting graffiti on the walls. Short of burning it down, they can't hurt much as you probably saw. The school corporation took everything usable to the new elementary."

Ellie asked, "Any way we could get some names and talk to these kids? They were sure watching us across the street. Maybe they saw something that might give us a lead, if not on the day of the murder, at some other time. We think the victim might have done what they are doing and taken advantage of an empty house and moved in. We can't ID him and no one seems to know how he came to be there. He was robbed but we think it was to deflect us, because the murder sure seemed personal."

The thin cop nodded, his face grim. "We heard about it from the officers who responded to the initial call. I'm not ashamed to say I'm glad I wasn't on duty. I understand he was pretty slashed up."

There were certain sights she couldn't erase from her memory as well and he was right, that happened to be one

of them. "We've worked a few brutal cases and this qualifies."

"As for the names of the kids, we can ask some questions. So far we've just told them to get out and stay out
but it wasn't worth hauling anyone in. We have enough real
problems out there."

Santiago turned to her, his blue eyes intent. "How about
if we just leave a note?"

"A note?" It was impossible to look at him as if he wasn't
insane.

"On the door. Attach our cards and ask them to come
forward. Mention we don't give a shit about them getting
into the school, but they could be heroes if they had info
we need."

"Oh sure, they're going to call the police voluntarily."

The thickset officer said, "Hey, worth a try."

Chapter 10

Georgia stirred her coffee and carefully set aside the spoon on a napkin. She said, "You're particularly troubled why?"

Rachel was an interesting patient. This was her regular appointment and today she seemed much different. More confident and less subdued, with a hint of gloss on her lips. She wore a tailored blazer over a much shorter skirt and shiny pumps with an actual heel. Today was obviously not a dark, worn flats sort of mood. She worked at a local hospital, she'd explained on her initial visit, in something to do with administration.

"I'm having more trouble with my roommate. I might ask her to leave. I'm just not good at confrontation. Maybe you can help me."

Maybe, maybe not. She hadn't decided yet if Rachel was a cooperative patient.

"What has she done that bothers you besides the incident with the shoes?" Georgia could believe the confrontation part. Rachel was not the personality type to enjoy an argument.

"She borrows things and doesn't ask."

"Have you considered talking to her about it?"

Rachel lifted her head and stopped restlessly adjusting her skirt. "I *have* talked to her about it. Nothing has changed."

After taking a sip of coffee, Georgia asked, "How do you think she'll react if you suggest she moves out?"

It was true her roommate sounded like a compelling study, but Georgia was more interested in Rachel.

Her patient took a minute but answered slowly, "I'm not sure. I'm afraid to actually do it."

"Because she gets angry?"

Rachel nodded and her voice was barely a whisper when she responded, "She might be."

An easy guess. All along she'd had the sense that Rachel was being manipulated. "Outline to me why you think so and maybe add why you'd put up with it."

"I'm not very strong."

She could beg to differ. Georgia's opinion was that the woman sitting in the chair so demurely across from her desk had more inner strength than she gave herself credit for, but a lot of patients hid behind their insecurities.

"Let's talk about that. Do you believe you will actually ask her to go?"

Rachel took a moment, but then shook her head. "No. I don't want the argument."

"Why? If you are in the right and it is your apartment, maybe you need to stand up for yourself."

"I think she'll just say no."

Unsurprised, Georgia reflected that this roommate sounded like a classic bully in the sense that she simply plowed over Rachel most of the time, but she might be just as much a prisoner in one aspect of their relationship. "Why do you think she would do that?"

"I don't know, but it worries me."

"Worries you in what way? Do you think she threw away the shoes to deliberately hurt or annoy you?"

"Her winter coat is missing too. I peeked in the closet."

Another non answer. Georgia rethought and tried again. "Can you tell me how you feel about her?"

This time Rachel stood and walked across the office, but a lot of patients did that to avoid the face-to-face confession. She stopped at the window. "I hate her sometimes and yet I still like her . . . her companionship. Does that make sense?"

"Sense is what you make of it. You don't wish to be alone?"

"Who does?" Rachel asked it simply, and Georgia couldn't disagree, so she tried another tack.

"If you didn't live with her, what kind of person would you choose?"

Rachel wasn't unintelligent, just uncertain personally. Her smile was cynical. "You mean if I didn't have to settle for her as a roommate? I might choose someone who wasn't so selfish. She does not compromise, and I mean that, Dr. Lukens."

This was why Georgia was sure sexual conflict was in the mix. Lea somehow represented a strong figure to Rachel, and she needed it, but without the threat of an actual male. "You don't often talk about your relationships with men."

"No."

It was a very predictable answer. Georgia asked gently, "Keeping in mind you can tell me anything, why? You are an attractive young woman. Surely they approach you."

"I only go out with Lea and men love her." Rachel turned and smiled thinly. "I'm invisible when I'm with her, so your question is moot. I go along, they ask *her* out, and that is the end of it. I learned that a long time ago."

"What about your date a few days ago?"

"I already told you he was really interested in *her*. I'll never see him again."

"Are you interested in dating *other* men?"

"Or do I like women, you mean?" Rachel's laugh was dry. "I'm not a lesbian, if that's what you're asking."

"I admit I am trying to define your interaction with Lea. Love/hate relationships are seldom healthy."

Silence. Rachel appeared to be thinking it over and dipped her head in a mannerism Georgia was coming to know very well, so that a veil of hair obscured her face. Eventually, she said, "I shouldn't have said I hated her. I'm afraid for her, actually. She's larger than life in a way. Impulsive and promiscuous; she drinks too much, dresses in provocative clothing, and she seems to be getting more and more reckless. One day I am afraid she just isn't going to come home."

"And then you'll be alone." That was the problem, Georgia understood. She'd seen it too many times with both men and women who put up with abusive spouses or domineering parents, or even employers who took advantage of them; the fear of solitude overrode their resentment and anger.

Something is better than nothing.

Rachel looked up. "Yes."

"This symbiotic existence the two of you share, is she aware of it? Has it occurred to you that perhaps you represent security and discipline to her, much as a parent cares for a child?"

"Quite frankly, I have no idea what she is thinking most of the time. Or if she's even thinking at all. She just dumped her last boyfriend."

"And you liked him?"

Rachel considered before she answered but she usually did. "She distrusts men who are nice to her. I've actually tried to convince her to make an appointment with you but she just laughs at the idea of therapy."

"Does she laugh at you for coming to see me?"

"I think she's worried I talk about her."

The evasion was typical and Georgia thought maybe her patient was becoming uncomfortable, which was not her goal. Besides she *did* talk about her. "That's possible. Now then, when you were here last week, you said you had some exciting news coming your way."

The subject switched then to Rachel's job, how she expected a promotion soon from the glowing review she'd just gotten from her supervisor, her normally passive expression becoming animated. When the session was over, Georgia jotted down a few notes in her chart.

Patient shows classic signs of dependency and denial, focusing on her roommate's behavior rather than examining her own lack of self-esteem. Once again did not bring up her childhood or details of her current social life. No overt hostility, but a blatant avoidance of whatever is truly bothering her.

Very unlike her next patient, she thought as the light on her desk blinked, indicating someone was in the waiting room.

Jason hated grocery shopping. It was up there with laundry and cleaning the bathroom in his opinion. He'd finally hired a housekeeper to do both of the latter, mostly because he could afford it since he lived a simple life aside from his sometimes really interesting job, and his apartment was cheap. He did eat out quite a bit, bachelor style, but he got tired of it, hence this trip to the closest supermarket.

The deli had a line, so he skipped that in lieu of the produce aisle, reminding himself some vegetables would not be a bad idea, and french fries did not count. He picked up some leaf lettuce, tomatoes, shallots, and tossed in an avocado, then bought fresh shrimp. He had about one recipe he could pull off if he discounted burgers in a pan on the stove, and that was a decent shrimp salad thanks to eight months of being stationed in Hawaii at one point in his military career.

Then he took out his phone and reminded himself he was an idiot.

Confirmed fact.

She answered on the third ring, her voice as businesslike as ever. "MacIntosh."

"Yeah, I know who I'm calling," he said, further proving his lack of any good sense whatsoever. "Don't you even look at the caller ID number?"

"*You* are criticizing *me* for phone etiquette? You must be joking. What?"

"I was wondering if you wanted to talk about the case over dinner. With Grantham out of town and all."

It took a minute, but then she said carefully, "What makes you think he's out of town?"

"Jesus, MacIntosh, I'm a detective and I heard half of your conversation. A kindergarten kid would have picked up on the fact he's not in Milwaukee right now." Jason stepped back to let a young woman push her cart past him, nodding in response to her murmured thanks. "If you are busy, that's fine, I just wondered if maybe you . . . weren't. Busy, that is."

Oh yeah, very smooth right there.

Another pause. "Well, actually, I'm not and the case is bugging me too. Okay. Where?"

"My apartment."

"You're going to cook?" She sounded irritatingly amused.

"Sort of. You're not allergic to shellfish, right?"

"No."

"Seven thirty." He ended the call, forgetting to say good-bye, which was just par for the course, and then he went off in search of frozen garlic bread.

It wasn't like they'd never had dinner together before. Several times, in fact, when they'd worked their last case and went north because it looked like a killer had a hard-on for him, thanks to his friendship with a murdered beat cop.

So, just dinner. Nothing. A blip on the screen, maybe.

"Excuse me again."

Jason glanced up, chagrined when he realized he was standing in front of the freezer and the same dark-haired woman was trying to get through the aisle. He moved back. "Sorry."

"We seem to have the same shopping list."

She was actually very nice looking and he noticed her figure was on the rounded side—hey, any guy would. Breasts that weren't big but still could pass for voluptuous—he'd always found that a hilarious word, but it applied in this case—and she wore, in January no less, some kind of clingy sleeveless shirt that showed off her assets.

He didn't miss the flirtatious smile either.

Not a bad boost because he was kind of apprehensive about his "date" with MacIntosh, so he returned it, reminding himself that while women were interested often enough in his external appearance, it was the sarcastic attitude and internal baggage that turned them off.

He was working on it, but the progress was slow.

"So, what do you think?" He pointed at the case of different kinds of garlic bread. "Got a specific one I should pick? I'm kind of lost. I could maybe make my own, but—"

"Too much trouble. I'm with you." She had even teeth he noticed as the smile widened. "Why do you think I'm picking up the same thing? I like that one. Some of them get too dry."

Good tip. He took it, opening the glass door. "Thanks. Want one?"

"Absolutely. Bread and pasta are my downfall."

"I think you're doing pretty good." He deliberately let his gaze wander. Facetiously, he asked, "What else is on your list, since we seem to be shopping together."

Her eyes weren't a striking hazel but dark instead, and she gazed at him very directly. "Um, I don't know. I like to wing it. How about you?"

The slight sexual innuendo didn't escape him. Noncommittally, he said, "I've been known to take a chance now and then."

"You look like the type that might."

Did he? Jason wasn't quite sure how to respond. He had no problem with a woman coming on to him, but he kind of had a date. If it even could be called that. MacIntosh was coming over for dinner only so they could talk about the case. He'd enticed her with the promise of murder.

They were probably both nuts, along with every homicide detective he knew.

"I usually get in and out as fast as possible."

"Is that so?" Her brows were arched and lifted a fraction.

He was almost impossible to embarrass, but he felt a tinge of it at the moment. "I'm talking the grocery store. By the way, I'm Jason."

She laughed and took his offered hand. "Nice to meet you. Maybe we could have a drink sometime."

It was ironic, he thought as he paid for the groceries, her number in his pocket, how he was simply not interested. Maybe he was learning something about love after all.

Chapter 11

It was interesting to see he'd bothered to set the dining room table because she'd never seen it without stacks of mail and carelessly tossed magazines, none of which, she suspected, he ever read.

Santiago's apartment building always gave her a sense that she didn't understand people as much as she thought she did, because he lived in a complex that was designed for families. He'd once told her having laundry hookup in his apartment was what made him sign the lease, but Grasso had suggested maybe Jason Santiago just plain liked children.

Who would think? She loved children too, but living in a noisy building full of families seemed an odd choice for a bachelor who also happened to be a homicide detective.

Ellie set down the bottles of wine she'd stopped to pick up. "You asked about seafood so I brought a Pinot Grigio and a Pinot Noir."

Santiago just laughed. "Yeah, you think my area of expertise is pairing wine with food? Whatever you want to drink is fine with me. At the moment I'm drinking a light beer that I'm proud to say is made in the great state of Wisconsin, but costs about ten bucks a case. College students won't even touch it, but then again, it is an acquired taste and I acquired it at about age fifteen. Old habits die hard. Let me see if I can find you a glass."

His kitchen was small but efficient, and she'd always been surprised by how tidy his apartment was in general. Maybe it was his military background kicking in again, but while there might be some clutter, it was pretty clean at all times in her experience. He went to a cabinet above the stove and took out a glass that he inspected before he handed it to her. "Will this work?"

"It'll be fine. Corkscrew?"

It was strange she felt a little awkward. They spent most of every day together and yet this was a bit different—maybe a lot different.

But the vibe didn't feel weird, it just seemed like their private lives were colliding a little with their professional relationship. It was impossible to work with someone so closely and not at least get a sense of what might be going on under the surface, but then again, they usually didn't talk about it.

Santiago opened a drawer and handed her the item in question. "Little used since Kate left. I might even switch to wine myself if you swear to me it isn't that sweet crap."

"It isn't."

"Sounds good then. All I have left to do is toast the garlic bread."

He moved around the kitchen easily, as usual in worn jeans and tonight a dark gray button-up shirt. As with anything else, he always chose his clothes for functionality instead of style, but he somehow managed to pull it off fairly well. Plain and without pretense suited him. The man might be at home at a rock concert in the pouring rain, but wouldn't be caught dead at the symphony. He wasn't a renaissance man by any means, but he didn't want to be either.

Ellie poured two glasses of white wine, and leaned against the counter, sipping hers. "I take it the brilliant note idea has not yet panned out."

"Give it time." He slid the bread into the oven and frowned when he turned around. "Help me keep an eye on that. My success level is raw or burned. That edible middle ground still evades me. Want to go sit in the living room? The instructions say twenty minutes, but I think my oven might be possessed by the devil."

"And here I thought that was you," Ellie said with a laugh.

His spontaneous smile was surprisingly boyish and maybe even a little charming. Charming was definitely not his style. "Okay, yes, guilty as charged most of the time."

He chose a chair she guessed was where he often sat because it looked well-worn and faced the television. Ellie wasn't sure if she agreed with the now-absent Kate about the place being adolescent. She thought it just looked like an unattached male lived there in a comfortable way. Bryce's house was better decorated, but then again, he had an ex-wife with excellent taste, so he'd walked away with a sense of how to buy furniture.

That was an interesting question. She asked, "Did you and Kate ever talk about getting married?"

That certainly caught Santiago's attention. "Why the hell did you just ask me that? Are you and Grantham thinking about it?"

"No." She said it too hastily, so she amended, "No, to the extent we haven't discussed that topic. I was just wondering since you lived together, and that seems to be a natural progression, if the two of you had ever talked it over. Never mind."

"This is pretty good wine." He drank some, and then added, "We did a little. You know, at the end of the day, I was just too edgy for her. I really think she liked the idea of damaged goods in theory, but she didn't like the reality. I hope that isn't what happens when she goes into practice."

As they never discussed anything but their cases this was different, but it did seem wrong to hash over corpses and then sit down to eat. "Damaged goods seems kind of a harsh way to describe yourself."

"I'm no walk in the park." He grimaced, lounging in his chair, his wineglass dangling from his fingers. "I work all the time, the subject matter isn't pleasant when we would talk about my job, and I don't have a lot of other interests. Maybe I should take up gardening, but guess what, I don't have a place to do that, and I'd be fucking lousy at it anyway, so murder tends to be my topic of choice."

It was hers too. Ellie raised her wineglass. "So let's talk about it."

· · ·

Dinner had been pretty good.

Delicious, in fact. It was kind of hard to go wrong with fresh shrimp Louie, but he'd even nailed the garlic bread despite his temperamental oven.

Jason set aside his fork, picked up his napkin, and consciously removed his elbows from the table. "So this is what we have? The university. Maybe the bank. Maybe the neighborhood . . . you have to do better than that, Detective MacIntosh. That's a lot of maybes."

She wore a soft sweater patterned in blue and yellow, jeans that clung perfectly to her hips—not that he noticed—and she looked fantastic sitting across the table from him. Ellie lifted her shoulders. "We both know the basic facts. If you have some hidden information, fork it over."

While he wished they didn't have the same problem, he was just as puzzled. "I'm afraid I don't know sh—er, anything." He swore in front of her to annoy her, but he could behave himself now and then and it seemed like maybe he should this evening. Then he changed the subject. "Who in your family is sick? Mother, sister, or aunt?"

She gazed at him in consternation, and then answered her own question. "How did you . . . oh, you saw the pamphlets about breast cancer in my car."

"And you didn't seem like someone who went on a relaxing beach vacation. You also have a printed form for a request for family medical leave with the dates blank in the drawer of your desk. Not snooping. I was looking for a pen. Can't seem to hold onto any of mine." He held up the half-empty bottle. "More wine?"

"I'm driving. One glass is my limit. I should probably go anyway."

To his dismay when she brushed back her hair from her face, her hand was shaking and he could see the liquid sheen of tears in her eyes as she got to her feet and turned away.

"Whoa," he said, rising swiftly and going around the table without even thinking it over. "Ellie, Christ, I didn't mean to make you cry."

"I didn't mean to cry," she whispered, and a tear escaped and rolled down her cheek. "I haven't cried yet and it just . . . happened. Don't worry about it."

This was one hell of a time for Grantham to leave her all alone. Jason was tempted to say it, but stopped himself. There was nothing the man could do any more than there was anything Jason could do, but he could at least do this. Tentatively, he slid his arms around her and she didn't pull her weapon and shoot him on the spot, so that was a positive sign. He said, "The first shoulder you encounter is rent-free and could probably use a good rinsing anyway. Go for it."

To his surprise she did, and of course he stood there like an idiot with no idea what to say, his partner, who could face a mangled body without flinching and hunt down ruthless killers, quietly sobbing against his chest. He'd had some specific fantasies that involved her in his arms, but not under these circumstances.

As his quest for something sensitive to say was met with no success whatsoever, he decided silence might be best. In the end, gently withdrawing, she thanked him for dinner, accepted a tissue from the box he kept in the bathroom, put on her coat, and assured him the storm was past and she was fine to drive. He walked her down to her car and she looked thoughtful when she turned before she got in.

"We didn't really discuss the case much, but, you know, something strikes me."

It was typical Ellie MacIntosh, he thought, looking down at her still-damp face. Hardly tough as nails, he'd never thought that, but smart as hell. "I'm all ears. What's that?"

"I wonder if they were related. Think about it. We have a picture of the professor but no idea what the second man looked like before the attack, but still it seemed to me they were about the same height and weight and had similar coloring. Brothers? Cousins?"

It was an interesting theory. He groaned. "Please don't make me go see that bitch Mrs. Peterson again."

Chapter 12

Georgia had taken the day off to paint the bathroom and had the television on for company when she caught a phrase or two from the lead story.

Another slasher murder?

Riveted, she set aside her brush because she hated painting anyway, and watched the broadcast clip.

She knew what her two favorite homicide detectives would be doing this cold morning.

He'd learned about the third murder via a text message at around six in the morning. Jason rolled over and groaned, reaching for his phone on the nightstand. The table rattled as he groped for the device.

"We have another body. Face slashed."

Levering himself on his elbow, he'd read it again, trying to clear his brain of early morning fog.

Naked. Right. He always slept naked. Maybe it was all those years in the military without privacy. He'd gone to the bathroom in front of other people in about six different countries, and was glad to have them there to watch his back but it was a gift to be able to sleep as he wished, comfortable and in his own space.

Coffee. He really needed caffeine to come awake enough to process this. He pulled on boxers and jeans, went into the kitchen and started a pot, and from there called Ellie back. "What the hell?"

"Good morning to you too." She'd sounded half-asleep also. "All I know is we have another body. Metzger was very charming on the phone, much like you, and he wants us right on it. I just got out of the shower. Want me to pick you up?"

What he really wanted was to go back to bed. "It's still dark out. Don't these maniacs ever sleep?" He exhaled and rubbed his face. "Yes, fine. Give me about twenty minutes."

She'd pulled up right on time.

He was sipping coffee at the window and saw the arc of her lights in the parking lot below just as the radio announced it was four degrees below zero.

Well, shit.

He grabbed his parka, because it was definitely parka weather, and took the travel mug with him.

"Who found the body?" He asked as he slid into the car and groped for the seat belt one-handed, balancing his beverage. "What have we got?"

"Some nut who got up early to do some cross-country skiing found the victim." She wore a stocking cap that managed to be feminine and still practical, with little snowflakes along the border. "From what I understand he saw splotches of blood in the snow and left the trail to give it a look. Called it in just about an hour ago. The news picked it up as a breaking story after he called nine-one-one."

"Skiing? On a day like today? You've got to be shittin' me." Jason took another gulp of hot coffee. "It's barely light out now. How early does this guy get up?"

"Santiago, you need to visit northern Wisconsin some-time. Those people view cross-country skiing like a reli-gion. Temperature or time is not a consideration."

"Bunch of freaks," he muttered. "Just thinking about it practically throws me into a cold- induced coma."

"Cold-induced? Never heard of that, but I agree it isn't my first choice of exercise, or at least not predawn." Ellie flipped the signal to exit the parking lot, though no one else was stupid enough to be up yet, at least not where he lived. "Anyway, from what Metzger told me, it sounds pretty sim-ilar to our two other bodies. The face is supposedly unrec-ognizable."

"The cross wounds in the chest?"

Streetlight illumination slid across her face. "His coat was frozen to his chest with blood like the one on the porch so until the medical examiner can get him on the table, we won't know."

"Male, then?"

"Yes. Follows the pattern."

It sure did. He rubbed his forehead. "Okay . . . we know what? A male victim with a slashed face dumped miles from here? Not much."

Ellie frowned at the road, taking an exit toward the free-way. "The killing was maybe done days ago and no one saw anything as far as I know. Metzger basically just told me that we needed to get there ASAP. The body was dumped in the woods, and it looks like it was dragged off the road on a sled or something like that. It was pretty windy the other night and the tracks are drifted over in places. Right now the state police are handling the scene."

It took them nearly an hour and a GPS device to get there but finally they pulled up to a line of patrol vehicles with swirling lights on a county highway. Jason wasn't really familiar with the area, but they were just there anyway to see if this victim might be part of their investigation. Jurisdiction issues would probably be a problem, but at the moment, linking the cases was top priority.

He stepped out into about a foot of an angular snowbank, sank in up to his calf, caught the cold blast of frigid air to the face, and flipped up his collar. Trees stood with snow-coated branches in a thick stand up to the edge of the winding road. A uniformed officer immediately walked over with a questioning look on his face.

"Milwaukee PD," Jason said shortly, his breath making puffs in the arctic cold. The sun was just starting to come up, the light struggling through the trees. "We aren't any happier to be here than you are."

"Right. I've been standing out here for quite a while. I can't feel my fingers." The trooper pointed toward the woods. "In this weather I can truly refer to the victim as a stiff. It isn't, by the way, a sight for the faint of heart, so I've warned you."

"If he's one of ours, I believe you." Jason's eyes were watering already from the cold. "And we've seen it."

"The skier lost his lunch, so to speak. Can't blame the guy."

Shoulders hunched, Ellie just walked past him, headed that direction. Jason followed, but he had to admit his level of enthusiasm was pretty low. For obvious reasons, this part of any investigation was his least favorite.

The body *was* pretty bad. He wasn't squeamish but this thing about utterly destroying the face might just give him nightmares.

There was ice crusted over the missing features and lacerated flesh, giving the wounds an opaque look, but they were still visible and disturbing. The victim was on his side, his hair matted with dark, congealed blood, and in contrast to their last grisly find, wore an expensive leather jacket.

"Let me guess, empty pockets?" Jason knelt down and reached with a gloved hand for the man's coat.

"No ID." An older man who had been introduced as the coroner said the words briskly, hands deep in the pockets of his long dark coat. "He didn't die here either. It happened somewhere else. I'd say between the time of death and when he was dropped off, not too long. He must have been wrapped up in something, bled all over that, and that's why we have blood here at the scene, but there's no splatter pattern I can see. It could be under the drifted snow though. It will help considerably when your medical examiner tried to give you an approximate time of death. I think that's going to be a challenge."

"So he could have been killed in Milwaukee?"

The coroner looked at Ellie with troubled eyes. "I suppose it is possible. Depending on what part of the city you are headed to, it can take less than an hour from around here."

Here was Jefferson County, sandwiched between Milwaukee and Madison. Did it mean something to the killer, Jason wondered as he squatted by the body, his eyes watering a little from the cold. Or was it just convenient? It could be their first real clue, or it could mean not a damn thing.

Ellie said in a businesslike tone, "I hate to tell you, but this looks familiar. Let's treat this as our case. Would everyone mind stepping back?"

Ellie had commandeered the investigation, but it was a justifiable conclusion. One look at the dead man told her this was the same killer.

The skier had hung around, which was nice of him since he'd given a statement already, but he didn't have much to add except for the name of the man who owned the farm and woods and had told him he could ski through the pasture if he wanted as long as he didn't spook the cattle, but in this weather, they preferred the barn, so it wasn't an issue. Ellie talked to him briefly, came to the conclusion he was just an unlucky passerby, and told him to go home and get warm.

The morning didn't get better.

She stood there, the wind whipping at her coat, chilled through, and it wasn't just the temperature. She'd knelt in the snow by the body and her jeans were wet, probably with both blood and melting snow. A crime scene team had finally arrived and at least she and Santiago weren't the ones digging through the drifts.

There was an inner feeling the murders were becoming more personal. Something big was going on . . . this was not a usual case. "Two significant things," she pointed out to Santiago as the body was zipped into a bag. "It bothers me once again that there isn't much attempt to hide the bodies. I don't think these are well-planned crimes. It isn't that the killer isn't smart, just disorganized. Lucky so far, but that rarely lasts long."

He swiped snow off his knees. "Unlucky describes those who have met up with him. I'm kind of hoping not to until the day we arrest his ass. What's the second thing?"

Her gloves were not doing the trick, probably due to the wind chill. Ellie wriggled her fingers to keep the circulation going. "More and more I am convinced the mutilation is personal, not just to keep us from identification. It's too savage to be deliberate."

"He loses control. I agree. Starts slashing and can't stop." Neither one of them wanted to talk about what had been done to the victim's eyes. Santiago squinted at the sky. "I haven't watched the weather in three days. We got some sort of system coming in?"

"A clipper from Canada," she confirmed. "You spend too much time on ESPN."

"You are entitled to your opinion. I think we're done here."

Neither of them mentioned the night before.

"Find out which deputy is going to escort the body, okay? I'll start the car."

She was cold to the bone as she slid in and turned the key, her hands shaking. They were in for some pretty typical January weather, but with lower than usual temperatures there was enough snow on the ground to blow around some. Not a huge event, but it didn't help when investigating a case in a rural area.

This was more her comfort zone. She was used to the woods, the terrain wasn't rough, but at least private enough that someone covered in blood—and they had to be, just like the other cases—felt they could come to this spot and dump off a body. She'd also been calculating since the minute they arrived how many cars came along this road.

Not many in the morning and even fewer if it had happened at night. Maybe five cars had passed by.

They *did* now know something about the killer.

When her partner opened the door and dropped into his seat, she said without preamble, "He's from right around here. I'd say he lives in the city now, but knows this area."

"Can you be more specific?"

"Our perp."

He buckled his seat belt. "Did he send you his former address or anything? If so, I missed that exchange of information."

She looked out the window. There was a line of trees and barren fields beyond, the snow in ashen waves of white and dirt, and in the distance a dairy farm. The frozen stream and bits of fallen branches on the road were indicative of a fairway the county didn't pay a lot of attention to, and she didn't believe for a minute this was just a lucky find.

"I'm not usually a big believer in coincidence." She adjusted the thermostat to high, since she was still pretty cold. The windshield was speckled with frosty stars and the tires made a keening noise as they pulled away.

"I can't say I am either." Slowly he added, "Local boy that

knew the spot? It's possible he just lucked into it, but I'm not thinking it was how it went down. That body could have started rotting away this spring before it was discovered."

"There's a pleasant thought."

He shot her a sardonic sidelong look. "If you expected this job to be pleasant, maybe you should work at a cosmetics counter in a department store instead, spritzing middle-aged women with perfume."

"Middle-aged men could probably use it more." There was a narrow bridge clearly iced over and she fishtailed a little on the black ice on the opposite side, glad she'd slowed down.

"Well, we agree on one thing then. Still, it must be good to know you have a career waiting for you if this one fails. All right, how about decomposing? Putrefying? Better words? Still means the same thing."

God, he could be annoying. What had been surprising was that the evening before he'd been on his best behavior. That had been a very strange dinner, all in all. In the natural course of doing their job they'd eaten together often enough, usually grabbing something on the go, but he'd gone to some trouble. He'd even tuned the obnoxiously big television in his living room to a soft classical station, and when she'd broken down—she still couldn't decide if she was relieved or mortified—he'd been very nice about it.

She was trying to figure out if it might have been a . . . *date*.

This morning, he was back to his usual irritating self anyway.

"So you think he knows the area?" she asked, pulling onto the snow-covered road.

"He might. I'm bugged by a few things."

"Like?"

Ellie really was interested in the answer. If there was one thing she could say about her somewhat brash partner, he rarely failed to surprise her. The way he operated was on a different level.

He never wore a hat, which was stupid in Wisconsin in the winter, so his hair was already starting to curl wildly because it was damp as the car warmed and the snow melted. His nose was pink from the cold and his gaze focused on the road ahead as he thought over the answer. "I think we are missing something small. Like double-stupid small. A nuance that would steer us the right way. I was going to speculate that the crimes were sexually motivated, but nothing in the autopsies of the first two victims indicated that and I doubt this one will either."

History showed that homosexual serial killers were just as deadly as the ones that preyed on women. She'd thought of it too. "I'm starting to think we'll never know who victim two is, but when someone reports this new guy missing, we could have a link."

"We sure need one."

"Double-stupid small?" She couldn't help but smother a laugh. "Where did you hear that one?"

"Hey, it's a saying from where I come from." Santiago grimaced. "Okay, I made it up, but it applies here. Think about it. We're really missing something."

The bleak landscape, stripped by winter, rolled by. She couldn't help but agree. "I think we are too."

Chapter 13

The symphony had been a mixed bag. Georgia had season tickets because it was one of the few things she did for herself. Once upon a time she'd considered a future as a concert violinist, but in truth, she had proven only adequate rather than brilliant, and the world of music required the latter. Yes, she could have taught with the passion of one who understood measure and bass and treble clef, meter and so forth, but genius performance required more.

It was undefinable.

It was something she'd been told, very gently to his credit, by a professor her first semester when she'd entered college as a music major. Very good could gain a position with a major orchestra with some luck, but she needed to evaluate what she wanted from a career in the arts.

All along she'd known it. The passion was there, but the natural talent was not. It didn't matter that she immersed

herself in the craft, knew the notes, practiced religiously . . .
brilliance was absent.

That was when she'd switched her major to psychology.
It was a logical transition to wonder what had prompted
her to pursue what she'd already realized was an impossible
dream. How fascinating to delude and deny even with the
reality right in front of her. It set her on an entirely different
path.

Good decision. She was far better at listening and offering what guidance she could than she was at performing a
concerto. Oh, she still longed for the latter, and played often, but it was not her true medium and it was a triumph
to acknowledge it and move on. Though she'd gone to her
dorm room and cried until she fell into an exhausted sleep
that afternoon, the honest professor had done her a profound favor.

Her companion took her elbow as they walked out the
doors with the exiting crowd. "Have a drink with me to
round out the evening?"

She liked Grant Rosenthal well enough, but even more,
she respected his academic background and credentials. His
interest was romantic—she got that loud and clear—hers
was more of colleague to colleague, but there could be potential for more. She wasn't going to rule it out, anyway.
He was graying around the temples but still fit the term
distinguished since he was a good fifteen years older.

The place he chose was a quiet martini bar with an elegant atmosphere and glass tables, comfortable leather chairs
completing the décor. Black walls held framed pieces of art
featuring vivid flowers.

"I'm not really fond of Gustav Mahler's style, but otherwise I thought the Albinoni and especially the piece by Jennifer Higdon were exquisite."

"An eclectic selection, I agree, but beautifully played. Thanks for coming with me." Georgia had ordered a cosmopolitan and it arrived in a frosted glass with a blue rim. She fingered the stem for a moment and then said, "However, I have an ulterior motive. I want to confer about one of my patients. I need some insight."

It wasn't like she didn't feel qualified to make an educated analysis, but it never hurt to ask for another opinion. He was well respected to say the least, and had more experience in general.

Grant smiled. So far, although she'd provided the symphony tickets, he'd paid for dinner, the cab, and now the drinks. They were still just colleagues enjoying an evening out.

His smile was affable. "Talking shop is fine." There was soft jazz playing in the background. "I'll help if I can."

He would. That was why she'd called him. She had no trouble going out by herself. Digging up another ticket had taken some time and she'd gone through the effort for a reason. "I have a patient that bothers me. You have waxed eloquent in your various published articles on how ignoring the inner voice is a mistake, and it isn't one I want to make. Can I get your take on it?"

"I'm reeling that anyone I know uses the phrase 'waxed eloquent,' Dr. Lukens, but please . . . ask away."

"Everyone you know uses that phrase. I've met a lot of them," she said dryly. "They listen to Scarlatti and drink

Grey Goose just like we are now. I have asked myself how many are really trying to help people, or how many just want to think they are."

"I don't think that's Scarlatti. More like Joplin." He pretended to contemplate his glass. "For that matter, I'm not sure this is Grey Goose but I get less picky as the evening goes on. What's the question?"

There was no question he was too old for her in some ways, and no question she liked his sense of humor. Georgia weighed her response. She took in a breath. "All right, I have a patient that seems to be in a relationship—not sexual—that is unlike anything I've really encountered before. It is fascinating in some ways, but disturbing in others. My initial diagnosis would be to call them both fairly socially dysfunctional and leave it alone, but they play extraordinarily well off each other and together achieve an odd balance. Both are women but quite different and the love/hate part of it is what drives their dynamic."

"I don't know the details but have encountered something similar before. Mothers and daughters in some cases, siblings; look at every case of domestic violence. Why are you worried?"

"I'm not worried."

He folded his arms on the table and looked at her intently. "Yes, you are, Dr. Lukens. Let's talk about why."

He was right. Rachel had seemed disturbed their past few sessions and fragile enough emotionally to begin with, so yes, she was concerned.

A martini bar seemed the perfect location to have this discussion.

There was a neon bear dropping a neon olive into a neon

glass above the bar. Georgia considered it and then explained. "You are a more experienced therapist than I am so I know you'll understand when I say that there's a secret this patient is keeping, not just from me, but maybe from herself."

"More experienced? What a very polite way to point out I'm somewhat older."

She looked at him directly. "Does that bother you?"

"You must be joking. Go on about this patient." He looked amused.

Good, they had that out of the way. She'd been wondering if they were ever, after several dates, going to say anything on the subject of their disparate ages. "On the surface she seems very composed and reasonable and I am not positive she remembers this secret. I've considered suggesting hypnosis, but I am not sure she isn't better off without the memory. Right now, she has a good job, which she seems to like, a nice apartment, and other than her uneasy relationship with her roommate, seems to be happy enough. She doesn't really date, or so she says, but she has not mentioned any problems with her male colleagues at work. My opinion would be she's ambivalent about her lack of a social life."

"Some people are, I agree. I take it you think she wants to remember, but is afraid of it. As her physician, so are you of that memory surfacing. If you encourage it, and it backfires, you might have done more harm than good." He pondered for a moment. "Do you think she'd agree to hypnosis?"

A waitress whisked by in a short black skirt with a tray of sparkling drinks for a table by the window facing the street, the patrons, from the way they were dressed, also part of the symphony crowd. Georgia answered the question. "I'm going to speculate one of two things would happen. She'd be completely puzzled as to why I would suggest it, or she'd quit therapy."

"I'm only a moderate believer in hypnosis myself and I think this patient needs to keep seeing you," Grant said decisively. "If you bring up the topic, you could do more harm than good if she stops her sessions and that is not what we strive for in our care. If this was my call, I would leave well enough alone and just give her someone to talk to openly."

She picked up her drink. "I think that is probably very good advice."

But she added, "I think she's dangerous and I haven't the slightest bit of proof."

The third murder set the news on fire, which wasn't really a surprise. In a lazy sprawl on his couch, Jason watched as a reporter stood on the perimeter of the woods where the latest body had been found and wondered just who had leaked the sensational details about the slashed face. He knew it wasn't Ellie; she didn't play the media game at all. If he had to guess, the source was someone on the crime scene team and Metzger was going to be pissed, but in truth, it didn't matter much to the case except the frustration of having exactly zero in the lead department.

Like zero degrees Kelvin leads.

That was, translated, negative 273.15 on the Celsius scale. The temperature where everything seizes up and stops moving.

They truly had nothing. The pattern was random, the

murders seemingly unconnected, and no one knew anything about the killer.

He stared at the television, watching only absently. He didn't share his partner's faith that the wooded area in Jefferson County meant a damn thing. It could, but—

His cell beeped. MacIntosh, no doubt, furious about the leak and watching the broadcast, except it *could* help them. He didn't even look at the screen before he answered. "I know, it's a piss off, but look at it this way, it might raise some flags."

Deadpan silence, and then someone said, "Hey, maybe I have the wrong number. I'm looking for a guy named Jason Santiago. Old-school, you know? He left this number."

Young voice. Like a barely there baritone with a potential for a bass in his future but that was a few years down the road. Jason sat up and endeavored for smooth calm despite his flicker of excitement. "Yeah, dude, you got him. Sorry, thought you were someone else."

"You're the cop?"

"Homicide detective." No use not to try and impress if he could. "I appreciate you calling. I take it you got my note and know what I want."

"We got it."

Score. Ellie was going to have to give in that he'd been right on this one. "You have some information for me?"

"Is there a reward?"

He wasn't surprised by the question. He'd met kids like this a hundred times. Hell, he'd been one what felt like centuries ago. "Yep. You get to do the right thing. We don't even know who the guy living across the street who was murdered was, so his family, if he had one, doesn't know he's dead. Law enforcement is supported by people like you and me. If you want to give yourself a dollar, go ahead. Just tell me what you got. What is it going to cost you unless maybe *you* killed him?"

"I didn't do shit."

"The neighborhood could be a little safer for you all to run around if you just speak up. Watch the news. It is an unsafe world out there with the guy hacking people up around."

The call ended abruptly.

He wasn't surprised. Ellie answered on the second ring when he punched in her number. "MacIntosh."

"Tossing out a line wasn't a bad idea. I just got a call."

"From?"

"If I had to call it, one of the kids breaking into the school. He knew my name but he didn't offer up his."

"What did he say?"

He told her and she sounded disappointed. "So it isn't a lead."

Jason knew she was smart, but they'd had an entirely different upbringing. Propping his feet on the coffee table, he said with utter confidence, "He's going to think about it and call back. I used to run the streets but I wasn't a bad kid. I kind of considered myself a rebel, and maybe that applied at the time, but I never lost my sense of right and wrong. That's where it breaks down. I knew kids that would have used the note for toilet paper. Those are the ones you worry about eventually getting letters in prison, but this wasn't one of them. My gut says we'll hear from him again eventually."

"You eat microwave burritos. Are you sure that isn't just indigestion?"

"He bothered, Ellie."

Her tone lost some of its brisk edge. "I get that, but we need something solid."

"The autopsy results might help us and fingers crossed we get a missing person report on our guy from the woods. He was pretty expensively dressed."

"But no wedding ring."

"Unless our killer took it."

"He didn't with the first victim."

She had a point.

"No, but our guy is getting better at it."

Chapter 14

Lea has a degree in anthropology but she doesn't use it." Rachel looked introspective. "She's taking night classes to get her master's. I'm not sure what she thinks she will do with it. Hopefully get a raise so she can buy a new car. Hers has some stains she can't quite get out on the carpet."

Her patient's tendency to share trivial information not pertinent to her own life was an avoidance tactic but Georgia wasn't sure strong-arm therapy would work with someone like Rachel, especially since she admitted to being at least borderline suicidal. She tried a gentle nudge. "You don't complain about your job and yet most people do. You must like it."

Rachel brightened. "I do. I just had my review. It went well. Lea kept telling me I was being stupid for wasting my time worrying about it, and it turned out, she was right."

"Do you socialize with the people you work with often?"

"Not often, no."

That was not surprising. "What do you do for fun, Rachel?"

"Hmm. I listen to music. In the summer sometimes I go to the lake cabin my family has north of here."

"Alone?" She was really interested in the answer.

Rachel shook her head. "No, my whole family has a get-together over the Fourth. My mother insists I go."

"You don't talk about your family very much." Georgia had in her notes that perhaps there had been childhood sexual abuse, but Rachel had not said anything yet to indicate that was the source of her anxiety and general introversion.

"They're . . . nice. I get along with them all pretty well if that is what you're asking."

"You have admitted to considering taking your own life. Don't you think that we should work together to discover why and maybe find a way to help you deal with the issue that makes you feel this way?"

"Discover why?" Rachel's face was entirely expressionless. "I already know why."

"We have a repeat of the methodology, and the tox screen came back the same."

Ellie wasn't surprised. One look at what was left of the last victim's face was so similar to the portraits of the other two, and unfortunately, that didn't help them much. "Stab wounds to the chest?"

All three crime scenes had been a less than pleasant experience.

The ME nodded, walking around the table, pointing with forceps. "You almost can't see them because it was so cold outside and done postmortem, but they are there. You have a cross pattern again. I am not a detective except in a medical sense, but if asked, I'd say the same person is responsible for this latest addition to our morgue's lovely collection. To be kind, the killer zipped the coat back up, probably to keep the deceased from feeling the cold. Some people are so nice."

"The coats on all three victims have been fastened back up." Santiago looked queasy but she already knew he disliked the morgue. Today he wore a white shirt under his dark blue jacket and his face was pretty much the same pale hue. "That probably means something, but this frickin' guy is off the charts. We all done here?"

"Just get Santiago out of here." Dr. Hammet's voice was dry as she looked at Ellie. "This place makes your partner so uncomfortable *I* start looking over my shoulder for dancing corpses."

"Normally, that would insult my manhood, but not now. And could you please never say dancing corpses in front of me again?" The man in question was halfway to the door. "Thanks, Doctor, we'll be in touch after the written report arrives."

Ellie followed, going up the cold staircase behind him. He didn't like elevators, but neither did she. "You didn't call her 'Doc.' Hammet was in shock."

"She hates being called 'Doc.' "

"But yet you usually do it anyway to annoy her. The light dawns. Do we have an agenda I am unaware of?"

He held up his phone. "I'm extremely popular it seems. Two calls. One from our resident upstanding citizen and drug-dealer informant and one from our young note-reader. Both are potential mother lodes, or could just be fool's gold."

"This is not an old western, Santiago."

"Hell, no, it isn't." He shoved open the door at the top. "In those they didn't put their phones on vibrate in the morgue. Want to hold on a second while I answer both messages?"

When she checked her phone, she saw she also had a few messages, one from the front desk, which was expedient since she was right there.

The other was from Bryce.

"I've got a couple to answer too." She murmured the words.

Santiago was already punching in a message with the swiftness of someone who did it often, but he glanced up and got her expression dead-on. "Lover boy? Did Ken call Barbie?"

"Shut up." She moved away for privacy, or at least relative privacy because the hall was fairly busy. She called back, but got voice mail, and left a message: *Sorry, in the morgue when you called. I'll be in touch later.*

No use sugarcoating her job. It wasn't like he wasn't well aware.

She walked over to the front desk then, leaned her elbows on the surface, and said, "Hi, Joan. If I kill my partner here in the hallway, will you report it or do me a favor and look the other way?"

Joan, who was about sixty and had a coil of gray hair at her nape and glasses too big for her thin face, answered without a blink. "No report if you agree to cover it up when

I murder my husband, who has just retired and is home all day. Every single damn day."

"Did someone say cover-up? I'm your man," Santiago drawled, walking up.

That was fast.

"Don't I wish you were mine, Detective." Joan gave him a wink. "I texted you both because you have a date with the governor and Metzger asked me to give you the details and time. Aren't you fancy."

He grimaced. "Not hardly. I think you've met me a time or two. When?"

"Saturday night. You have hotel reservations and transportation, all arranged courtesy of the fine state of Wisconsin."

Santiago looked at Ellie with his signature smartass smile, propping an arm carelessly on the counter. "You'd better hope we got a king-sized bed. I'm kind of a restless sleeper. Word has it I snore too, but I've never believed that. Now you can put that nasty rumor to rest."

Ellie muttered, "I know you *think* you're funny."

Joan offered up a piece of paper. "Sorry cowboy, separate rooms. The state is cheap, but apparently not that cheap. It's a bummer, I know. There's a cocktail reception before dinner, and the chief suggests you get a haircut before you two leave for Madison and he isn't talking about Detective MacIntosh."

He took the itinerary. "I've been meaning to, but I keep forgetting."

"I personally like the lead-singer-in-a-rock-band look, but the chief can be picky. Did you know that our governor's

mansion is one of only a handful of states that is not actually located in the capital? It's actually in Maple Bluff right
on Lake Mendota."

"Aren't you a font of interesting trivia. Tell me more."

"Let me know when the two of you are done flirting, will
you?" Ellie said mildly. "I have three homicides to solve that
are getting more high profile all the time, and a pile of paperwork on my desk. Thanks for the information, Joan."

"She's just jealous," Santiago said in a theatrically lowered voice as Ellie started to walk away, before he caught
up in two long strides. "Hey, I texted the kid back and said
for him to meet us at the deserted school. Our drug informant apparently is not answering his phone, but give him
a break, selling drugs illegally is a time-consuming business."

All along she'd thought getting a lead on who was buying rufilin off the street and connecting it to the crimes was
not going to pan out anyway, but the kid—that was a different story. That could mean something. "When?" she
asked.

At least this time they didn't have to go inside.

Jason got out of the car. The predicted clipper had brought
not only colder temperatures, but it was snowing. Again.

The school looked more dreary and broken down than
ever. There were two bikes propped against the flagpole,
one on either side, and he had to think with some amusement that only in Milwaukee, well, maybe Minneapolis or
Fargo, would kids ride bikes on the streets in this weather.
Duluth—it got shit-cold there—and Chicago—anyway, he'd

ridden his bike all winter long too. He'd never liked the school bus and it was cold riding your bike, but not as cold as walking. At least it went faster.

The first crime he'd ever solved was when his bike was stolen.

God, he'd been pissed. The kid that had taken it had never stood a chance. Jason got suspended for fighting, but he also retrieved his bike, so voted the entire episode worth it. He'd mowed a lot of lawns to save up for that bicycle.

"I'm guessing the stairwell of the entrance we used," he told Ellie, who was wearing the little snowflake cap again. "At least it offers some shelter and privacy."

"Tell them to come around to the front." She refused to budge. "I'm distrustful of going down into that well with anyone I don't know, even if we both have weapons."

"Not a bad call." He reached for his phone and made a call and minutes later two boys—he'd guess twelve or thirteen—came around the corner. They looked scared underneath a definite swagger, and Jason also remembered being *that* kid.

One was fairly tall, but still obviously young, and the other one was short and pudgy, but there was every chance from the width of his shoulders he might grow out of it.

"MacIntosh, let me do the talking, okay?" Jason said it pleasantly as the two of them skirted the sidewalk. "Pretty blondes rattle boys their age, so just don't say a word. Hey." He held up his badge briefly. "It's damn cold out here so we'll keep it fast and you can get home." He lifted his chin briefly. "We appreciate you calling in. How can you help us?"

"Dead guy across the street." The pudgy one wore a dark

blue parka and a gray skullcap and might have been trying
to grow a mustache but wasn't old enough yet for success.
"We can tell you exactly when he bought it."

"Bought what? The house?"

"No. Like . . . died."

"Oh. *Bought it.* This isn't a cop show, this is real-world
stuff and we need for you to say exactly what you mean
instead of what you think are cool phrases, okay? So you
saw him being killed?"

God, that would be the ultimate break . . .

"No. but we might have heard it."

Jason glanced at the two bicycles and remembered what
it was like to be that age. Long summer nights, sidewalks,
mud football . . .

"Okay, go ahead. You heard something that bugged you,
right? Like what?"

"Screaming. It came from that house, or that's how it
seemed." He pointed across the street. "We were just coming out of the school." He looked wary over that admission.

The other one added, "It didn't last very long and we
didn't see anything, but it was, you know, kind of freaky
so we took off down the block."

"The police didn't occur to you?" Ellie evidently couldn't
help that question, her hands stuffed into her pockets.
"Someone screaming? Maybe call the police?"

Both the boys looked at her as if she'd lost her mind,
which he could have predicted. Jason asked smoothly instead, "Can you give us a time and a day? That would help
a lot."

True enough. Forensics hadn't been able to pin time of

death down with any conviction because of the temperatures so they still only had a vague time frame.

"It was a Friday." The tall one said it positively. "I go to my dad's on Saturdays and I remember thinking about telling him. But he's, like, ex-military, and would probably kick my ass for the breaking into the school thing."

Okay, they had a time frame. Excellent. The body wasn't found until Monday.

This *was* gold.

"So after school then? Was it dark out?" Ellie asked.

They both frowned. "Kinda dark," the pudgy kid said. "The old lady, the one that walks her dog all the time, had her front porch light on already."

"Did you realize someone lived in that house? Had you seen him?" Jason did his best to keep the urgency out of his voice. He didn't want to spook them or have them make something up just for the attention.

"Didn't think about it." The boy shrugged. "Lots of people that live around here stay inside most of the time or work all day. That's why we hang around here so much."

Jason could get that. For instance, riding your bike was sure easier if there wasn't much traffic so this quiet street was perfect. "Was there a car parked on the street out front?"

"Most people park off the alley out back."

They'd discovered that during the initial visit to the scene, and the neighborhood was within reasonable walking distance of public transit. Considering the general lack of affluence, he suspected a lot of people opted to not even own a car. "Which means you might remember it even more," he urged, glad he'd worn his heavier parka for this outside discussion. The wind was really picking up.

The tall kid wiped his nose with the back of his hand and brightened. "Hey, there was a really nice car parked in front of that house, not that night but a few days before. I remember thinkin' it was kind of out of place."

"Can you tell us what kind?"

"Black."

Not helpful. The days of boys their age being car crazy seemed to be over. Now it was video games and surfing the Net. Jason still mourned his vintage Mustang. He inquired patiently, "Four doors or two? Expensive old-person sedan or an SUV?"

"Um . . . okay, lemme think. Four. Pretty sure. Hey man, I just noticed it, you know."

They were getting restless, and probably cold, and that really was the sum total of what they knew, so Jason said, "Okay, thanks for calling and meeting with us. We owe you one. Stay out of trouble."

"Just one more question," Ellie said. "Very quick. When the man was screaming, could you make out a name or any words, or did he just scream in pain?"

Pudgy shook his head. "You've got it wrong. It wasn't a guy screaming. It was a woman."

Chapter 15

Ellie rose and switched off her phone. It was office policy anyway, and it wasn't too much to ask for half an hour now and then of strictly personal time, especially when she was off duty. Dr. Lukens came to the door and opened it—she always did. Today she wore her usual tailored dark slacks but her blouse was a brilliant turquoise and the vibrancy suited her coloring.

"Good morning, Detective. Have a seat."

They both settled into chairs and Georgia Lukens asked, "Not as your therapist, but as a concerned citizen, how is the investigation going? I read in the paper there's been another murder. The article said the police department believes they are linked together."

"We've had a small break," Ellie acknowledged, because she had, after all, shown her the picture of the second victim. Neither did they have a typical doctor/patient relationship. "It is possible there is a witness to the second murder. All we need is for them to come forward."

"Promising, but I find it disturbing they haven't done so already."

"You aren't the only one who thinks that's strange, but then again, the victim was living illegally in the house where he was murdered. This case seems to be riddled with people breaking trespassing laws. We are cooperating with the media a little more than usual to make sure the word is out that we are looking for this person."

"I truly hope you find them soon. Now then, how is Ellie MacIntosh the woman, not the police officer?"

That was a good question. To her, the best part of therapy was being able to just speak freely and never have it leave the room. "The woman is very unhappy living in Bryce's house without him there," she said frankly. "It makes me uncomfortable in about a dozen ways."

"List a few of them for me?"

"It's his house, for one. My house is still up north. That's my home, the house I chose and paid for, and my furniture and personal taste are part of it. I would never have moved in had I known he was going to move out, even if it is temporary. If you want to talk about trespassing, that's how I feel when I walk through the door each night."

Dr. Lukens regarded her thoughtfully. "Do you think you would feel better if the two of you had bought a house together instead of your current circumstances?"

That was a pretty good question. Ellie wasn't sure. On the one hand, she was happy for him, and even understood why he'd gone to New York. Some aspiring writers never completed that book they dreamed of writing, others wrote many and never sold them, and to have a book deal like the one he'd been offered was the culmination of his dream and a lot of hard work. There was absolutely no way she could—or would—stand in the way of that. She was smart enough, she hoped anyway, to know that it would not improve their relationship but probably destroy it.

"No." Ellie sighed and tucked a strand of hair behind her ear. "I think I'd probably have a sense of living alone in a space that wasn't mine anyway. Maybe if I'd sold my house already, it would be different. I disliked living in the condo I rented when I first moved to Milwaukee, but I was adjusting to a new job and a new place. The job is a good fit, so I am comfortable with that decision. Maybe I overthink things a little too much, but in many ways, especially now, I feel like Bryce and I live two very different and separate lives."

"If he asked you to move to New York, would you go?"

"He isn't there permanently."

"That isn't really answering my question, is it?"

With a sigh, Ellie admitted, "I doubt it. Not as it stands right now. This past year I embarked on a new life as it were, and it certainly seems like he is doing the same thing. We care about each other, but is it the right fit? We just couldn't be more different, and sometimes I know that is a good thing, and sometimes it flat-out doesn't work long term."

"Have you talked about marriage?"

"Around it, maybe. We're just both cautious. I only want to do that one time. He's already been through one divorce and I know he doesn't want to do *that* again."

"Seems logical."

It did, but was love supposed to be based on logic? "It's probably just as well Bryce is out of town now. My partner and I are pretty focused on these cases."

Georgia Lukens kept her usual neutral expression. "And how is the sometimes irritating Detective Santiago? Your description, not mine."

"As usual." Ellie reconsidered her answer. "Maybe not quite. He made me dinner the other night. That is unprecedented, I admit. I think he feels sorry for me that Bryce is gone."

"And why do you have that impression?"

Dryly, she answered, "I'd guess frozen pizza is his normal source of nutrition if you can call it that, so he went to the trouble for some reason. Besides, we are talking Santiago here and he is about as subtle as a bull moose usually. He actually exerted himself to be nice."

"You spend a lot of time together and depend upon one another in a way I would compare to the camaraderie of soldiers. Maybe he cares about how you feel but is uncertain of how to express himself."

"Trust me, he has no problem expressing himself." Ellie laughed ruefully and shook her head.

Jason had absolutely no idea what to say.

He sat at his desk and stared at the woman sitting across from him and tried to formulate a decent answer that would not get him fired.

Because what he wanted to say sure would get his ass in deep trouble.

"Mrs. Peterson," he said after careful consideration,

"there have been two other murders very similar to what happened to your husband, yes. We are working all three cases diligently and with almost single-minded purpose, both on and off duty. Detective MacIntosh and I are very determined to apprehend whoever killed your husband."

That sounded a lot more professional than: *Stop wasting my precious time you pretentious bitch.*

But . . . it was tempting to say the latter.

"No one feels you have made any progress. I repeat, I would like to see your notes." She sat in the chair by his desk in elegant pumps, a black dress, and had her perfectly manicured hands clasped tightly in her lap.

"No one?" he repeated, staying remarkably polite but it cost him. "I was unaware there was a meeting over how we are handling the case. It would have been nice to have been invited. And I'm sorry but my notes are on my computer in a file at this time and I am not only reluctant to give you access to it, but I am fairly sure that violates policy. If you wish to discuss it, that's fine, but it would be better if you would just let me get on with doing my job."

Her mouth tightened. "Where is the other detective? The woman."

"Off chasing bad guys, I expect."

"I don't appreciate your sarcasm."

"I was being sincere. Detective *MacIntosh,*" he said with emphasis, as he knew perfectly well Mrs. Peterson remembered Ellie's name since he'd just said it, "takes this as seriously as I do, and that is very seriously."

The murdered professor's wife stood stiffly. "I do not want this matter being sensationalized in the media."

Her husband's death was a "matter"?

Was that what this impromptu and not exactly pleasant visit was all about? Jason regarded her steadily. "Have you seen me or my partner on the news, talking about it? I can answer that, no, you haven't. Some facts are public record and we can't help that, and sometimes the police department shares details with reporters that might make someone with information come forward, but that is not my decision."

She slapped a hand on his desk, her expression venomous. "Let me make it clear that I do not want the Milwaukee Police Department to attempt to make anyone come forward."

"Excuse me? Didn't you just accuse us of not making enough effort?"

She turned on her heel and walked away instead of answering, leaving Jason sitting there perplexed. As luck would have it, Carl Grasso happened to be walking by and heard the exchange, and he turned and also watched the departing widow. "Isn't she a little old for you, Santiago? Usually you make much younger women furious."

"I'm not positive what just happened." Jason rubbed the back of his neck. "But that is one unhappy woman and I happened to be handy. Where's MacIntosh when you need her? Maybe she could have talked Peterson's wife off her ledge. I was fighting the urge to tell the woman to fuck off."

Lieutenant Grasso whistled. "And you won the battle? I'm impressed. What's her problem?"

That was a valid question. Around them the station was busy, people passing by, the smell of coffee left a little too long on the burner in the air. Jason said slowly, "I'm not exactly sure but it seems to me that if I dissect our conversation, what I come up with is that she wants nothing about her husband's murder on the news. It really ticks her off. She arrived and demanded to see my case notes."

Grasso looked thoughtfully down the hallway, his hands casually in his pockets. "It makes you wonder what it is she's worried you've uncovered."

His thoughts exactly. Grasso was a crack investigator, so his insight was usually gold. "We've uncovered nothing," Jason admitted, leaning back, punching up a screen. "So she's getting all in a twist about the media for no reason I can think of at the moment, but now I'm starting to wonder."

"*I've* been wondering how it was going but busy with that triple homicide we think is gang related. Luckily, we've got someone ready to roll over on his kind and softhearted friends." Grasso took the chair Mrs. Peterson had just vacated. "What do you have so far?"

It never hurt to exchange ideas with someone who knew the ropes like Grasso. Jason looked at his screen, but he didn't need to read the words. "We've nothing on Peterson except that he was drugged before he died and his face mutilated. Good finances. By all accounts a solid marriage, though how he could stand her escapes my ass, but apparently he could. Maybe she was nice to him if he paid for that big house and all. A possible eyewitness to the second murder, though no idea who the victim is, and we are hoping for a missing person report on our third vic. That's about it unless you count the pretty brutal way all three had their faces hacked apart, the fact that they were drugged, and those cross-like stab wounds. Oh yeah, the professor and the second vic ate something similar, some sort of cake with apples in it."

Grasso's gray eyes held a hint of careful consideration. "That's one of those small things that can break open a case. That could be a real lead. Same killer, no doubt about it. Methodology does not lie. Tell me about the witness?"

Jason briefly told him about the boys at the school and the screams they'd heard.

"I worked vice for five years." Grasso didn't mention he'd been reprimanded and just reinstated to homicide, but he didn't need to, since Jason knew the details anyway. "I'd say you might have a prostitute witness. She isn't coming forward because it would just get her in trouble, or worst-case scenario, she can't come forward because he killed her too and she is just someone no one will ever report missing."

A depressing thought for both their case and for the witness.

"It's a pretty dicey neighborhood." Jason needed more coffee but he'd already had three cups. "So you could be right. I'm working on the rufilin connection too and my informant actually called me, but now I can't reach the guy. I've been sitting here expecting a call."

"Drug dealers are not the most reliable sources."

"Maybe I should go find him. I did it once before. I know the bar he uses as an office."

"Maybe." Grasso lifted his shoulders. "It couldn't hurt. Any lead is better than no lead. I've had informants turn a case like gang killing, but your dealer could have relocated."

At that moment his phone rang and Jason answered, recognizing the number. "Where in the hell are you?"

Ellie said, "I'm looking at a dead man that I'm wondering

if you might recognize. Your number is programmed into his phone on the contact list."

"Shit," he muttered. "Tell me his name isn't Gurst."

"We don't know yet. No ID, but yours was one of the last numbers he called. This isn't our case, by the way. It belongs to Rays and Johnson."

"Mind telling me why they didn't call me instead of you?" His hand tightened on the phone at her testy tone.

"Because they called Metzger first in case he's your buddy or something. This guy called you, you called him back, and now he is dead. The chief isn't into surprises by the way, and wants to know why you might be associated with the dead man because he has two bags of heroin on him. All of us are standing around scratching our heads and wondering, if the killing is drug related, why the drugs were left behind."

"What, they're wondering if I use drugs? Jesus, give me a break. He's an informant."

"I didn't say anyone thought that." Her tone was pragmatic with an edge of sympathy. "There are cops out there with dirty little secrets. This is nothing like the other crime scenes, by the way, so it probably isn't related to our investigation, but who knows at this point."

It was, though. If a cop talked to someone who might have information about a murder case and then that person ended up dead, well, it wasn't much of a stretch to assume the events were connected.

Grasso was looking at him, his expression extremely interested. Jason said succinctly, "This is entirely screwed up. I'll be right there."

Chapter 16

T wo bullets to the back of the head."

Ellie could see the holes, so she didn't need the play-by-play, but she simply nodded. The man was sprawled on the concrete of a parking garage—never a safe place to be—and he had not experienced a happy day.

The deputy medical examiner was young, male, and very professional. "He didn't see it coming, so maybe that means something to you. They walked up behind him and shot him point-blank at a very close range. If you have a suspect, they would have residue on their hands. Forensics will be able to provide trajectory, but I'd say the person was shorter. That doesn't really limit the number of possible perpetrators of this crime very much since he was a tall man, but on an initial examination, that is an educated guess."

No suspect. No, they sure didn't. She didn't want to dwell on it.

"All right. Thanks." She noted Santiago pulling into the

parking lot. "I think we might have a positive ID coming up here."

Her partner got out and slammed his car door, hatless as usual, in a hurry as he came toward the taped-off area in long measured strides. His first words were predictably, "What the fuck?"

She pointed at the corpse. "Gurst?"

"Shit, yeah, that's him." Santiago irritatingly looked like he wasn't even cold even though it was freezing outside and he was wearing a leather coat that was open over a denim shirt, jeans, and cowboy boots. No gloves or scarf. No wonder he constantly grumbled about the temperature. He drawled, "I think I can see why he didn't return my call. I guess I'm not going to hold a grudge just this once."

The deputy ME laughed and gave them a nod as he picked up his bag and walked away. Crime scene techs were scouring the parking lot, their breath sending little clouds into the stale air.

"This *is* part of our case." Santiago said it with conviction.

Detective Rays, in a long overcoat and polished shoes, looked interested, his partner off to see if they could retrieve surveillance tapes. "The slasher thing?"

Ellie wasn't buying it . . . except for the phone number. "He's a drug dealer. It happens that in the course of doing business with people not known for their high moral standards, sometimes it goes south."

"He is one hundred percent a drug dealer," Santiago agreed, staring at the body superimposed on the cracked asphalt. "And this shit does happen. But I don't like the timing. There's only one reason he'd call me and it has nothing to do with two bags of heroin."

"It is a very different crime." Ellie stepped aside for two men with a body bag and a stretcher. "It's somewhat interesting he called you and then was killed, but only *somewhat* since I'm guessing he was just another guppy in the food chain and a bigger fish gobbled him up. Happens every single day. The call and the murder are probably unrelated."

"Quite the coincidence though. What if our boy here decided to shake down one of his customers, letting him know the police were sniffing around about rufilin? Gurst was not a genius. He might be stupid enough to see if he could extort money from the wrong person." Santiago's blue eyes were unfocused in a way Ellie recognized meant he was thinking swiftly, sorting it out. "If so, it was a really bad idea. But no way he'd meet them here and not be on guard. He didn't like the crime scene picture I showed him at all."

Before he started to walk away, Rays said, "Maybe the tapes will help us all out. We'll let you know if we find anything."

"Thanks."

Ellie and Santiago both watched the body being loaded into the van as the other detective wandered off, talking on his cell phone. Light snow swirled around them in erratic patterns. She said contemplatively, "He could just be a drug dealer shot in a garage."

"He could be a drug dealer *I* got shot in a garage. Why the hell would they leave the heroin if it was a deal gone south?" Santiago's expression was unreadable and he finally seemed to feel the cold. "I need a cup of coffee or a beer, but beer is chilled unless you're in England, and this is Milwaukee, so I'm thinking coffee. I'll buy."

She did realize Seattle was known as the coffee capital of the US, but Milwaukee could hold its own. Considering the climate, people drank a lot of coffee. "Good idea. Maybe we can make some sense of this—"

The sound of tires squealing caught her off guard and scattered the crime scene unit as a car skidded around a corner, going way too fast and glancing off the bumper of a minivan, knocking the vehicle sideways and narrowly missing the ME van. The two men loading the body dropped the stretcher, and the sound was sickening as it hit the pavement. The dead man rolled when they dived out of the way. The car careened in the opposite direction, grazed a post, and sped off down the ramp.

Santiago swore, his weapon drawn but it happened so fast getting off a shot would have been impossible.

Next to her, he muttered, "What was that?"

Ellie, still standing by the pool of drying blood, had to admit her heartbeat had picked up a little. Rays was running, and they could hear the screech of tires on concrete as the car moved too fast to a lower level.

Then she called out, "I got a couple of numbers on the license plate and it wasn't Wisconsin-issue. Anyone see more?"

"I think it was North Carolina." One of the techs was swiping at his knees with gloved hands, his face pinched. "I swear it said First in Flight. NC, right?"

"That would be it." She hadn't caught that, but just that

it didn't look like something she saw every day and he was closer. "Let's get them picked up."

"The asshole nearly hit me," the technician said bitterly.

"Why would someone from North Carolina meet a drug dealer in a parking garage in Milwaukee?" Ellie mused out loud, her mind racing.

"Want my guess? He wanted to buy two bags of heroin and instead witnessed a murder." Santiago glanced around, digging in his pocket. "Shit, of course they did. Then they decided as cops started to pile in, that they were nervous and should get the hell out of Dodge."

He could be right.

Her partner grabbed her arm. "Crown Vic. Black, new model. I didn't see the plate, but I'll take your word for it. Let's go. My car is right here."

A high-speed pursuit was hardly on his agenda for the afternoon, but then again, it seemed wise to hit the pavement running if possible. Ellie clicked her seat belt and didn't even object as he took the corner at almost the same speed as the escaping car. The gate on one side was broken through so that bought them some time, but he did slow down a little to make sure it was clear before he gunned the vehicle onto the street.

"We don't even know the direction they turned," MacIntosh said reasonably, apparently unfazed by how he changed lanes three times in about forty seconds and was driving like a stunt man in a movie. "What if they went left?"

"Easier to go right." He dodged a truck and pushed a

button so the system on his vehicle was activated to his cell phone. "Call in and tell them where we are and what we're doing. I don't want to get pulled over for speeding or reckless driving, plus I want them looking for our first possible suspect too."

She did it, reporting a chase in a possible homicide investigation, and then grabbed onto the passenger-side grip above her door to balance herself as he sped up.

No car ahead.

Well, fuck.

Then, there it was. He caught the gleam of black at the same time as Ellie pointed, and again did a harrowing lane change, cutting off a Mercedes, but it brought them closer. He said tersely, "You get the entire plate and I make it possible, then we stop pursuit. That's the deal. I think they already know we're following them from the way they are driving, and this is not a face-off we're doing without backup."

"What is this? 'Err on the side of caution' from Jason Santiago?" Ellie turned to look at him incredulously.

It was impossible to explain. He couldn't risk her. A part of his brain told him he wasn't entirely doing his job, and another part understood how the men riding guard on the wagon trains over a century before circled around to defend the women. It wasn't selfless. Quite the opposite. He just wouldn't be able to forgive himself if it went all wrong.

Never mind that Ellie would probably strangle him if she knew what he was thinking.

The black car took a right, and no way, considering how the driver was acting, could they not know they were being followed just as he'd predicted. He took the same route, fairly sure two wheels came off the pavement he made the turn so fast. He said, "Our kids from the school said it was a black car."

"There is more than one or two in the city of Milwaukee."

"Come on, get out of the way," he muttered urgently to the windshield, referring to the car ahead. "We just need one clear view."

They didn't get it. Instead a driver in a blue sedan switched lanes in front of them, oblivious apparently to their pursuit. The black car took advantage and ran a light, red taillights coming on as the car between them stopped.

Jason rested his head briefly against the steering wheel after he slammed on his brakes and narrowly avoided an accident. The car disappeared into traffic. "There they go. Home free. Fuck."

MacIntosh was on her phone now, reporting their location since they were stopped. "This is where we are and I've got a partial plate."

By the time she hung up the light had changed and they pulled through, but Jason had no faith at all that he might pick the trail back up. "That sucked. We were close."

"I took a picture with my phone. Maybe forensics can do something with it." Ellie put the phone back in her pocket. "You sure it was a Crown Vic?"

He'd gotten a good look and he had an eye for cars. "Oh, yes."

"Federal agents?" She looked puzzled, the fall of hair under the rim of her hat gold in the light.

"I don't think so." He'd seen that kind of driving before; these people knew the streets. The car had disappeared by now, into a driveway somewhere if he had to guess. "Locals, and not new locals, and not good locals. They picked the car on purpose because it looks like a cop car, and they disappeared because they knew they could dodge us."

"The heroin buyers. This isn't our murderer."

"Maybe, so we shouldn't get our hopes up over them ever coming forward either." Jason pulled through the intersection behind the still clueless driver of the car ahead. "I feel like I'm wandering around in the dark with my hands tied behind my back. I don't mind going on record saying it is fine to tie me up—I'd let you do it to me anytime—but this is bullshit."

That won him a scathing look. "You *so* need to work on your sense of humor."

"You've mentioned it. And quite a few of my other problems." He would have added a lewd wink for effect but he was still looking for the car and the streets were not busy, but slick.

That comment at least made her reluctantly laugh.

"It might not be our murderer that we were just chasing, but obviously they weren't upstanding citizens." MacIntosh was looking too, her gaze scanning the area. "We aren't going to repeat our luck with the boys from the school. These guys are not going to come forward about the murder, even if they didn't do it."

"Nope." He agreed completely. "Now we have several sets of possible witnesses out there that could help us, and yet apparently none of them will."

Traffic streamed by, the treadmill apparent.

"It's snowing again." Ellie rubbed her forehead. "Can I mention I am sick of winter?"

"It is a popular pastime in Milwaukee to gripe about the weather. Go ahead. You always get on me about it."

"What do we do now?"

"Go for that cup of coffee I could really use? Just an idea I have swimming around in my head."

"Always thinking of yourself."

"I'm afraid so."

If there was one thing he'd learned about Detective Ellie MacIntosh, it was that her brain moved forward in a linear, focused fashion so she probably didn't even hear what he'd just said. In profile, she was very still. "I'm going over this. His body had been there for a while. That bothers me. I think he was there to meet with whoever took off in the car and the heroin was part of that deal, but what if the reason they were still waiting was because he was already dead in that corner of the garage and they didn't know it?"

He signaled left. The suspects were long gone. There was a time to admit defeat and start regrouping. The car they were pursuing could have pulled in anywhere, or simply caught a break and made half a dozen lights by now . . . cruising around wasn't going to solve their problems.

Making an executive decision, he headed for his favorite dive that served not just coffee but cinnamon rolls. "We aren't catching them right at the moment and I propose a change of venue."

Chapter 17

We have a missing person report that might match the third victim."

Ellie glanced up and registered that Santiago not only had a file he tossed on her desk, but was dressed in the tailored black suit they had selected, his unruly hair at least comparable to fashionably tousled, the dark narrow tie and white shirt doing some nice things for his coloring. He added, "You look good."

She certainly hoped so since she'd spent about an hour getting ready and her usual routine was brushing her teeth and running a hairbrush through her hair, maybe some clear gloss for the evening, and if she was in the mood, a touch of mascara. Considering she'd opted out of the little black cliché and instead chosen a form-fitting scarlet dress she trotted out on special occasions, she expected at least one suggestive comment, but he seemed more interested in the most recent murder than the length of her skirt.

"Thank you." She opened the file and glanced over it. There wasn't time at the moment to study it, but during the drive she could at least get the details. "Lance Young. Thirty-eight and single. He worked for a pest control company and he's not been seen for days. How strong is the possibility he's the one found in Jefferson County?"

"Right height, right weight, and a missing appendix all match up. The last time he was heard from is pretty accurate as well." Santiago's voice was somber. "I sure hate like hell asking his parents to come try to identify him. I'm hoping Hammet can do it from family DNA but that takes a long time. If it is Young, he has a sister."

"I don't think it would be possible for anyone to recognize him anyway unless there's a birthmark or scar or something definitive like that."

A grim reality. She didn't want to think about that body in the woods with the ravaged face. Or any of the victims for that matter. She'd worked some tough cases and this one was pretty bad. If it was someone she loved, that would be beyond awful.

"We have a black car. We have two witnesses that are still in middle school so reliable is a questionable word when used to describe them. We have three victims with slashed faces and a dead man with two bullets through the back of his skull. Please tell me how to connect a guy walking around spraying insecticide to a college professor and someone who seems to have decided to just take over a house? And where does our drug dealer tie in, if he does at all? There's something else, but I don't see it."

There so was. She couldn't see it, but she could *feel* it.

"Maybe the media can get our witness to come forward.

I'm sure Mrs. Peterson will blame me, but if it works, I can handle it."

"If the witness is still alive." Ellie had really thought about it. "The boys said the screaming stopped abruptly." It had bothered her then when she'd first heard of it and it bothered her now. "Maybe there's another cross-country skier who's going to get an unpleasant surprise."

Her partner admitted, "That's occurred to me too, and Grasso also mentioned it as a possibility. I don't like it when we all are thinking along those lines."

A passing uniformed officer gave a low whistle and grinned as he tapped Santiago on the shoulder. "Wow. Am I in Hollywood or something?"

"Fuck off, Wagner." Santiago reluctantly laughed as he said the words. He turned back to Ellie. "We'd better go. The traffic on ninety-four can be a bitch and we need to check into the hotel. Bring the file and read it in the car. I'm driving."

Normally she'd take issue with the presumptive male tone but Ellie knew he was nervous about the upcoming evening, whether he showed it outwardly or not. "Fine with me, but we are taking my car instead of your pickup truck. Crawling in and out of that thing in heels sounds like a recipe for disaster. I don't mind getting shot at for the citizens of the state of Wisconsin, but I do draw the line at breaking my leg."

"I don't want to be responsible for a shoe dysfunction." Her partner held up his hands in a mock gesture of surrender. "Your car it is."

"Glad you agree."

"I save my arguments for things I really give a shit about."

"Could you try and not say 'shit' in front of the governor?"

"I can try."

She took the file and picked up the handbag that was half the size of the one she usually carried but matched her dress, and stood up, giving him her keys. "We'll talk about this on our way to Madison."

"I had no doubt of that." The words were said dryly. He stepped back to let her precede him. "Does it bother Grantham when you get really focused and talk about dead people, crime scene photos, and possible motives over your spaghetti and meatballs? It used to drive Kate crazy. In her somewhat expert opinion, she thought I was . . . how did she put it? Morbidly obsessed with my job. Yeah, those were her exact words."

It was a valid question—if a little personal—but Santiago never had trouble with being blunt.

She hadn't talked to Bryce in several days. It was easy to picture him sitting in his hotel room in front of his computer, no doubt forgetting to eat lunch. It brought on a pang of unwelcome emotion that she didn't want to analyze. "If he minds, he's never said so. Let me get my coat."

Jason was sweating.

It had nothing to do with the temperature in the car and everything to do with the evening in general. It didn't help how Ellie looked in a red dress that distracted him, and the

sucky weather had gotten worse and he was driving an unfamiliar vehicle.

When they pulled into the hotel parking lot it was a relief.

They checked in—separate rooms of course, that had
been the truth unfortunately—and he dropped his bag on
the floor of his generic room and absurdly enough wondered
what his mother might think if she knew he was going to
have dinner with the governor.

Why he'd care was a mystery even to him as he dismissed
the thought. Maybe it was just not really remembering her,
having that inner curiosity over what she might be like, and
this was one hell of a time to examine his feelings about it
all. Maybe Lukens could unravel it, but he was coming to
terms with the reality that therapy didn't work that way.
He said something, she shot it back at him, and he was
forced to think about it and dissect it himself.

Not his favorite pastime.

Somehow he'd thought seeing a shrink involved them
telling you what was wrong. Not the way it went unless
Lukens was a hack, and he didn't think she was. In his opinion introspection was worthless but he was being forced
into it anyway.

Why does the idea of commitment bother you?

"Because life is not a damn television show," he'd answered in their last session. *Commitment involves serious
risk and there is no promise from God or anyone else that
the person you've just decided is an important part of your
life will stay in it. Whether it is their choice, or someone
just takes them away.*

Impossible to get more honest than that. Lukens had nod-

ded and he wasn't sure if it was because he'd just told her
something profound that she'd already guessed or if she
just agreed. For some reason he kind of thought it was
the latter.

When he went just one door down in the hotel hallway
and knocked, MacIntosh answered wearing a long grace-
ful wool coat that extended to her ankles. She'd added some
lipstick to the ensemble and he caught a subtle whiff of perfume.

Limousine.

Lights across Lake Mendota.

Cold night but not snowing at the moment. He'd drank
a beer in his room in about five seconds flat because he
needed it, and while in the past he'd wondered if he had a
problem with alcohol, he was pretty sure he didn't, he just
liked it. No crime there. He'd had plenty of time to ponder
addiction and it wasn't one of his many sins.

"Please tell me we won't be drinking red wine all evening with our pinky fingers sticking out," he said as he gazed
out over the water. At least the shoes they'd picked out were
comfortable. It was doubtful he'd ever wear them again, but
they weren't bad.

MacIntosh laughed softly as the driver opened the door
for her. "If we do, you'll get through it."

As tense as *he* was, she was perfectly relaxed in the car
as they pulled away, legs crossed, her profile remote. Why
should *she* be nervous? On the other hand, social graces
weren't his strong suit. It was more a lack of experience than
anything innate, or so he liked to think anyway.

He just said it flat out. "I might embarrass the crap out
of you."

"How sweet you are to be worried about me." Her tone was saccharine on purpose. "Nicely put too."

Okay, now she was just trying to tick him off. "I've been called a lot of things, but not sweet. Fine, so that statement was an example of how I might embarrass you, got it now?"

"Not really. I am me, and you are you. If anyone confuses us, then they are an idiot, and I do not care what idiots think."

The lights of cars in the other lanes went past and he glanced over, moved to *almost* say that she'd basically pinned down his outlook on life. "There are times I actually like you, though I am still confused over whether or not that was supportive, or an insult. I'm going for the latter."

"Really? The next thing you'll do is kick me on the playground."

All right, now she'd made *him* laugh. He stretched out his legs. "All this protocol and stuff . . . I don't know. If I could have figured out a way to get out of this shit, I would have."

MacIntosh didn't disagree. "Yes, you would have, but Metzger would have pushed back and at the end of it all, it's just one night. Besides, come on, you helped the man's niece and his zealous cause—which I agree with—just give the governor the chance to thank you. Any man in his position would want to, so don't treat him differently. He deserves the same consideration you'd give anyone else."

That was such backhanded logic he turned his head and stared at her. "You think I'd be rude to our governor?"

Her serene poise was unruffled. "Anything is possible. You said two seconds ago you might embarrass me."

"Oh, for Christ's sake, MacIntosh. Not like that."

The smooth swing of her hair brushed her shoulders as she shook her head. "I think you'll do your best and that is all anyone can ask."

The mansion was built with palatial columns and well-lit. Security people came out as the car pulled up and they were hustled out of the limousine. He'd already been told he couldn't carry a weapon and that had not helped how he felt about the entire evening. Relinquishing his sidearm to someone he didn't know chafed. He handed it over with a tight jaw to a dark-haired guy dressed in what was probably a more expensive suit. "Loaded and the name is Santiago. I want it back."

Ellie showed more grace, but she would. She let them open her door, got out, and took her .45 from her purse. Handle first, she handed it over. "Detective MacIntosh, MPD."

The security detail was polite, nice, admiring Ellie, and she was worth looking at when she pulled out the stops. Jason had the irrational—and he knew it was—urge to go all possessive even if he knew he had no right to it, and take her arm, but he consciously did his best not to touch her.

So he motioned at the door. "Shall we?"

Just then his phone began to vibrate. Luckily, he'd been smart enough to silence it, though he certainly was not expecting a call of any kind. He pulled it from his pocket and saw the display, but didn't recognize the number.

That was weird. He allowed himself to be screened and casually pocketed his phone, but waited until they were inside to check the actual message. It was a text, not a call.

"Jason, where are you?"

"Problem?" Ellie looked at him inquiringly.

"I have no idea," he said truthfully, but before he could explain someone laid a hand on his arm.

The governor's niece was as pretty as he'd imagined she'd be when she wasn't shaken and pale and her smile was warm. A shimmery blue dress set off her dark chestnut hair. "Detective Santiago, I'm glad to see you under better circumstances." She held out her hand to Ellie. "I'm Lauren."

"Detective Santiago's partner, Ellie MacIntosh."

"Oh." The young woman's eyes widened slightly. "I saw your name on the list but when you walked in together I assumed you were his wife or girlfriend."

"No sane woman would put up with him if not ordered to do so by the chief of police." Ellie ignored Santiago's sardonic look. "This is a beautiful place. And I'm looking forward to meeting your uncle."

"I'd love to give you a private tour. Let me introduce you first."

So this was hell.

He'd kind of always wondered since he anticipated he'd end up there eventually. Jason viewed the array of forks with resignation, guessing most people did the same thing, because no one would ever intentionally dirty this much silverware for one meal.

Luckily, he was decently observant—he should hope so considering his job—and he just did what everyone else did with their cutlery, so that part wasn't difficult.

Other aspects of the meal were not as comfortable. Lauren sat next to him and she wasn't what he'd call animated, but she did flirt a little, and he had to wonder what Ellie was thinking.

Right. She was thinking nothing about him, he decided after the salad course was cleared away. In that red dress, she sat next to one of the governor's aides engrossed in what appeared to be a deep conversation. Jason was honestly experiencing a frustrating jealousy that he couldn't even justify since she lived with Grantham. End of story.

Hell, he should call Grantham so they could commiserate. The entire thing sucked.

At least he'd have something to talk about with Dr. Lukens on his next visit.

It only got worse.

"My uncle told me you've been shot twice in the line of duty." Lauren looked at him with what appeared to be admiration. All around them the elegant dining room hummed with conversation and the subdued clink of silverware on fine porcelain.

Actually, he'd been shot on two occasions, but taken three bullets and had the scars to prove it. "Yeah, you'd think I'd be a little more careful," he said wryly. "Makes me sound like an idiot."

"Not at all." Lauren sat back so a waiter could put a plate of what looked to be sautéed chicken in a sauce that had mushrooms and tiny translucent onions in front of her. "It just means you are willing to risk your life for the public. Not all people can say that."

His plate was served next and whatever else could be said of the evening, it did smell fantastic. He should at least make an effort to be cordial because normally he'd be pretty interested, but just like he'd felt with the interest of the woman in the grocery store, he was finding it hard to overcome his personal stupidity at lusting after another man's girlfriend.

A serious impairment to his already lackluster personal life.

So he said with what he hoped was convincing interest, "Tell me about you. What do you do? Have you always lived in Milwaukee?"

"I'm from a small town, actually. Word of warning, by the way, since I don't get the sense you're having the time of your life tonight, my uncle is going to ask you a favor."

Well, apparently he wasn't good at hiding his feelings, but then again, he'd rarely practiced. Jason carefully cut off a piece of chicken but didn't put it in his mouth. He had a tendency to eat too fast, both from a childhood desire to wolf down his food and keep his time with his father to a minimum and his stint in the military that demanded efficiency of time. "Like what?"

"I'll let him tell you." Her gaze was earnest but held a hint of laughter. "I think I got you dragged into it."

"You're enjoying this," he said with a rueful laugh. "But then again, you're right, you got me into this situation."

Lauren laughed but then sobered and said in a very quiet voice, "You have the bluest eyes. Has anyone ever told you that?"

Chapter 18

Ellie knew all evening her partner wasn't happy, but it was hardly part of her job description to keep him that way. Still, she did feel amused sympathy when the governor, in front of everyone at the dinner she knew Jason didn't want to attend, made him stand to a round of applause, and asked him in front of the guests if he would be willing to go on camera for a public service announcement about cell phone misuse. A classic deer-in-the-headlights moment if one ever existed. Metzger would kill him if he said no. To Santiago's credit he recovered fairly well and mumbled something that was probably agreement but she wouldn't swear to it, and he came back to sit down as quickly as possible. Then he looked at her and his expression said: *Just get me out of here.*

The least she could do. More than once during the course of the evening she'd met his eyes and tried to convey a silent message of support. Hopefully she'd succeeded since as far as she could tell, he'd done just fine. He looked outwardly relaxed and pulled off the pretense anyway of enjoying himself. So she was the one who excused them, shaking the governor's hand, citing the current case. Not a lie. The clock was ticking and someone was out there, maybe thinking about the next victim.

They walked through the lobby of the hotel and caught an elevator going up. "Ordeal over."

It was just a comment. Jason appreciated that he'd been the man of the hour in some ways, but that was a dubious distinction in his mind. Luckily Ellie had evidently caught the edge of desperation in his gaze and theatrically checked her phone and declared a lead had come through in this latest case and they needed to leave. It worked effectively, since the governor was not going to stop them from catching the killer gaining the most momentum in the press, so it was a pretty good angle.

The downside was that now they *needed* a lead. As if they didn't before, but now it was expected.

"It ended up better than I thought it would be." Ellie looked a little drained, but they had the case, the drive, getting introduced to what seemed like a thousand people but was probably only a group of thirty or so, and he was wiped out too as they rode up in the elevator.

He watched the buttons light up as they ascended floors. "It wasn't too bad. Kind of like flying. I hate it, but when I arrive at my destination and we haven't crashed into the ground, then it was a good experience. At least they had booze."

"That's you. Always seeing the bright side."

"Ours is an occupation that inspires a cheerful disposition."

"I rather think Lauren might have a mild crush on you." Ellie's hazel eyes were amused as the bell dinged, signaling their floor.

He'd gotten that vibe as well, loud and clear. She admitted she was the one who had texted him, afraid he might have had to cancel. Nice, but they'd really only barely met. He was about as bad at flirtation as he was at small talk. "The governor's aide seemed to find you interesting." The doors to the elevator opened. He said, "Lauren is about a decade too young, for your information."

And about a century or so in life experience when he thought about his past.

"I thought that's what men were looking for." Ellie stepped out and he followed. "Anyway, it ended up being a nice night and his aide and I just talked about the new state health care plan. It was a very stimulating conversation, as you can imagine. I'm just glad we're back here."

He didn't disagree. There was something about taking the girl of your dreams to the governor's mansion for a first date, especially when she didn't even realize it was a date.

Or even that she was the girl of your dreams.

Ellie went on. "I liked everyone fairly well, even the attorney general, though I don't always agree with her politics."

God, she's beautiful. Ellie, not the attorney general,

though maybe the AG was, he just didn't notice because he'd been busy trying not to ogle his partner all evening. Jason leaned an arm on the wall next to the door of her room and just *looked* at her.

It startled him that he'd never really made the distinction before. Pretty girls and hot women, he'd met quite a few, dated some, slept with his fair share, but he really thought she was *beautiful*.

So he stood there awkwardly—and he was a lot of things, but not usually awkward with women—and it was, infuriatingly, a lot like a prom date. A suit, a slinky dress, the whole tongue-tied, uncertain package.

Or like the ones he'd seen on television. He'd worked pretty much all through high school in the afternoons and evenings, though the one thing he'd ever done that his old man had approved of was take time off to play football. But he'd gotten kicked off the team his senior year for getting caught drinking beer and smoking weed. Before the school year was even over his father had thrown him out anyway, so he'd struggled pretty hard to even graduate. There was no money for the luxury of a fancy date.

Jason said in a voice that was only a little off-key, "I had a better time than I imagined too."

"Come on in. We can talk about the case." She swiped her key card and turned the handle of her door. "Forensics could do nothing with the picture from my phone of the car we followed. That was the message I actually got, not a lead. We really need to figure out if it fits in."

The case was important to him too, but was that the only possible topic they could discuss?

It pissed him off. Like totally. Not because she wanted

to talk about four unsolved murders on what had turned out to be the most meaningful night of his life, but because MacIntosh didn't *understand* it was the most meaningful night of his life.

So he did what he did best and was a jerk.

"No thanks." He shoved his hands in his pockets.

She turned around, her expression perplexed at his abruptness and short tone. "All right. I brought my notes, so that's what I'm going to do. It's not that late."

"Yeah, it's not that late, but once again, no thanks." He tried to picture himself being in the same room with her, a convenient bed at hand, and concentrating on those damn notes. *Nope, not happening.*

"What is the matter with you all of a sudden?" She stared at him. He probably was acting strangely, because it had been such an unusual evening in the first place and he was, quite frankly, torn between being glad it was over and not wanting it to end.

Who he was mad at escaped him. Not her really, she'd been poised and lovely, but seemed like she absolutely did not get it.

Get him and how he felt.

Maybe he *was* a little ticked at her. "I'm surprised you aren't tired from flirting all night with what's-his-name, the aide guy."

"He was sitting next to me, and I told you, we talked about the health care changes." The words were slow and maybe, finally, she was starting to catch on, her head tilted back as she gazed up at him with a newfound wariness that indicated on a feminine level she recognized the source of his angst. "Were you *jealous*?"

He didn't mean for it to happen. Not planned, not scripted, but just one of those moments. He stepped forward and planted his other hand on the wall by her shoulder as she stood by the open door, definitely invading her personal space. She retreated too, which was not her style, stepping backward, but she was essentially trapped.

Yes, he'd been watching her all evening.

"Fuck yes," he answered flatly. "And this is what the hell is the matter with me." He bent his head and she guessed what he was about to do at the last moment; he caught it in the way her breathing changed before he kissed her.

The only thing he could say in his favor was that other than the element of surprise, he did nothing to prevent her from pulling away. Her lips were soft and smooth and warm, pretty much living up to his fantasies of this moment, and while he wouldn't say precisely that she kissed him back, she didn't stop him either.

So he took his time about it, a voice in his head telling him maybe this would be the only one, so get it right, buddy . . .

When he lifted his head and looked at her, she seemed unnerved. She just stood there in her coat and that killer dress and stared at him like he'd lost his mind. He had, so the look was justified.

He might have just seriously fucked his career, and even worse, his life. He'd worked hard to redeem himself with Metzger and thought he'd succeeded pretty well, a lot in part because of Ellie, and now it was possible he'd screwed it all up. If she cried sexual harassment and complained, the chief might just fire him.

Brilliant move.

But *worth it*. And she wouldn't do that, or he didn't think so. Request a different partner maybe, but she wasn't the type to screw him over that way.

Silence. A little too prolonged. Ellie MacIntosh at a loss for words for once.

He was a little shook up himself. He fumbled in his pocket for his key card and turned away. "I think you can see now why maybe we should just talk about the case tomorrow on the way back. Don't ever expect me to apologize for what I just did, by the way."

Ellie tossed her coat on a chair and sat down on the edge of the bed before kicking out of her shoes, the turn of the evening a little surreal.

What just happened?

Jason Santiago had just kissed her and actually, it had been quite a memorable experience, done with a surprising amount of finesse for a man who was much more action-oriented usually, his edginess one of the things that made him such an effective police officer. In bed she imagined he would be more passionate than tender and the pace would be about a hundred miles an hour, more like a high-speed drag race than a moonlit walk on a beach.

And he was fooling himself if he thought she expected him to ever apologize for anything. She knew better. Definitely not Santiago.

This wasn't a complication she needed. She exhaled and stared at the ceiling as she flopped backward on the generic bedspread.

Had she imagined him in bed?

No.

Well, maybe in the back of her mind. It wasn't a betrayal of her relationship with Bryce, she assured herself, just a commentary on the dynamics of how women and men interact. Sexual attraction happened, that was how the world stayed populated. She'd always just interpreted her partner's suggestive remarks as his idea of cracking a crude joke but maybe on some level she'd known he *wasn't* joking.

As luck would have it, Bryce called at that moment. She recognized the ring and stared at her purse for a moment before snapping it open and taking out her phone. "Hi."

"I hope it isn't too late to call. How was the big night?"

That was quite a question. Answering it would take a great deal more reflection than she'd had time to do just yet. Analyzing her feelings at this moment was a bit of an overwhelming proposition. Ellie said, "Interesting."

"Interesting good or interesting bad?"

She could picture him, probably at the desk wherever he was staying—he'd sublet an apartment—no doubt in front of his computer, his dark hair hanging over his brow.

"Fine. Dinner was this six-course thing . . . very good. I've been bad about cooking for myself lately. So it was kind of a treat. I had a nice time overall."

Not completely honest but close. She'd enjoyed herself until the very end. Now she was just confused and not very happy about it. "We just got back a few minutes ago. What's it like in New York?"

"The weather? It's snowing. The city looks like a jewel with the lights in the buildings and a veil of white."

He did have a way with words. Ellie adjusted her position so she was propped against the pillows. What she really wanted to do was remove her pantyhose but it was almost impossible one-handed. She tried it anyway. "I bet. The book?"

"Going pretty well. How about the murders? My parents keep me up on what's in the paper."

"The leads we have so far are kind of all over the place. The good news is we have a few."

"That is good news. I miss you, just in case you were wondering."

"I miss you too." She did, but they were still at cross purposes, no illusions there. Maybe now more than ever. "Going to New York still feels like the right thing to do?"

"I think so," he answered, his voice casual, though Bryce wasn't casual about anything. His intensity was different than Santiago's but it was there. "I was crowding you, this book is important to me, and logistically, you would never come with me, I knew that. I don't mean that like it sounds either, your life just wouldn't allow it even if it was what you wanted."

Even if it was what she wanted? It was so close to the conversation she'd had with Georgia Lukens she was stuck there without a reply until she finally came up with a careful comment. "That is an interesting way of putting it. I don't think there is a right way to respond."

"I'm not asking you to." He smiled, she could hear it in his voice. "If there is one thing I learned from being married to Suzanne for five years, it is that having your own life is really important. Self-reliance is a virtue, not a sin. Okay, now that sounded a shade too philosophical for a phone conversation. Tell me about the governor's mansion. Nice?"

"What do you think? Very."

"I know Santiago was dreading it. He survive?"

"Made it through, but he's glad it is over is my impression." Her voice was a little stilted. "There are times I think I understand him, and times I am not so sure."

An understatement, so she changed the subject. "The one thing I'd do if I was in New York is catch a Broadway show. I'm not much for crowds but I'd have that on my list. Have you been?"

He had. He'd caught *The Phantom of the Opera* and it was, according to him, wonderful. She relaxed a little at the change in subject, opening the bottle of water the hotel had provided, physically and mentally tired but glad he'd called by the time they hung up.

She might be a detective but she hadn't the faintest clue what to do about Santiago. Or Bryce, for that matter. Or her mother's illness . . .

Or the murders.

The case notes sat in her briefcase by the side of the bed. Ellie changed into pajama pants and a T-shirt, had another sip of water, and propped the file on her lap.

She used a pad of paper and pen instead of her computer. Sometimes she thought better that way, just musing it out. First she wrote: *Dead professor.*

Peterson was an enigma to the extent that he seemed like a boring, maybe even pretentious man with a wife who was, in Ellie's opinion—like Santiago's—more bitter over losing her source of income than her husband. Why kill him?

Exhibit one.

Squatter. Exhibit two. They still knew nothing except

he'd never rented the house, and the kids heard the woman screaming. Possible black car, no idea of the make or model.

Exhibit three. *Body in woods*. Maybe an identity, but it didn't connect anything except the slashed face, the drug, and the postmortem cross in the chest.

Exhibit four. *Dead drug dealer*.

She still wasn't sure how it fit in. Gurst could easily have just been a casualty of his dubious profession.

Maybe ticking off the boxes would help. Except for the shooting victim, all of them were done by one killer, of that she had no doubt. The signature was there in the form of the drug, the way their faces were cut up, and the cross in the form of stab wounds in their chests.

Wait a minute. Remember?

She riffled through the papers and pulled out the autopsy reports to compare them. There were similarities besides the cause and manner of death. According to the medical examiner's reports, they were all about the same height and weight, blond-haired, and as disturbing as it was to read how their eyes had been destroyed, blue-eyed.

She wrote down: *physical characteristics?*

Under normal circumstances she would call Santiago and ask him what he thought about that theory since he'd never had any trouble calling her at odd hours, but she had absolutely no idea what to say to him on this particular evening, so it would be a good topic tomorrow when they drove back to Milwaukee.

Better than the alternative conversation certainly.

Chapter 19

Her first two appointments had not shown up, but that was not unusual. One of the warnings professors had given everyone who aspired to her choice in profession when Georgia was still in college was that patients were notoriously unreliable, and needed to be treated for it.

She'd laughed at the time—everyone had—but it had proven to be true, so resignation now better described her attitude. It was protocol to bill their insurance anyway if they didn't at least call, but rarely did she take that route. After all, she was supposed to be their only friend in oh-so too many instances.

Mrs. Markinson was a chronic hoarder. Neat, elderly, polite, and a woman with a house that had stacks of plastic jugs, piles of papers, and according to her children, enough canned food to feed most of the African continent. Georgia listened to the classic excuses and denials and kept a pleasant and nonjudgmental expression on her face.

"They don't understand." Mrs. Markinson was deferential and would have been a perfect candidate for grandmother of the year. She wore a high-collared dress with a prim bow at her throat, slip-on rubber boots over her sturdy shoes, and had a pious look on her lined face.

It was tempting to believe her, except there were rats in her house and her children refused to take any of their children near their mother.

Irrefutable fact. It was a very real problem. One of her sons had shown Georgia the exterminator's report.

This was their first session. Georgia said, "I completely understand your desire to not throw anything useful away. Have you thought about recycling?"

A hesitation. Short but telling. "Oh, yes. But who would do that for me?"

"Your sons say they have offered."

"I would have to go through it and I don't really have time."

"Mrs. Markinson, you are retired. True?"

The older woman said defensively, "I worked for fifty-two years. Cooked, cleaned, raised children, and kept house."

"That is extremely admirable. Are you still keeping house? Your children don't think so."

"One of my sons is a lawyer, and the other does some kind of financial work. They do not understand that I can't afford to throw things out."

This was going to be a long road.

"Emotionally can't afford it?" Georgia kept her voice gentle. One of the challenges as a therapist was to understand and treat behaviors that were personally incomprehensible to her as an individual.

"I don't know what you mean." Mrs. Markinson had a stubborn tone.

But she did. She knew full well, and Georgia stifled a sigh. Therapy was like quitting smoking. It only worked if you wanted it to work. She was not sitting in that chair voluntarily.

Forty-five minutes later, when Jason Santiago sauntered through the door, it was a relief to see him. Evasive was not his usual way of dealing with therapy. He wore the usual ensemble of jeans and leather jacket and though she always found the courtesy amusing, politely waited for her to sit down before he took a chair.

He began the conversation with the declaration, "I fucked up."

An interesting statement. "How so?"

"Totally."

He was pretty funny sometimes. She laughed. "The governor thing? What did you do? Step on his foot? Or more likely yet, put *your* foot in your mouth?"

She found it refreshing to talk to him because he didn't pull punches so what she got she was fairly sure was always the truth. She had no illusions—he was seeing her because he knew MacIntosh saw her and had some secret hope of insight into his partner's private life that he was not going to get—but his basic honesty was likeable. Did Georgia ever think he'd be capable of crossing the line of the law? Yes, she did, but was convinced only for a good cause.

"No feet. Just shook his hand." Jason laughed ruefully. "I'm talking about Ellie."

Ellie? He'd almost always referred to her as MacIntosh until lately, so that was interesting. Georgia had been waiting for him to personalize it beyond his sexual attraction to his partner himself, not just because of her observations. A small milestone, but progress.

"So?"

"I kissed her."

Had he now? She did have a front seat on an interesting relationship journey. "Her reaction?"

"We are basically not talking about it."

"Denial. I see."

"Oh, hell no. Not denial. It happened, we both know it happened, but we aren't hashing it over." He shook his head, sprawled in his chair in his usual careless pose. "I really don't know what I was thinking. I mean she looked great, but that wasn't it. I see her almost every day anyway and always think she looks great. It was more that she didn't get it. How is it possible that we work together, literally risk our lives for each other, and she had no clue as to how I feel? She's the smartest woman I have ever met."

"No offense taken, by the way," Georgia said dryly. "I have to wonder if your evident frustration is really with her, or with your inability to just tell her the truth."

"Ouch, I think you just jabbed me back." His mouth curved. "I just meant how can it be that someone so intelligent could be so clueless?"

Georgia propped her elbows on her desk and gazed at him. "Do you think maybe you are interested in shifting the responsibility? You've been on your own for a long time. You take care of Jason Santiago and no one else. Suddenly you find yourself wanting to take care of her and it bothers you that you are not certain how to do it. What you'd like is for her to step in and teach you, but she is not fulfilling that expectation, and being on even footing with you professionally, she really doesn't need you to take care of her anyway."

"Is emasculation supposed to be part of the therapy process?" he asked irritably after a moment. "Okay, fine, I'll own that she can handle herself. In fact, of the partners I've had, she holds her own, or maybe is better than any of the others. I trust her."

Georgia settled for murmuring, "Tell me about the kiss."

Predictably, he looked even more irritated. "What kind of question is that? You want details? It was a kiss. I shouldn't have done it probably, but I did. I wanted to. Do I think it was a mistake? Obviously. You're the one who keeps urging me to tell her, and actions speak louder than words, right?"

"I don't think every embrace is created equal." Georgia stifled a smile because his reaction was so typically male. To a male, action was so much easier, and to a female, talking seemed to make the most sense. "How did she respond? That was my actual question."

He blew out a short breath. "I don't really know."

"Let me ask you this: Do you feel better?"

He felt like shit.

Articulating it wasn't quite so easy, but that was the basic vibe.

MacIntosh wasn't talking to him. Their exchange earlier had been a brief update on the positive identification of Young as the third victim and she'd avoided even really looking at him. The return drive to Milwaukee hadn't been awkward in that she had just never referred to the kiss at all, talked on her phone most of the way and checked messages, and he'd also left it alone. It was going to be difficult for them to work as a team if they didn't resolve this in some way.

In short, he was an idiot, and so be it, but did he feel better? No.

Jason considered Dr. Lukens and raised his brows. "I think I just mentioned she isn't talking to me. How am I supposed to feel better?"

"She isn't talking about what happened, but I'd guess that's because she's still processing it. You know, like a detective might."

He liked Lukens. Had she been some earnest know-it-all scholar he would have gritted his teeth to make it through the evaluation for the department, but never have set one foot back through her office door. So he regarded her with a look he hoped said he was serious. He didn't take this lightly. "Very funny. So you're saying back off until she says something?"

"You know full well that she and Bryce Grantham are at a sort of crossroads. I am not betraying confidence by pointing that out because you have mentioned it to me before, so I know you are aware of what is going on." She tilted her head a little, studying him. "I want to ask you another question, Detective. I would like you to carefully consider the answer, understood? No knee-jerk response, please. If Ellie came to you tonight and said she'd sleep with you this very evening, one encounter, but absolutely no strings because she's waiting on what Grantham decides to do next, what would you say?"

His instinctive reaction would be to point out flippantly that it meant that had been one hell of a kiss then, but she'd asked him directly to not be a smartass. He started to respond, "I'd . . . ," trailed off, and then after thinking it over, said simply, "I guess I'd say no thanks. Don't get me wrong, I have some pretty wicked fantasies about the two of us naked in a nice, soft bed, but not under those circumstances."

"Why?"

"Because I think about Ellie naked often and—"

"Stop that. We both know you are just avoiding the answer."

He moved, shifting his entire body. "Look, Doc, I think you already know the answer to the question. Can we skip this?"

"I do think I know the answer, but until you tell me, it is just a guess."

Fine. "I'm not really interested in a glass that is half empty," he explained rapidly, resisting the urge to shove his fingers through his hair because she probably knew by now that he did that when he was pushed and she was definitely pushing him on purpose. "Sex is great, but sex isn't everything. I can find someone for that if the itch gets bad, but meaningless sex is just that. I'd probably take it, but I'm pretty sure I'd hate myself in the morning."

That joke certainly fell flat.

"Are you finally admitting that maybe this is important to you?"

"Have I ever said it wasn't?"

"Have you ever said it was?"

What kind of a question was that? Kate used to tell him

an argument for the sake of the argument was counterproductive and he was starting to believe that. "Did Ellie tell you we have a decent lead on the slasher case?"

Georgia Lukens looked interested. "I am not going to tell you what she did or did not tell me, but go ahead, please, since you want to change the subject. I watch the news and haven't heard you have a suspect."

"We don't. All the victims have similar characteristics in a physical sense, but nothing else in common as far as we can tell. We're not sure what it means, but possibly something. Coincidence is not a term we use often with a case like this one."

"So your killer is targeting males that possibly remind him of someone? From a psychological standpoint, that's quite fascinating."

"I don't think the victims would agree. Hell, it could be me. Blond and about my height. We don't have much more."

"It is a possibility that whoever is murdering these men in such a heinous and violent manner was the victim of abuse at the hands of an authority figure such as a father or teacher."

"Or minister or priest." Jason thought about the postmortem cross pattern on their chests. "That's a viable theory, but only helpful if we can find someone and dig into their past. Other people would have to know about the abuse and be willing to tell us about it. When it comes to sexual abuse especially, men don't exactly open up. My father never did that to me as a kid, but he was pretty free with his fists. I had a few parents of friends and some teachers who asked me about the bruises and I just lied."

He'd never really told anyone else that before now.

Dr. Lukens clearly contemplated her reply. "Why would you lie?"

He shrugged. "Didn't want to be a foster kid. The devil I knew was at least familiar and I learned at an early age to stay away from him when he was drunk. Otherwise he pretty much left me alone. It wasn't bad, all in all. I sure as hell have seen kids who had it worse than I did."

"But surely painful, just the same."

"I didn't really know anything else, so no, not really." True. And if he'd gotten his only parent in trouble, he might go from only pretty bad to worse.

"Would you ever treat children of your own that way?"

"Jesus. Hell no."

It came out more vehemently than he'd intended so he modified the tone of his voice. "I happen to love kids but my old man didn't. Not everyone who becomes a parent should be one. I think he knew it too, which is why I really didn't take it personally. At least we had that understanding between us."

"A healthy attitude."

The light on her desk glowed and so he got up. "Next patient is here. Thanks for the insight on the case. I'll pass that one along to MacIntosh."

Georgia Lukens shot back at him a final bit of observation. "So she's back to MacIntosh when you mention the case? Ellie is the woman and MacIntosh is your partner? You are going to have to reconcile that the two are one and the same."

"The problem is, I have. It would be easier to separate the two," he said as he left the room.

Chapter 20

Fergusson wants an update on the cases." Ellie spoke shortly. "Let's go."

Santiago glanced up, nodded, pressed a button on his computer, and shut it down. He was remarkably quiet for him as they walked down the hallway to the chief detective's office, but then again, they were both being distant, and she wasn't sure if it was cause and effect. She was really avoiding him and since he was smart, he knew it.

Life really could change in the blink of an eye.

Fergusson, hefty and keen-eyed, did not appear to be in a good mood, and that was not unusual, but she had the uneasy feeling they were about to get reamed. He didn't even tell them to sit down. He said with false pleasantness, "I'm going to keep this meeting simple. I want some good news, okay? Metzger is getting pressure from the university, for one thing, to solve a murder that happened on its campus. From your reports, I'm pretty disappointed in the progress being made. Your problem is this face-slashing deal is catching the eye of the media again, and the citizens of this city seem to have a high opinion of your abilities to solve this kind of case, but *I'm* starting to have some doubts. The leads you do have are all over the place and no point A leads to a point B, much less a point C. Peterson's widow just did an interview with the university paper, and I realize that is not a nationwide publication, but she expressed in not very subtle terms that she believes our homicide division is overrated. If the city papers don't pick it up, I'll be surprised, and be aware it is unflattering."

"Look—" Santiago started to say heatedly.

"Shut up." Fergusson gave them both a flinty look. "I also think she's a bitch, I talk to her on the phone about every other day, but she is entitled to her opinion and she is the widow of a man who died horrifically. The public will feel sorry for her, and to a certain extent, they should excuse how she is acting. So should we."

Santiago rubbed his taut jaw. "She knows something. First she came to me and told me explicitly—ask Grasso—to not let this case be sensationalized, and then she does a newspaper interview and slams us? What the fuck?"

Fergusson put his beefy hands on the desktop, fingers splayed. "How do I know? If you think she knows something, go after it. Or I'll send Grasso. He solved his last case in two days. She might like him, or at least his *GQ* look."

Ellie said caustically, because the implied criticism stung, "His last case was a drunk and disorderly that only turned into a homicide because the victim was so intoxicated when he was shoved during a bar fight, he fell and hit his head.

Manslaughter at best. There were about twenty witnesses. That gang case before it doesn't count either."

"I'm not picking on you, MacIntosh. I'm pointing out he's free right now."

"Oh." She stopped and compromised because she was angry too, but she'd met Mrs. Peterson. The woman disliked her, and Santiago was certainly a little intense for most people. So she settled for a more civil tone. "Grasso is good, no denying it, and you might have a point. He's pretty upper crust and that is definitely her thing. Sure helped in our last case. If he is free, my vote is, we'd appreciate it if he'd try to talk to her."

To her surprise, her partner caved pretty easily. Usually he was opposed to sharing an investigation. Santiago muttered, "Fine by me. If I never have to speak to that woman again, it won't have me crying in my beer. She's a . . . well, I'm going to use some self-restraint here, but bitch is too mild. Use your imagination and supply the word."

Ellie refrained from commenting. She didn't really disagree. Mrs. Peterson had been antagonistic from the beginning.

"She isn't the killer, but maybe a lover is the reason she seems to be panicking?" She threw it out there because she'd been thinking about it—a lot. "It doesn't take great deductive skills to assume it is possible she demands to know how the investigation is progressing more because she wants to be abreast of what we know and don't know."

"There's a problem with that theory," Santiago said with a hint of his infamous sarcasm, "she *can't* be a good lay."

In open disgust but unwillingly amused, Ellie said, "I

meant her *husband* was having an affair. She's figured it out somehow and does not want us to do the same thing."

He brightened theatrically. "Possible he was cheating . . . I would."

"Now, see, that kind of statement might be why you are still single, Santiago."

"Maybe." His face went shuttered. "Hey, you're single too."

Fergusson intervened. "Go talk it over with Grasso and you two keep me informed, right?"

They left, walking down the generic hallway. Her partner said coolly, "I think we need to interview Lance Young's coworkers as soon as we talk to Grasso. Monday is a business day. Someone will be in the office."

"I agree." Her tone matched his.

Maybe a shade chillier.

He caught it, but then again, she'd intended it that way. It was ridiculous, but having had over a day to think about it, her initial confusion had turned to resentment. When she'd been assigned Santiago as a partner he'd absolutely rubbed her the wrong way with his abrasive remarks and he definitely had not been secretive about how he disliked working with a female detective that did not have his level of experience. During their first big case they'd discovered— both of them were surprised—that they worked well together, and formed a truce.

In her opinion, he'd ruined that relationship.

"Look"—his hand shot out and shackled her wrist, stopping them both right in the middle of the hallway—"is the cold-shoulder treatment necessary?"

He'd said he wasn't going to apologize and she believed

that to be true, but he did at least look a little repentant and obviously it was bothering him too. There was a hint of regret in his blue eyes as he stared down at her, but she doubted it was for the kiss, but more for her reaction to it. Whatever his faults, they did have one thing in common and that was a passion for the job.

"You were pretty unprofessional."

"I wasn't a cop at that moment. I was a man."

She didn't really have an answer to that, but with unfortunate timing, Metzger's secretary walked by. He had a new one and she was brusquely efficient, much like her boss. She said, "What's this? Lover's quarrel? I just dropped off the ballistics report for our drug dealer. The chief pushed it through fast and Rays wanted you to have it too, so I made copies. On your desks, Detectives."

To his credit Santiago let go of Ellie's wrist right away, and might have even seemed chagrined, if that was possible. She said, "Thanks, Liz." She glanced at her partner. "Let's go take a look."

The office itself was a generic cinder block building in an industrial district that was being renovated bit by bit, and since the only people that worked there were management in the extermination company, Jason wouldn't call the visit a success. Lance was a good employee, they'd learned from his earnest boss, had been with them for several years, always serviced his calls, and very rarely called in. He'd passed the yearly drug screening with flying colors and unfortunately didn't talk about his private life, if he had one.

One way or another, everyone had a personal existence

even if it meant watching reruns of sitcoms from the fifties with your mother while eating microwave popcorn. It was a life away from work. Lance actually *had* lived with his mother, but according to her, he wasn't home much and it was a temporary arrangement as he switched apartments.

"He had charges on his credit cards from two different bars." Ellie opened the door and got into the car. "Let's go check them out."

Jason was driving and he went around to the driver's side. "If he was a regular, they might remember him if it is a local place. I don't recognize the names of either of them, but this city has a lot of bars."

"I'm sure you've visited your share."

A hint of the normal Ellie. He'd take the gesture toward getting everything back to normal, at least while they were working. "And I'm always willing to expand my horizons." He pulled out and they headed for a district right off downtown, a mixture of older, nice neighborhoods and urban amenities including, apparently, a place called Joelle's. It was pretty full even on a Monday afternoon, probably because of a happy hour special, and the clientele was a mixture of young professionals sprinkled with blue-collar types with their names embroidered on their shirts. Loud, busy, trendy.

A flash of Young's picture yielded nothing but a shake of the head from the bartender, but he did wave over a waitress who obligingly showed it around to the other staff.

Dead end.

The second place, however, was quieter and only about a block from his mother's house. Dark, smelled a little like stale beer, and the music was subdued. Old tables lined the walls, and there were pictures of sports stars on the walls, most of which were no longer in this world, and televisions tuned to ESPN mounted in the corners. Of the two, Jason would prefer this one for a quiet drink, but probably Lance knew his job hung on being able to drive from house to house, so the lure was that he could walk to it.

The white-haired man at the bar was the owner and he recognized Young right away. "Right, yeah, know him. He hasn't been in since last week and I'm kind of surprised. Doesn't usually come here on Friday or Saturday, but is pretty regular during the week. What's he done? Seems like a nice guy."

"He's a nice *dead* guy." Jason leaned on the bar. "Help us out. He ever come in with anyone? A girl or a buddy? We'll listen to whatever you can tell us."

"A young woman was with him the last time he came in. He's . . . dead?"

"Can we get a description of the woman?'

"Um, dark hair. She had long brown hair. Give me a sec." The owner waited a minute to think about it even though a phone was ringing somewhere. He had a diet soda sitting on a paper coaster patterned with a pig's face, and took a drink. "I'm good with faces. Probably thirty, no . . . maybe younger, I'd say. Around his age, pretty, and might have been a knockout under the layers of makeup. I don't like women who do themselves up too much." He eyed Ellie. "Taller than you, but not by much. Not as slender, but close. She had on a short skirt and heels I thought were risky in this weather. Black ice isn't just on the roads. The sidewalks aren't too friendly."

"When was this?" Ellie asked it with a friendly smile but

her gaze was razor sharp. "We certainly appreciate your help. He came here often and we have the credit card traces, but if you could pinpoint when she was with him, then maybe we can track her down and find out if she has information."

"Last visit." The proprietor sounded positive. "I mean, he came in here alone a lot. I remember thinking to myself it was nice to see he had a girlfriend."

"Ever seen her before?"

"No."

"He buy, or did she pay for anything?"

"He paid like he usually did, with his credit card. She had a cup of coffee and he had a beer."

"Would you recognize her again? You seem to have an above-average memory."

It was true, but still pleased the guy. He inclined his head. "I think I would if you brought me a picture or if she walked through the door."

Jason handed him his card. "If you see her again or remember anything else, even something that seems insignificant, can you give us a call?"

"Sure." He tucked the card in his shirt pocket after looking at it, and wiped the bar, unsmiling. "So, he was murdered? It isn't part of that thing I saw on the news, is it?"

"I'm afraid so," Ellie confirmed as they turned away and walked toward the door.

"Find who did it," the owner called out. "That was a nice young man."

When they emerged onto the street, it had started to sift fine white particles from the sky again, courtesy of the winter in the northern climes. Jason considered opening her door but thought better of it. Anything at this point that might topple over the tenuous understanding they had to put the other night behind them was not worth risking. "I take the position that anyone is too young to be stabbed to death and dumped in the woods. Anyway, his mother didn't say anything about a girlfriend."

"His mother," Ellie said as she looked down the street, a light frosting of snow landing on her hair, "was so distraught and incoherent when we talked to her, I am surprised she could string two words together and I can't blame her. The living back home thing is obviously not what he wanted for more than a few months. Dismiss the idea she would know his life."

Jason didn't disagree. "So where do you want to go next?"

His partner eyed the darkening sky. "Peterson's wife is now up to Grasso, and I think that's a good call. A woman screamed when our second victim was killed, and there was a woman with Lance Young on the night he died. Peterson might have been having an affair. The thread is starting to bother me."

"They were stabbed," he protested. "That isn't a woman's crime." But he understood her unease.

"It isn't a woman's crime because a man is usually stronger." MacIntosh now had snowflakes on her eyelashes. "But, if fed rufilin, they might not be as able to defend themselves."

Jason put his hand up and rubbed his forehead. A part of him didn't believe it. But a part of him did. "Holy shit, what if we *are* looking for a woman?"

Chapter 21

Lea never talks about her mother."

Georgia considered her patient across the polished surface of her desk. Another conversation with Grant had her convinced that a switch in how she handled Rachel's therapy might be beneficial. "And why do you worry about that? All of us avoid topics that make us uncomfortable. Not everyone is lucky enough to have a good relationship with their parents."

"I care about her and her problems," Rachel said defensively. This morning she was back to a plain mousy gray sweater and a straight black skirt and the worn flats. "We're friends."

"Yet you've talked about trying to get her to move out."

There were times when Rachel seemed unfocused, but she sent Georgia an almost combative look. "I realize we have a dysfunctional relationship and you've been trying to figure out how to say it diplomatically, Dr. Lukens. I'm here talking to you because I already know that. I just want some advice on how to handle it."

That was very assertive for Rachel, so maybe Grant's angle was effective. "You've told me that you are a little afraid of her, that you think she won't consider your wishes, that she borrows things without asking, and yet you prefer her to be there so you don't have to be alone. I think you should weigh the benefits of having a friend that doesn't take you into consideration very much, and am curious about what problems have you so concerned."

Rachel smoothed back her hair. "She sometimes follows men."

"Follows them?" Georgia had to admit that was a startling revelation. "Follows them in what way?"

"If she's interested in them she follows them around for a while. So she already knows where they work, where they live, that sort of thing. It's weird, isn't it?"

"It is certainly unusual, yes." That kind of behavior definitely gave Georgia pause. "Tell me something, have you ever asked her why she would bother to do that? Obviously the two of you have talked about it."

Rachel visibly shivered. "No, we haven't. Not really. I just know she does it. I think I'm a little afraid of the answer if I ask directly."

"I get that, but you brought it up, so it is bothering you. Is there any reason for you to be afraid of Lea?"

"No, but maybe the men she chooses should be afraid. I think they remind her of someone." Then she added in a very emotionless voice, "She has a gun. I've seen it. But now it's gone."

. . .

The house was pretty cold and empty as usual. Ellie dropped her keys on the hall table, and then went into the kitchen. Maybe it had been a mistake to move in with Bryce and maybe it had been a life lesson. Certain people were not cut out to share their life. What if she was one of them?

She went to the refrigerator and took out some sliced cheese she'd bought earlier in the week, ate it standing there, and then shut the door. That really was not dinner, but she wasn't in the mood to cook.

So she changed, took out her cell phone, and called her sister. Jody answered pretty quickly, which either meant she was stirring something delicious on the stove, or just got done reading someone a bedtime story. Jody was pregnant again, this time with a boy. Ellie did ask, "Good time or bad time to talk?"

"I'm not throwing up, so hey, take advantage of the window. If I start to gurgle and drop the phone, you are just going to have to forgive me. They call it morning sickness, right? Why do I have it constantly?"

Ellie laughed softly. "You don't really do a lot to glamorize pregnancy."

"Let's see. My butt is probably bigger than it has ever been, I have to eat two ounces of food at a time or there will be trouble if you are between me and the closest bathroom, and I'm pretty damn tired before the baby is even kicking me in the ribs. Let's not mention how I can't color my hair so I have roots that make me look like a reverse skunk. If you need more glamour than that, you are just plain greedy. What's up?"

The beauty of Jody was her ability to make everything funny. "Not much compared to you. Just the average murder stuff."

"I contemplate murder each day. But then they pick up their toys and I allow them to live."

"You adore your children."

"I do. Hence their continued existence, and you haven't answered my question."

Ellie was sitting on the couch in the living room in flannel pajama bottoms, wool socks, and a long-sleeved T-shirt, sipping a glass of Merlot. "I talked to Mom earlier. She sounded pretty good, but I'm glad Aunt Clare is there with her."

"I know. She told me they had a hysterical time picking out wigs. There's nothing wrong with her sense of humor and when those two are together I sometimes laugh until I cry. Talk about two squabbling older ladies who love each other dearly, but snipe at each other constantly. I suppose that's our future, sis. Only, can we move to Bermuda instead of Florida? I've always wanted to go there but somehow end up at Disney World instead. The kids think lying on a beach is boring. Whatever happened to sand buckets and cute shovels? I keep telling them that back in the olden days that was good enough for us, but they still prefer roller coasters and dancing mice with giant plastic heads."

"Olden days? Hey, I take exception to that." Ellie set down her glass. "Speaking of moving . . . I'm thinking about it, but not to Bermuda. I might start looking for another condo to lease until my house up north sells."

"I wondered. On the one hand, it seems wrong to let that big fancy house sit empty, but on the other hand, I could see where you might feel awkward living in someone else's house when they aren't even there."

That very accurate observation made Ellie feel better—and worse. Half-jokingly she said, "Jody, you were supposed to talk me out of it and tell me how Bryce and I are perfect for each other."

"Honey, I like Bryce. A lot. He's the catch of the century in some ways, but what I see is the two of you amicably living your separate lives pretty much like you do now if you stay together, and if that is what you want, fine, it's your life."

"But?"

"Did I say 'but'?"

"Yes, you did. It was implied." Ellie picked up her glass again and took a large mouthful.

"Sorry. How about, for once, I don't know what advice to give you. Forgive me. Want me to come down and look with you?"

Did she? No. Then she'd be tempted to spill out this new problem with Santiago and Jody would have an opinion and she wasn't sure she wanted to hear it. "No, I need to talk to Bryce first. It's hardly fair to him if I have plans set in place to move before I even tell him I'm thinking it all over."

"He went to New York without consulting you."

"He had good reasons to go there. The book deal, research, meeting with his publisher and agent—"

"I'm not arguing that, I am just stating that you are the one who told me he didn't exactly advertise when he was going."

True. She shut her eyes and leaned back. "I need to get through this case before I do anything."

Her sister said somberly, "So I understand. They are really starting to talk about it on the news."

"We're doing our best."

"Of course. There's no doubt here."

After they hung up Ellie contemplated watching a movie, but decided silence was better, just sitting there, half-reclined on the couch. Outside the windows it was dark and cold.

The killer *could* be using rufilin to disorient the victims for a specific reason. Was it less physical ability to carry out the intended crime?

Why would a man need to do that?

He probably wouldn't. Santiago was right, a knife was not usually a woman's weapon, but she was starting to think that a female was involved in the murders in some way.

The knock came as he was putting his plate in the dishwasher—how long had it been since he'd run it? Probably three days, but Jason tended to cook with the least frequency possible. In the summer he almost exclusively used his outdoor grill, a stainless steel indulgence that had a side burner and was on his outside balcony. Tonight he'd baked a frozen chicken patty and ate it on bread with some ketchup. To his credit he'd been out of potato chips, so he'd eaten some canned green beans with it. Seemed almost healthy . . .

When he opened the door, the young woman on the other side smiled at him with uncertainty. "Hi."

Lauren. He'd gotten the impression she might be interested but not that she'd just show up out of the blue. She didn't seem the type.

He said uncertainly, "Uh, hi. How in the hel . . . Um, how did you find me?"

Her expression was a little embarrassed and apologetic. "I have my ways. I feel kind of like a stalker, but I don't have your number. I wanted to know if you cared to go out for a drink or a cup of coffee."

Jason was rarely at a loss for words, but had to admit he wasn't sure what to say. It wasn't very late, maybe nine o'clock, but as usual he'd already had a couple of beers.

It wasn't like he had big plans for the rest of the evening, and he was flattered, if a little off balance by her boldness. But then again, what could it hurt?

"Sure. There's a place a block away. Do you mind if we walk?" He took in her jeans tucked into boots and casual coat. Women worried about how they were dressed. "It's just a bar, but it's close."

"Not at all. Sure, let's walk. It's cold, but not bad."

"Come on in. Let me get my jacket."

She followed him into the apartment and looked around. "This is nice."

He laughed, but was still puzzled as he opened the small hall closet that held about three things: vacuum, windbreaker, winter coat. He took out the latter. "It's generic and geared toward families, but you know, it has a laundry hookup in the apartment and a lot of parking. That did it for me. I signed the lease the day after first seeing it. How did you get the address anyway?"

"I found you through my job, not my uncle. His staff is pretty security conscious."

"Your job?" He truly was curious.

"I work at a hospital and you've been shot twice in the line of duty, remember? All those records at my fingertips." She laughed lightly.

"Abuse of power. I like that."

As they walked out the door, she glanced back at him. "Ever done it?"

"What?"

"Abuse of power?"

With a cheeky smile he responded, "Of course not. I'm sworn to uphold the law. I don't even jaywalk." Actually he'd been reprimanded for strong-arming a punk who'd needed a reality check a year or two ago, but he didn't advertise it. That incident got MacIntosh stuck with him.

"Don't tell on me. That might get me fired." She shot the words over her shoulder.

They walked down the hallway to the stairs, and she was right, when they stepped outside, the night was chill, but there wasn't any wind, and for once, it wasn't snowing.

"The governor's niece? I'm finding it doubtful you'd get fired."

"You never know who might get up in arms over nepotism."

She had a point; he'd just never been in that position. Well, not true, Metzger had cut him slack for being ex-military now and again. A former marine, the chief might have fired someone else for breaking some of the rules Jason considered to be suggestions, not carved in stone. "True. So, how long have you worked there?" he asked as they skirted the parking lot.

She pulled a pair of mittens from her pocket and slid them on. "The hospital? A few years now. I got a different job right out of college, but was still looking around. We started to talk about it the other night but got interrupted. Is being a detective your dream job?"

He walked beside her, hands in his pockets. Gloves, and more so mittens, were an impediment to drawing his weapon if necessary. "Yep. A detective with MPD is exactly what I want to do, especially homicide, but you've probably already figured that one out. I'm single, and don't have any other family obligations, so why not? The married detectives have a harder time balancing the job and their families."

She slanted him a glance. "Single. I like that."

Jason had to reflect ironically that since Kate moved out his love life had been pretty much like a flatline on a heart monitor, but suddenly he seemed to have a measure of popularity—with everyone but Ellie. It figured.

"You saw my apartment. Did you doubt it?"

"True. No artificial flowers in painted vases anywhere."

"They get dusty," he said, but appreciated her sense of humor. "I can scrub a toilet, but I hate dusting."

"I knew we had something in common."

"Item number one." He saw the lights of the bar down the street. With a giant jug tilted sideways on the neon sign, it really wasn't exactly a classy place, but it had good food and served cold beer and some decent wines.

Lauren gave him an amused look as he opened the door and held it. "What a good start."

It wasn't the start of anything—he really didn't think he could do that now, but it was a nice diversion.

He wasn't thinking about the case and he wasn't thinking about Ellie at the moment. Win-win.

The bartender knew him. "Hiya, Detective. You two sitting at the bar or in a booth?"

Normally Jason just chose a stool, but a booth certainly offered a little more privacy. "The booth in the corner?"

"Help yourself. You want your usual? What about the lady?"

She ordered a glass of Chablis and slid into the booth, smiling. "Obviously you're a regular."

"I admit to not having much of a social life."

"Me either. Besides my job I take a few night classes because I want to get my MBA." She wore dark eyeliner tonight that gave her eyes a slant and he could see under the low-hanging light either her lotion or foundation had a faint hint of glitter in it. When she removed her coat she wore a tight top in a deep purple and the plunge of the neckline nicely showed off her curves.

Completely different from the other two times he'd been around her. It sparked a certain curiosity.

Of course, the first time she'd just been in a car accident, and the second was at a fancy, formal dinner, so maybe this was more the real her.

He gave her cleavage the appreciative glance it deserved, but was subtle about it, though he was pretty sure she noticed from the deepened dimple in her cheek. "It sounds like you keep busy."

She thanked the bartender nicely for her drink as he set it down on a little napkin. "I do. What about you? What do you do in your spare time, Mr. Detective? Do you have family around here? What's your story?"

Eventually every woman asked that. He was just never sure how to answer it.

"City kid, no picket fences in our neighborhood, and the only dogs were the ones who tipped over the trash every Wednesday. No family around here."

"Street boy, eh?"

"Pretty much."

"With a good sense of humor. I like it."

She had one too, he decided as they sipped and talked, and after he paid for their drinks—she tried but he insisted— they walked back to his apartment building. Even though it was weird as hell to just have her show up, it really had been a welcome distraction.

"I'll walk you to your car," he insisted, noting the ice crystals on the windshields. By now it was getting close to ten thirty and the parking lot was quiet.

"Over there." She pointed at her expensive car that had evidently been repaired because it looked sleek and polished. She turned and offered him her hand. "I had a nice time, Detective Jason Santiago. Would you mind if we did it again sometime?"

Would he? No, it had been a nice diversion. Why not? "I'd mind if we didn't."

"Let me give you my number."

Chapter 22

Georgia was in the bathtub when the phone rang, neck deep in bubbles, a cup of tea on a small stand. It was her one true indulgence—a long hot bath at least twice a week in contrast to the quick showers she usually took in the mornings before heading to her office. It gave her time to think, and of course, that usually involved her patients and their problems. She really needed to do something about her dead-end personal life.

She'd been reflecting on how she was looking forward to her next session with Ellie. It was a bit of a muddy spot ethically to be seeing both her and Santiago even though the department had done the initial referral. Ellie obviously didn't know he'd decided on private therapy past that one initial evaluation, and if he chose to keep that to himself, Georgia couldn't violate his privacy. If they were just two ordinary people who worked together it was hardly an issue, but Jason's deepening feelings put her in a some-what tenable position.

She had to admit she was extremely curious to see if Ellie would mention the kiss.

Drying off her hand, she picked up her phone and lis-tened to the message from her service, and then called them back. "This is Dr. Lukens. Did the patient mention suicide?"

"No, just was extremely insistent she see you right away."

That was interesting. Rachel was unstable, in Georgia's professional opinion. However, any mention of possibly treating the symptoms with medication was firmly rejected, so she'd left it alone. "I do know my ten o'clock canceled, so tell her I can see her then. Thank you."

All hopes of catching up on her notes were now gone, so she'd better get to the office early. Reluctantly getting out of the bath and wrapping herself in a fluffy towel, she had to wonder what Lea had done now. It seemed that more and more the focus of their sessions involved Lea's prob-lems much more than Rachel's issues with trust and men in general. Georgia had treated asexual patients before—it was more common than people realized—and she was fairly sure Rachel fit the category, but whether it was a simple matter of a hormonal imbalance or some past trauma, she still couldn't say.

She doubted the emergency included a male, so Lea or her work seemed the logical choices. As devoted as Rachel seemed to be to her job, if she was in a panic over some-thing, losing her position would be paramount, but Georgia found out she was wrong when Rachel walked in precisely at ten, her face drawn.

She sat in her usual fussy manner, brushing off the chair

first, settling down, and crossing her legs. Very rarely did she set her purse on the floor but preferred it in her lap, and this morning her fingers clasped it tightly. "Dr. Lukens . . . I . . . I . . ."

Behind her desk, Georgia said calmly, "Take a breath. I admit I am curious over the urgency when we have an appointment in two days, but if you need to talk to someone, that is exactly why I am here."

"I know Lea's secret." Rachel leaned forward earnestly, and her eyes glistened with tears. "I have to talk about it. I think I now understand why she is the way she is, promiscuous and selfish and taking risks that could hurt other people, even those she loves."

How to handle this was a delicate question. There were breakthrough moments in all therapy that worked, and Georgia took a second but not too long, because she didn't want her patient to back away. "She told you?"

"I discovered it."

At least the snow was melting a little, she could hear the swish of the spraying slush as cars went by on the street outside the office. "Maybe you could define for me what that means exactly."

"I usually respect her privacy." Rachel took off her coat in a gymnastics exercise that still did not involve her setting her purse on the floor. "But I was looking for something of mine since we frequently share—remember the shoes?— and I found some pictures in a drawer. So I asked her about them."

It was a measure of progress to have Rachel stand up to Lea. Georgia asked, "And how did she react?"

"She doesn't like me in her room, and I don't like her in

mine, so I respect that, but truly, she had not returned something that belonged to me, and though we argued a little she finally admitted she'd thrown it away just like the shoes."

Their bizarre relationship wasn't the most unusual Georgia had ever dealt with, but it was certainly beginning to climb to the top. "Did she explain why?"

Rachel did that thing with her head when she bent forward enough so her hair hid her face. "Not exactly. We talked about the pictures instead. She said she'd been waiting to tell me for a long time."

"Tell you what?"

"There's a little boy in the photographs. About ten or so. He was her big brother."

Was had an ominous sound to it. As Georgia watched, Rachel actually dropped her purse down on the carpet and wound her hands together. "This is so awful . . . I knew there was something in her past that explained why she is the way she is, but this is *shattering*."

Grasso's desk was a lot neater than hers, but then again, the man spent a lot of time at it. Not that she didn't spend time at hers as well, but not like him. His gray eyes were as direct as usual when he glanced up and saw them coming and his faint smile was full of triumph.

Next to her, Santiago muttered, "Oh shit, he looks smug, or as smug as he can ever look. If he breaks this case instead of us, I'm going to be extremely pissed off."

She murmured back, "You're always extremely pissed off." To Grasso she said, "You rang, Lieutenant? I take it that means you've got something."

Grasso leaned back in his leather chair, the one he'd purchased himself and brought from home. "You were right, Peterson was having an affair. It took two glasses of expensive scotch to get his lovely wife to admit it, but according to her, and I quote, 'That asshole was cheating.' You owe me by the way, because I was then subject to the history of their marriage and how she still couldn't believe it, because in her objective opinion, she's pretty wonderful. They met in college. I can tell you the rest if you'd like."

"No thanks. Okay, so let's powwow." Santiago motioned Ellie to the chair by the desk and went over to drag one from the desk of another detective who shot him a reproving look. He sat down with the back forward, his arms resting on the top. "So who is this siren who could possibly lure the esteemed professor away from his charming wife?"

"Siren? Have you been watching PBS again?" Ellie asked caustically, turning to give him an incredulous look.

"I'm a cultured kind of guy."

"Yeah . . . well, that's debatable." She asked Grasso, "Despite how it was originally phrased, that's my question too. Got a name for the mistress?"

"Only a first, I'm afraid. Mrs. Peterson never saw them together either, so no description. She thinks they met when he was doing some research for a professional article on the economic impact of health care reform, hence the tie to biology. I am told a lot of his students go on to med school. But that's a dead end since I checked with their personnel department and there is no employee there with that first name."

"Health care again," Santiago murmured not quite under his breath.

She ignored him. "In other words, a dead end. Did she cooperate enough to at least offer the name of a *few* close friends who might know who this woman is? You sure got more out of her than we did."

"Therein lies the problem. She doesn't want us questioning their friends in case this shameful secret leaks out." Grasso looked frustrated. "So, the answer is no. She claims none of them would know anything anyway."

"How did *she* find out?"

"Eavesdropping on a phone call. She called it accidentally listening, but let's face it, eavesdropping."

"I suppose she's far too ethical to nab his phone later and get a number?" Ellie's opinion of Mrs. Peterson wasn't very high. "Surely if it made her suspicious enough to think it was the other woman, she would."

Grasso said, "She did. I asked, and she says she called it and got the hospital's main desk, that's where she got the idea it might be someone from there. But he was doing an article so he had a legitimate reason to call there and if he was smart, he deleted the number anyway."

"And our killer has his phone and has probably disposed of it." Santiago looked reflective. "But we could check with the phone company that handles the hospital and see just *who* he called during the course of his research."

"I'm on that one already. They are going to get back to me."

Of course he was, Grasso was thorough. Ellie sighed. "Just because the brilliant Mrs. Peterson thinks it is someone at the hospital, it doesn't mean it is. It could be anyone, and completely unconnected to the murder. He worked at a university with pretty coeds everywhere, and since she's been so uncooperative, I'm kind of skeptical of any information coming from Peterson's widow anyway."

"I think going back to the university, questioning the other people in his department and maybe getting a roster of names for the classes he taught would not be a bad idea now that we have a first name." Santiago stood decisively. "Please tell me it isn't Mary or Susan or something else pretty common."

Grasso said, "No. Lauren."

"We'll go check it out but let us know about the hospital lead." Ellie also stood but when she looked at her partner, he had a very strange expression on his face. She asked slowly, "Something wrong?"

"I don't know." The words were measured and his eyes had that abstracted look she had come to know pretty well. "Before we go to the university, I want to look at the autopsy reports again, okay?"

Chapter 23

The walk across campus was cold as an unforgiving wind had started to pick up around noon and the snow was a gentle fall but it swirled around them in small waves. Jason wasn't a big believer in scarves any more than gloves but at the moment wished he had both. "I wonder what the damn wind chill is."

"For the last time, get over it," Ellie replied, wearing her snowflake cap. "This is Wisconsin, we don't do wind chill here. Real temperature usually scares you enough." She pointed. "I think that's the building we want."

"This place is a maze."

"Every big university is." Huddled in her coat, she went up the steps in front of him. It wasn't until they were in the hallway of the student center building that she turned to him. "Are you going to tell me what was new and enlightening in those autopsy reports or not? You've been very quiet."

"I'm still trying to decide if I am drawing a very crazy conclusion—which we are not supposed to do without enough evidence."

"True, but—"

"Ellie, you have your process and I have mine," he interrupted, his voice brusque. "Let's sniff around here again and I'll tell you this much, what we find might sway the vote on whether I tell you or just decide I have a naturally suspicious mind."

"All cops have suspicious minds." She stopped in front of a door with an opaque glass panel. "It defines who and what we are."

"Great news. Some of us are assholes," he murmured, following her inside into the office of admissions.

The person at the desk initially sent them an unfriendly stare until informed they were police detectives, and then her broad face reflected dismay but also curiosity. "What can I do for you?"

"We haven't talked to you specifically before, but we are the ones investigating the death of Professor Peterson and would appreciate the cooperation of the university in following a lead. Could you give us a list of any students who took his classes in the past year? We are especially interested in anyone who might have been taking one of his lectures or worked directly with him in the biology curriculum."

The receptionist, middle-aged and harried, at first nodded, but then frowned even as she reached for the keyboard of her computer. "Don't you need a court order for this kind of information?"

What? People watched entirely too much television, Jason thought irritably.

"Employee information in a public institution is already available, but it would be a lot simpler if you could give it to us. We can get a warrant for the student roster, but this is not invasive information, just a list of names. As I said, we are following a lead. There is no actual suspect as of yet."

In the end, a short call to Metzger, a twenty-minute wait, and one fax later, they had the information they wanted. He tried to decide if she admired the woman's stubbornness or just found it annoying since this *was* a murder investigation. Ellie stayed pleasant, but he wasn't nearly as patient. Then again, ever since their conversation with Grasso he'd been tense.

"No one named Lauren in the same department, but she could easily be other faculty," Ellie said as they walked toward the car, students streaming past, shivering against the cold. "In the past year, only two students with that name, but then again he taught upper-level classes and it isn't *that* common of a name."

"We know someone named Lauren." Jason pushed a button on his key chain to start the truck. "Just met her recently."

The offhand tone of his voice obviously set off alarm bells. He was not an offhand kind of person. Ellie looked at him sharply, "Go on."

"Pretty, wouldn't you say? She seems kind of interested. I mean she just showed up at my apartment the other night. We went out for a drink."

"Lauren, as in the governor's Lauren, just showed up? And she asked you out?"

He slanted a sardonic look her way. "Your level of surprise isn't very flattering. Yes, she asked me out for a drink and I went. Man and woman sharing a booth and having a beverage. Not a first in the history of mankind."

"True enough." She opened her own door before he could get it for her and clambered inside the vehicle. "And I'm not really all that surprised given the way she was flirting with you at the dinner. Get in and tell me why it's bothering you."

"I never stated it was bothering me." He stood there in the snow, flakes drifting onto his coat, a few clinging to his lashes. *So, she had noticed . . .*

"Bullshit," she said inelegantly and slammed the door.

She had a point, since it *was* bothering him. He went around and got in, flicking up the heat, slamming his door even more vehemently. "It was more how she acted than anything . . . I don't know. She said she was studying for her MBA, and she works at the hospital."

"She wasn't taking any of Peterson's classes."

"But what if she saw him there?"

"What if? Keep going."

"It seemed contrived." He didn't pull out right away, still thinking, staring at the snow-flecked windshield. "She really flirted with me, but there was something forced about it. I'm not doing a good job of describing it, but let's just say I had a drink with a very nice-looking young woman who went through some trouble to make it happen and I was uncomfortable for some unknown reason."

"That certainly is not you."

"I'm trying to tell you a serious story, dammit."

Ellie looked interested and that was good, but he would have preferred at least some measure of annoyance based on jealousy. "Go on. I'm listening, believe me. So a pretty woman who just happens to have the same first name as the one who might or might not have been seeing Peterson asked you out. Give me one solid reason that is pertinent to this case."

He put the truck in gear and looked over his shoulder as he backed out of the parking space as he said, "Because, FYI, I'm blond and about the same age, height, and weight as the other three victims. She also drives a pretty nice black car. During the course of casual conversation about our routine lives, she even mentioned the hospital cafeteria served some killer apple cinnamon muffins."

"You can't be serious."

"I know," he said grimly, "but yet I kind of think I am."

As she watched the white-dusted buildings as they drove past, Ellie digested this new twist to an already unusual case.

He could be delusional.

Only Jason Santiago was a lot of things, but that wasn't one of them.

He was thinking, she was thinking, and they didn't talk for a while.

In profile she studied his slightly Roman nose. There were Italians that were blond, especially from the northern part of that country. "A few more details would be appreciated for this insane theory. It could be coincidence. We are talking the governor's niece here."

"I agree, but . . ." He trailed off.

"But?"

"The name is hardly significant, I agree," he said, turning into the station parking lot. "And the muffins . . . has there ever been a murder case on record solved by a link to baked goods? It was more *her*. I'm trying hard to figure out how to describe it. She even said she felt like a stalker, and you know, it rang true. She might have been exactly that. I just have a hunch. Jesus, I hate that damn word. No, she wasn't one of his students, but there is a clear tie between Peterson and the hospital."

A hunch. And Peterson had eaten something that resembled an apple muffin. So had the second victim.

The problem was, he could be right. The link was starting to strengthen. Peterson and the hospital. Lauren and the hospital. Maybe they could link victim two as well.

He turned the truck off but Ellie didn't make a move to get out, mostly certain he was dead wrong, but not convinced enough to tell him to just go get a life. Her gaze was searching and he looked right back. "So, you are trying to tell me that a possible murderer sought out the officer who is investigating her crimes and invited him out for a drink?"

"Oh, hell no. I'm saying we stumbled across each other because of that accident and I fit what she seems to be looking for. Maybe that we're looking for *her* is a secondary thrill of some kind. Don't ask me for a motive, I don't even have a theory on that one. All I know is it seems like she went to some trouble to make sure we'd meet again, first at the dinner, and then when she came to my apartment."

"It's possible she just thinks you're an attractive guy."

"Thank you. I accept the heartfelt compliment."

He was, as usual, impossible. "A professor, a squatter, an exterminator, and a homicide detective? That's quite a range of dissimilarity."

"It isn't what we do, Ellie, it's how we look."

The parking lot resembled something out of a dreary movie, snow-covered and not yet plowed because so far they only had maybe an inch of accumulation on top of the piles of existing snow. "It sounds pretty far-fetched," she said, but her voice didn't carry the earlier conviction. God, maybe he was on to something. "All we have is a first name with a tentative link to Peterson. Admit that's very, very thin."

"I have her phone number."

"What are you going to do, call the governor's niece up and ask her if maybe she murdered three men—four if she shot Gurst—and if she says yes, we can make an arrest? Great plan."

He lifted his shoulders. "Look, we think we're looking for a woman. Possibly someone named Lauren, and there is a thread with the physical descriptions, the car, and even those muffins link the second victim. I admit it's thin, but my instincts tell me something is off. Why don't I just call her and make another date?"

"Maybe because she could be a potential murderer? Just a thought."

"How nice to know you care."

Despite the sarcastic drawl of that observation, she actually did. "I'm being serious. The whole world thinks there are successful serial killers crawling around everywhere, when in truth it is very hard to get away with it. That means the good ones are not just dysfunctional but also smart. Don't be stupid."

He said mildly, "I think I've just been insulted. Luckily I'm too stupid to be insulted. Tell you what, let's put this in front of Grasso and get his opinion. A forum is better than an argument."

"Forum?" She opened her door. "Really? You *have* been watching PBS."

Georgia sat and contemplated the fire.

Ethics were a pain in the posterior, and she'd known it going in when she chose her profession. There was a reason they had to take classes on that subject and on the legal ramifications of falling asleep during the part about patient confidentiality. She'd stayed wide awake.

She liked her living room. It had warm wood floors and the mantel was polished wood wide enough to display several vases she'd collected over the years, and vintage family photos. She'd made sure her couch was comfortable enough she could slip out of her shoes and relax before the fire. At the moment, however, she was immune to the inviting atmosphere and focused on her current dilemma.

It was clearly part of her professional responsibility to divulge information revealed in therapy that, if she felt it was pertinent, threatened the safety of an individual.

But, she pondered as she sipped a glass of wine, her feet up on an ottoman, the flames leaping and giving out welcome warmth, when an unstable patient speculated on the emotional state of a person Georgia had never even met, she was not obligated to report that to anyone. She might even be violating any number of rules and costing the taxpaying population money if the police chose to pursue the tip.

It wasn't like she enjoyed being in this position, and in a moment of self-contemplation, she wondered if two of her patients weren't homicide detectives would she even be having this inner conversation.

In the end, she picked up her phone and called Grant again.

She cut his warm hello short. "I need your help."

"If this is a flat tire, I'll come get you right away, but I have a feeling it isn't."

The man was entirely too astute, she'd always known it. "No, I'm sitting in my living room drinking Merlot."

"Wearing?"

She laughed. She couldn't help it. "Fully clothed. Sorry."

"I'll just pretend I got a different answer. I'm very curious about the question at hand. Shoot."

"Remember our recent conversation?"

"Certainly. Your fragile patient with the roommate issues."

She crossed her ankles and closed her eyes. The fire crackled. "I think I have a new problem. I just want you to tell me what you would do, and then I'll make a decision and never tell you what it is. Agreed?"

"How can I refuse an offer like that? My pompous opinion and no ramifications? I'm in."

"I want to know if I should go to the police. All I have is the speculation of an unstable patient about someone I have never met or evaluated. It feels to an extent like repeating unreliable gossip. On the other hand, if half of what this patient has told me is true, this person could potentially be a true threat."

"To?"

"Random victims. That's my impression. There's a transference problem from a past occurrence that maybe has the roommate acting out her rage. She's acquired a gun, I know that much."

"That's quite a leap. A lot of people in this country have guns."

She briefly outlined what Rachel had told her about Lea following men around.

"It sounds dangerous." Seriousness replaced his earlier teasing tone. "But I'm not sure what you can do. This is not duty to warn because it doesn't sound like there is anything concrete enough for that. This is a feeling a patient has because she is at odds with someone she knows. Georgia, tread lightly on this. First of all, the police deal with facts, not suppositions, and you have no facts that I've heard so far."

"It is possible there's blood in Lea's car. Rachel has said she thinks it might be. What if by DNA they could link it to a crime?"

"Oh." He audibly blew out a breath. "That's a little different, but still, if you only *think* you have it . . . this is tricky. Your first concern should be the welfare of your patient. From what I've heard so far, she has a very involved relationship with this person and should you bring her suspicions to light it would probably shatter it. What would that do to her, especially if it proved not to be true?"

Rachel never talked about other friends, just Lea. He had a point.

"Agreed."

"Dinner soon?"

"I'd like that. Thanks." She pushed a button and went back to watching the fire. She really owed Ellie MacIntosh.

But paybacks could be hell.

Chapter 24

Jason parked the car and wondered again about the vagaries of fate.

Grasso's house was in a neighborhood built by old money, set well back from the street, the manicured lawn indicative of the fortune he'd been left when his parents had met with an accident when he was still in college. He answered the elegant front door without his suit coat, his tie discarded and his shirt unbuttoned at the neck and yet Jason wondered if he ever actually relaxed.

They came from very dissimilar backgrounds but had one thing in common. Both of them had a unique dedication to their job.

"Come on in." Grasso stepped back to let them into the foyer. "The one evening I leave a little early and work comes to me. Good. Saves me from going back. The message you left sounded pretty interesting. Let's go sit down and you can fill me in."

Both he and Ellie had been to the house before and Jason was fairly sure that Lieutenant Carl Grasso hadn't changed the expensive but dated furnishings one bit since he inherited the pricey property, but that was his choice. His place might be decorated like a college dorm room, but it was a lot more comfortable in his opinion than this big rambling house.

To his relief they sat in the kitchen, which was the size of his entire apartment but at least cozy compared to the rest of the house. The table was polished mahogany, the floor marble, and he wasn't exactly an expert, but the chandelier looked Tiffany. Still, more cozy than the rest of it, and that said it all.

Grasso asked, "Who wants to go first? I don't have a lot on my end, so maybe we should get that out of the way. The hospital was a no-go. I talked to the woman who had been helping Peterson with his research numbers and she knew nothing helpful. I wasn't surprised, but it was worth a shot. She said mostly they e-mailed back and forth, and quite naturally, he didn't discuss his private life. In her memory, she never saw him with Lauren Levine."

Ellie didn't blink an eye at the disappointment, but Jason knew she was always moving forward and every setback just meant there was a need to rethink and reconsider. That was good, he operated that way himself. Looking backward had never been his thing.

She settled her arms on the table and gazed at him. "Okay, you want to talk? This is your theory, not mine necessarily. I'm still undecided if you are the lunatic of the year."

"There's a vote of confidence." Jason had been considering the facts the entire drive over. "Look," he said to Grasso, "maybe I am crazy but we can link her to Peterson through the university and the hospital, and I am a body double for all three of the men who have been killed by the slasher unless you want to throw in Gurst, who may or may not be part of the equation and supplying her with the drugs. It isn't we're all twins separated at birth or anything, but pretty close to the same build and coloring. The last time Young was seen alive, it was with a woman with long, dark-brown hair. She qualifies. That's a tentative lead, but she has also made an effort to pursue me. We also think we are looking for a woman."

Grasso's brows rose and he actually looked surprised, which did not happen very often. "All right, didn't see that coming. What? Start over if you don't mind."

Jason did. He recounted the story of the car accident again, and as he spoke he became more and more sure that he really could be right, especially when he recalled his conversation with Georgia Lukens. "Lauren engineered the dinner with the governor, I'm sure of it. At the least she had to have told her father to tell her uncle about what happened or he never would have known. Was it altruistic or motivated?"

After he was done, neither Grasso nor Ellie commented and so he waited, slouched in the chair, thinking about it himself. Finally, Ellie brushed back her hair and said, "Picked apart it sounds improbable, but then again, the sum of the parts has me wondering."

Jason said, "It all kind of chafes my ass, because here I thought she was just into me."

He was joking. What it did was bring up memories of those ruined faces.

And Lauren knew where he lived. Nice. The impulse existed to move to a tropical island and call it a day. Only he knew himself too well. He'd be bored by noon the first day, fly back, and get on with the job.

"So," Grasso said finally, "it seems kind of simple to me. Santiago calls her up and they go on a date, and we shadow. The worst thing that can happen is that she is not the person viciously killing men in our fair city and he gets to have drinks on the taxpayers' dollar."

"That's the worst? Or," Ellie countered, "she spikes his drink and plunges a knife into his back and then proceeds to use him like a pincushion right after she mutilates his face."

"Ah, shit, now you're taking all the romance out of it," Jason murmured. He asked Grasso, "You have any beer? This conversation is making me want one."

"You drink too much."

Santiago turned to look at her. "You're like a nagging wife without the benefits. Now if you'd care to include the benefits—"

So much more like him to crack that kind of joke. It was a relief.

"I still think it's a bad idea." Ellie was annoyed and overruled. The sun had set and Grasso had turned on the lights, but the room was shadowed, and to her, even though she knew he lived there, the house always smelled slightly disused. "You two really think this is a decent plan?"

Grasso was pretty impassive, but that was usual. "I think it is a little out there, but here's my take on it. The recurring theme is the drug. If we can catch her slipping something into his drink, then we've got something solid. A possibility she was seeing Peterson? There's just nothing there, MacIntosh, and you know it. Putting rufilin in a man's drink that fits the description of the other victims suddenly makes the circumstantial evidence compelling. With a little luck, she'll be carrying the same knife used in the other murders."

"That does sound extremely lucky." Her smile was sardonic. "I'm trying to figure out if a clever lawyer could finagle an entrapment defense."

"No way." Santiago sounded firm. "She tracked me down, remember? Offered me her phone number voluntarily. Before we left for the university I asked our guys to run it. Burner phone. I'm sure she has a regular cell, so why give me that one? So no one could trace a call from my phone to her? No law against that but another tiny bit of circumstantial evidence. Let's see if we can get enough to make a case for at least detaining her for questioning."

She wasn't convinced but it was better than anything else they had. "Her uncle is the *governor*. We can't screw this up. We already have Mrs. Peterson maligning us in the press. Imagine what would happen if this theory is way off? We'd look like complete idiots."

"There's nothing to screw up," Santiago argued, his tall body sprawled in a chair, his face taut. "Look, I'll go on a date with her and if she makes a move, we'll have enough to take to Metzger. If she doesn't, the worst thing that happens is I have cocktails with a pleasant young woman."

He *must* be certifiably nuts.

Ellie argued, "Gurst was shot, remember? If he tried to blackmail her because he'd sold her the drug, she doesn't like being threatened. You have a thick skull, that I'll admit, but it isn't bulletproof. She has a gun."

"I don't think shooting me would give her the right buzz."

That echoed what Georgia Lukens had said, so she finally shut her eyes briefly and agreed. "Fine, it's your neck on the line. We'll do surveillance. But either we're wasting our time, or else you're risking your life."

And . . . don't. She didn't want him to do this. Why she felt so strongly about it, well, she was afraid of the answer to that volatile question.

"Nothing ventured, nothing gained. In case you missed the memo, risking our lives is part of the gig." Santiago took out his phone. "Let's see what she says. I've got fifty bucks that says if I offer to pick her up she'll suggest we meet instead."

"You have fifty bucks? You're so much more responsible than you seem."

Her partner gave her a sardonic look as he tapped in the number. "I was going to say a hundred but I need money for beer."

The phone conversation was brief, but it was at least productive. When he hung up he informed them, "Called that one. I'm going to meet her at a place called Number Nine near the lake at eight thirty."

"We'll arrive first," Grasso said. "Two people on a date. We'll order drinks, and hopefully sit with a clear view of where you end up."

"Get a table," Ellie said to Santiago. "We'll sit at the bar.

It'd be nice if we could have someone else there too. Maybe Rays would handle that for us. The garage homicide is his case, after all."

"Wish I'd thought of that the other night, but even though I wasn't sold on the situation, I hadn't made a connection yet like we have now." Jason rubbed his jaw. "Damn, I forgot to shave this morning. I'd better take care of that."

"I'll call Rays. Backup never hurts anyway." Grasso already had his phone out. "He has a vested interest in this."

Ellie stood, trying to maintain a professional attitude but there was already a small knot in the pit of her stomach. "Let's go then. You can drop me off and Grasso can pick me up. This seems like it might just be a long night. I'm going to get something to eat and change."

"Fine with me. I need to change too for my hot date." Santiago's grin was irreverent as he followed her out of the room, which was no surprise. "Any suggestions?"

She wasn't sure how he could be so calm about having a drink with possibly a very vicious killer. "This isn't dinner at the mansion on Lake Mendota. Keep it in mind."

"I know. Give me some credit. That was a nice night though, wasn't it?"

It wasn't a secret he tended to always push things to irritate her on purpose. The indirect reference to the kiss fell into that category.

Not to mention she didn't like being afraid for him. It was uncomfortable, and she was rarely uncomfortable with her job. Ellie looked him in the eye. "I do, actually, give you credit for being a good cop."

He pushed a button on his key chain to unlock her door. The night had thickened, with low clouds obscuring the moon. "That's nice to know, but I wasn't talking about the job."

"Let's not get our personal relationship into this for God's sake."

"I wasn't sure we had one."

"This conversation is now over," Ellie informed him and climbed in.

Chapter 25

Her computer screen stared at her accusingly.

Georgia had taken out her phone twice, set it down without making a call, and now she just sat there with it on but unused.

Listening to your inner voice was something she preached, but apparently taking her own advice was more difficult than she realized.

Her notes were encapsulated into various behavioral columns usually, and with Rachel she'd certainly had plenty to work with, but it was Lea that really concerned her. Through her patient she felt like she knew her pretty well.

Selfish. Deceptive. Manipulative.

It seemed unlikely that in a city the size of Milwaukee she would be the single therapist that would be seeing two homicide detectives investigating a series of murders and also have for a patient the roommate of the actual killer.

Highly unlikely.

Beyond improbable.

But, the inner voice argued, what if the series of events was not as random as they seemed? Rachel didn't use her insurance to pay for her sessions. She always just paid cash. She'd said once that since she worked at a hospital, she didn't really want anyone to know she was seeing a mental health specialist and they would certainly know if she billed it through that department.

Logical.

But . . .

It was all bothering her. She was reviewing notes and going over sessions in her mind and something really did not add up.

So she picked up the phone yet again and this time made a call.

Ellie didn't answer but she called right back. "This is kind of an unusual time for a call."

"This is kind of an unusual call."

"Oh?"

"I don't do this."

"Maybe you should define what it is you don't do."

Georgia contemplated the request and then said succinctly, "I don't betray patient confidentiality lightly."

"Good to know as I am a patient." Ellie sounded curious and yet tense, her voice low. "Why are we having this conversation?"

"You aren't going to believe it."

"That blanket statement does not intimidate me at all. I've seen some things in my life that would make your toes curl."

Now that was undoubtedly true. Homicide detective equaled unusual situations.

"I have a patient who I think might know your killer in the slasher murders. I can't swear it, but this person is definitely a sociopath in some ways, and female, and there are some disturbing signs."

Someone said something in the background and MacIntosh answered the question and then was back on the line. "Want to clarify? Because I am definitely listening."

The place had low, seductive lighting, high tables, and jazz playing just a shade too loud for his tastes. The expensive glitter of steel and glass was modern and sophisticated.

A far cry from the place he'd suggested the other night, but she'd seemed to not mind the shabby establishment. Lauren was certainly dressed for this trendy spot: white silk blouse unbuttoned so that if she moved just right, he could get a hint of a lacy bra and the shadow between her breasts, short leather skirt, black hose with a tiny pattern of some kind, and calf-high boots that were her only apparent nod to the winter temperatures.

Jason imagined that in this place, most of the patrons greeted each other with a kiss on the cheek or some such pretentious bullshit, but he wasn't interested in being someone he wasn't and doubted he could pull it off anyway, so he just took a seat opposite. "Hi."

His date had on the catlike eyeliner again and her lips glistened with a ruby-red gloss that she managed to pull off very well. Her hair was loose and there was a silver bracelet on her wrist. "Hi back. I'm glad you called. I already ordered, but my drink just got here."

He was still trying to figure out if his suspicions were just ludicrous. Could this fairly slender young woman possibly drug and stab three grown men to death and shoot a drug dealer? MacIntosh was right, they were stretching it.

Then again, Young had been transported by a sled of some kind. That indicated planning and that the killer couldn't directly carry the body. Once again, inconclusive.

MacIntosh and Grasso were at the bar, Ellie's back to them because Lauren would certainly recognize her. Grasso was leaning forward as if talking to her, his usual scotch in front of him but probably untouched.

Jason admired the shining fall of his partner's fair hair before he returned his attention to what he was actually *doing*. This was their problem. He was too aware of her, it made him less of a cop, and wasn't productive.

It was a thought to ask Metzger if he could transfer partners, but then he'd have to explain why and he wouldn't see her except in passing. *No go*.

The waiter came over. Jason ordered a draft beer, was told they didn't serve beer, and so opted for the simplest drink possible, just gin and a twist of lemon. He wondered how to play it. Carefully, that was for sure. If he acted strange, that would spoil the deal but undercover was not his usual persona. He'd done it once when he was coming up through the ranks but he hadn't enjoyed it particularly, and this was an entirely different situation even though the goal was the same.

So . . . focus. Lauren wasn't a drug dealer or a member of organized crime. She was potentially a psychotic killer.

"I'm glad I called too." He made his smile slow and let his gaze drift downward to her chest because he knew she dressed to provoke just that response and this was about finesse. "You look great."

"So do you, Detective."

He laughed. "I'm wearing jeans and a shirt."

"Not the clothes, but the man." She took a sip of her drink, her eyes assessing. "Why'd you call me?"

Was this a cat-and-mouse test? He couldn't be sure. "Had a nice time the other night. Why'd you accept?"

"I like a little walk on the wild side now and then."

"I think you've got that backward. I work *for* law enforcement."

She leaned forward. "I know. It doesn't make you a safe choice necessarily."

It was possible, given the circumstances, that she was absolutely right there. He took a sip of his drink before commenting. "Well, you know where I live and where I work. I think you're safe enough."

"None of us are ever safe." She laughed softly. "Besides, don't you carry a loaded weapon?"

"At all times," he replied blandly, surveying the high glass windows. "This is a nice place. You come here often?"

"Never. A friend recommended it to me."

Was she high? He wondered. The conversation had a slightly surreal feel to it and her pupils seemed a little dilated, but that could be the lighting. If they were aiming for mood, in his case it was wary and he was afraid she'd sense it. "Not quite like the corner tavern I suggested, is it? What can I say? I'm a peasant, I guess."

"Well, it's a martini bar and you tried ordering a beer, so that might be true."

He grinned. "I've never claimed to be cultured. How are things at the hospital?"

If she had any suspicion he'd checked on her employment, it didn't show. "Hectic." She fished an olive from her drink with her fingers and popped it in her mouth. "How are things in the murder business? Keeping you hopping?"

"Pretty much, unfortunately. You'd think it was too cold here in the winter to go out and kill people, but that's not so."

She pursed her mouth. "Yeah, but keep in mind that it happens on beautiful sunny summer days also, when you think you don't have a care in the world, are happy and full of life, and then suddenly, someone just takes it away."

It struck him. Hard. That remark meant something.

His response was subdued. "For some reason, I think that's the voice of experience speaking."

Looking convincingly pensive, she said, "A little bit, but let's move to a more cheerful subject."

At that moment, right on cue, his phone vibrated. Jason pulled it out, and said apologetically, "Speaking of work, I'm sorry, I have to take this. I'll be right back."

He walked toward the back of the bar, phone to his ear.

It was Ellie. "Since half the people in here are on their cells and my back is to her, I doubt she'll get suspicious. Grasso is watching your unattended drink. If she makes a move, we'll catch it. Go into the bathroom or something, okay?"

"Fine. Are we going to arrest her here?"

"I've been on the phone with Metzger and he says to bring her in for questioning if it happens, but otherwise he doesn't think we have enough and I think we all agree on that point. He'd like to be able to say we have a suspect, so he's got his proverbial fingers crossed but he wishes like hell it was someone else."

"Send me a text about the drink, will you? Though I admit I hate to be the rude bastard who constantly checks his phone."

"You could always be the dead polite bastard instead. I'll text. Check your phone if it beeps." Ellie ended the call and he had to give an inward choked laugh.

Dead polite bastard.

But she had a point.

She didn't do it.

Lauren simply sat there until Santiago came back, occasionally lifting her drink to her mouth, idly drumming her fingers on the table. Not a single move toward his glass, not anything more suspicious than resting her elbow on the table. When he returned, a provocative leg cross was in order apparently—which he noticed—and she said something, and lifted a brow.

"We're barking up the wrong tree." There was a certain sense of resignation in Ellie's muttered words. "That was a wide-open chance. She passed."

Grasso agreed. "One of two things just happened. Either she's a woman who is simply interested in Santiago, or she's playing a very careful game. Maybe she made us."

"You're wearing a thousand-dollar suit." Ellie didn't keep the skepticism out of her voice. "The average police officer doesn't do that, and women usually can tell the difference. I don't think she's even glanced at us."

"This place isn't all that crowded. I find that interesting because I don't know about you, but I normally look around."

"Maybe, but then again, you're a police officer."

"If I were a murderer I'd look twice."

"So would I, but hopefully most of them aren't as smart as we are."

"Hopefully," Grasso said with a hint of amusement as he leaned in. "I'm going to put my hand on your knee and I'd really appreciate it if you don't pull your service weapon and shoot me. You are about a decade younger than I am so we should be on an older man–younger woman sort of date. This is a trendy place, so let's pretend we are on one and we can talk without being heard."

"Good thing you warned me." She picked up her glass, which had iced tea in it, not whiskey, though it looked the same, and took a sip. "Or I really might shoot you."

His touch was respectful at least, if a little too intimate, warm as he squeezed her knee. "Like I wouldn't hedge my bets to protect myself," Grasso said dryly, his mouth near her ear. "You've taken out a killer before."

"You've taken out two."

"Self-defense."

"I'll buy that if you say so." The popular opinion was that he'd done a bit of vigilante justice, but the world was a better place without the two men he'd killed, so she wasn't going to judge.

"Thanks for the vote of confidence."

"I don't encourage gossip but I listen to it."

He whispered in her ear. "This is interesting; they're leaving together."

It was maddening to not be able to swivel around and look. "What? He's got to know better than that."

"One would think so, but then again, she didn't touch his drink. Don't panic yet." He removed his hand and his voice was normal now, his brow slightly furrowed.

"I'm not panicking," she retorted, laying several bills on the bar, listening to a saxophone solo. "I'm preparing us for a quick exit."

"I have my keys in my hand. Walk out arm in arm?"

"Sure . . . yes . . . fine."

He helped her on with her coat and she let him, anxious to get out the door. This case had been confusing from the beginning and she was not all that sure it was getting any clearer. Grasso opened the door and she stepped onto the chilly sidewalk in time to see Santiago getting into a black car, settling into the passenger seat.

BMW, check. Expensive car not usually seen in the neighborhood by the school.

"This is great. We can't show up at another bar if that's where they're headed. If it's her apartment, we are really in trouble." Apprehension tightened Ellie's throat. "Two minutes ago I was pretty sure she wasn't our suspect, but right now I've got a bad feeling. If she's our girl, why didn't she slip him the drug when she had the chance?"

Grasso's breath made frosty puffs and his gray eyes were somber. "Gurst is dead. Maybe she decided trying to buy it was too risky with all the publicity. I'm not happy either but she knows he isn't doped, which is how, if it even is her, she is able to kill healthy men considerably bigger than she is. He can handle himself. Let's relax and follow them. This martini bar is hardly something Santiago would choose. It's possible she suggested someplace where he could get a beer instead. Much more his style."

"Maybe," Ellie said tightly as they walked toward Grasso's expensive vehicle, which he'd already started with the push of a button. "And that worries me. What if she picked a martini bar because she has already figured that out about him, and this way, she can get him into *her* car?"

"That would be premeditated and well-thought out." The lieutenant opened her door. When he'd walked around and was settled into the driver's seat, he added darkly, "The question is: Is she that smart?"

"We sure as hell haven't caught her."

"Not yet." He buckled in.

That was what she liked about Carl Grasso. He was a matter-of-fact person, not nearly as argumentative as Santiago, and yet just as focused. They had different ways of how they handled an investigation, that was for sure. Santiago was much more a seat-of-his-pants sort of cop, ready to go in guns blazing, but Grasso was more methodical.

At one time in their careers, they'd each crossed the line. Santiago was always a cowboy and got reprimanded when it happened, but Grasso had done much more collateral damage and yet walked away with nothing more than a transfer. He'd even kept his rank.

"I hope you have better success trailing them than we did with the car leaving the parking lot crime scene after the dealer was shot." Ellie also fastened her seat belt, her eye on the luxury sedan. "In the movies they make it look so easy, but there are some pesky problems, like trying to not kill yourself and civilians by running traffic lights. Rays is in the blue compact parked on the street, right? At least he can go in if they choose another bar."

"Always nice to have backup."

"I agree."

A thin veil of snow spiraled behind the departing vehicle and Ellie called Rays. "We think maybe they're going to another bar. She passed on the chance to spike his drink at Number Nine, so if they go in somewhere else, you get the honors. If she sees us twice she'll catch on, and she knows me anyway."

"Got it." He sounded collected but terse.

She pressed a button to end the call as they pulled out onto the street and watched as Rays followed in her side mirror. Ellie murmured, "I still have a bad feeling about this."

Unfortunately, Grasso agreed. "I do too."

Chapter 26

She came at him out of the blue.

Jason wasn't quite aware of what happened at first. He was on his guard, but not for this. All through a pleasant drink he'd been telling himself he was maybe wrong, no one like Lauren could possibly have anything to do with the murders. He'd looked into her eyes and she'd looked back and this was one giant dead end.

He'd thought he was just wrong.

Then she'd suggested they leave.

And almost the moment they were in the car, she'd done it. Leaned over with a laugh and taken him entirely by surprise.

It had hurt like hell; that much he was cognizant of as he swam dangerously close to losing it, his body still humming. Not once but at least twice. Right to the side of his neck.

Stun gun.

No wonder she hadn't bothered to put anything in his drink.

Their killer was evolving, and he wasn't too happy to be part of the process. His arms and legs were leaden and though he was aware he was still breathing, it wasn't an easy exercise. Slumped against the door he clung to consciousness, but only barely. *Dammit . . .*

Lauren calmly got out at a service station, put gas in the tank as he tried to recover, and then got in and used the stun gun again. A matter of minutes, but she was a bright girl, he might have been able to come out of it a little anyway if she hadn't gone after it again.

Son of a bitch that hurts . . .

His world went away again.

She leaned over and whispered, "Where is he?"

What the fuck? The most he managed was an inarticulate gurgle of sound that embarrassed him.

Her face inches away, she asked again, "What did you do with him?"

He wanted to ask what the hell she was talking about, but his brain seemed to be moving as slow as his body, and that was like a snail stuck in the ice, though if that had ever happened, he'd never heard of it. Apparently snails were smarter than he was.

Well, he wasn't completely stupid. He'd figured it out but had no idea what might happen next. On his guard, but not bright enough to avoid the bullet.

Pretty stupid still. . . .

What just happened?"

Parked across the street from the gas station with a steady stream of traffic going by, they didn't have a clear view of the car, but Ellie realized that she could no longer see Santiago, even though he hadn't gotten out of the car.

Grasso muttered, "I don't know. She's surely not going to kill him in her car."

She normally wouldn't think so, but Georgia's call was in the back of her mind. Lauren perfectly matched the description of a patient who was so unstable and unpredictable Dr. Lukens had taken the time to point her out against all standards of her chosen profession.

Not something to ignore.

"Yeah, let's not count on her good manners. I'm going in." Ellie was already out of the car, wondering if she was going to blow the whole thing, if he'd maybe dropped something on the floor and was looking for it, and if that was the case, he'd give her grief for ruining his cover.

Raft of shit. In his own words.

So be it.

Her shoes hit slush in the gutter first, and she cleared the first lane, but a car honked from the second and narrowly missed her, careening into the other lane, and she said a bad word and tugged at her gun.

Closing at a hundred feet, maybe a little more, she still couldn't see her partner in the vehicle, but knew he hadn't been dropped off anywhere. Besides, Lauren, seemed to be talking to the passenger side of the vehicle.

Ellie reached the driver's side window in time to see Santiago half-sprawled against the seat and door opposite, Lauren fumbling in a small duffle bag. His eyes were half-closed.

She rapped on the window. "Police! Open your door."

Lauren paid no attention, still talking to what appeared

to be an only partially conscious man until she found what she'd been looking for.

The knife gleamed as she lifted it.

Talk about an oh-shit moment.

Not even two seconds to decide. Ellie knew if she fired through the window from this angle, she might hit Santiago as well, so she took four steps to the back of the vehicle and fired through the rear window, using the silhouette as a target.

Glass shattered, her ears started to ring, and she stepped back two more steps.

Got her?

There was a moment where the world drifted in the surreal aftermath. She could hear Lauren screaming.

Then the car lurched backward, tires squealing, sliding on the ice and Ellie dived out of the way, not quite fast enough, the collision of vehicle and flesh and bone brought home by a suspension of the world as she knew it.

It hurt, and she hit the ground hard, sliding across the ice, her face stinging. The car roared backward and she was aware she should crawl out of the way, but there wasn't time and the bumper brushed her hip before the vehicle surged forward and fishtailed toward the exit to the street.

With one hand she shoved herself up and winced just as the passenger side door to the vehicle opened and a body spilled out onto the street. The door swinging, the black car left her line of vision, but she'd bumped her head pretty hard on the icy concrete when the car had hit her and she went down, so her eyesight was not really all that clear anyway.

Body.

Santiago.

He was facedown in the gutter, literally, as the car sped off. Grasso ran across the lanes of traffic and then kneeled next to him as she sat up, and to her relief, her partner also sat up and shook his head. *Cars are stopping on the street . . . people getting out . . .*

Still alive. They both were, but that had been close. Relief washed through her even as she figured out her right leg hurt like hell.

Their suspect was on the run.

As Santiago staggered to his feet and Grasso ran toward her she was already saying, "Go, go, go! Follow Rays. I'm okay, I'm okay. She's the one. Get her."

If he was one thing, Grasso wasn't indecisive. He turned back toward his car and said something to Santiago as he passed, just a word, and then sprinted through the confusion of traffic and was in his expensive car, pulling away.

Ellie found that trying to stand was not an option. She'd dropped her weapon and crawled toward it, mainly because she didn't want anyone else to touch it, and realized not only did her right leg hurt, but it didn't work very well. There was a claustrophobic sense of vulnerability she didn't like as people came running, both from the street and the gas station attendant emerged as well, then there was a moment when each one of them realized she had a gun and stopped cold.

"Police officer," she identified herself, dipping into her pocket for her badge. "Can someone please call nine-one-one?"

"Hurry." A familiar voice chimed in as Santiago elbowed his way through the crowd, weaving on his feet, his face pasty. He dropped to his knees next to her and she wasn't sure it was on purpose. "I could use some TLC myself. El-lie, you all right?"

About half a dozen people were calling from their cell phones, which was good because she didn't know exactly where they were. "Been better. At the least a sprained ankle. At the worst, broken. I'm kind of hoping for the sprain." Her smile was probably forced. "You seem to be bleeding."

"I am?" He looked vaguely down at his jacket and registered the blood on his sleeve and dripping from his hand, crimson droplets coloring the snow. "I guess you're right. You know, that was the worst date ever. I doubt I'm asking her out again."

"Ah, and you looked so cute together. I'm sorry it didn't work out. Help me up. This parking lot is freezing."

It didn't go well. Maybe broken went to probably broken in regards to her ankle. She couldn't put any weight on it, had a vague idea of the bruises she was going to have, and went down on the ice again.

In the end Santiago simply picked her up though she wasn't sure he was more capable of walking than she was, and carried her into the gas station where he promptly sank down on the floor and leaned back against a display of different types of chips, propping his back on the shelves. Ellie rested her head against his shoulder because there wasn't any way to insist they change their position and her ankle was swelling so fast she could feel it happening. With effort, she said jokingly, "At least Grasso didn't grope your knee tonight and whisper in your ear."

"Saw that. I need to give him some pointers."

"Um, yeah right, because you're so smooth? What happened?"

Santiago's eyes were closed, but at least his body was warm. "She Tazered the shit out of me. Three times. I want to go on record as saying that really is not the best experience on this planet. Then she tried to stab me. I think the screaming the boys heard from the school is explained. Did you hear her as she came after me?"

"I think people across the Canadian border heard her. What was she saying?"

"I vaguely remember her asking me what I did with him. None of the rest of it made any sense, not that that does either. Luckily, I didn't fasten my seat belt on purpose and was able to get the door open after you shot the back window out."

"Sorry I missed her." It was vehement declaration.

"If it's any consolation, that's a pretty tough shot." His mouth grazed her temple and his arms tightened a fraction. Then he bent his head and whispered against her mouth, "Thanks."

She would have objected, but it was an insignificant transgression compared to the events of the evening, and was over so quickly what was the point. "I couldn't use the driver's side window in case I hit you too."

"See, I knew you cared. Thanks, since I'm not a fan of being shot. Been there, done that."

"I'm kind of not a fan of being hit by a car either." Her whole leg was throbbing.

"Let's just cross those off our bucket list. Deal?"

"Fine with me."

"All this and we aren't going to be the ones to make this fucking arrest. It pisses me off."

Ellie was in serious pain, but she had to laugh. "This is

redundant. Haven't we established that everything pretty much pisses you off? Besides, don your cape. We are on the side of justice, not of glory."

"Did Grasso get a stun gun to the neck or run over by a car? I don't think so." His lashes lifted. "We earned the arrest. I think I hear sirens. You doing okay?"

"If you say one word to anyone about me sitting on your lap, I'll shoot you. I need a little practice and you are the perfect target."

His arms tightened. "I'm sure if you could get up and kick my ass you would. But if you want to talk redundancy, I think my ass has already been kicked tonight."

They were both lucky.

That is if ten stitches from several knife wounds, a ruined leather jacket, and Ellie's two broken bones counted as lucky. Besides her definitely broken ankle, she'd cracked her wrist trying to break her fall, just as he'd reflexively thrown up his arm when Lauren came after him with the knife.

Damn, Jason really had liked that jacket.

Chief Metzger, no tie in sight, in creased slacks and a plaid shirt, came into the waiting area with a cardboard cup of coffee and sat down on a gray upholstered chair. "How is it I seem to visit the hospital more for you and MacIntosh than anyone else?"

The room smelled like antiseptic and Jason was tired, his arm was numb, and he was pretty scraped up in general from falling out of a moving car onto an icy street. "It's just our way of getting your attention."

"How is she doing?"

"I am informed she'll be fine. A bit banged up, but okay. Something about a clean break that really didn't need to be reset, a fiberglass cast, and they are just about to wrap her wrist. What happened? I've tried to call Grasso twice but no answer."

"We have her car. Lots of blood in it, some of it fresh, which I assume is yours, and some of it not so fresh. We are treating it like a crime scene and the lab guys are processing it." The chief rubbed his jaw which had a serious five o'clock shadow. "The suspect has not been apprehended. She pulled into a parking garage evidently, and it took them a while to even locate her vehicle. So she escaped on foot. What we are hoping is that she caught a cab and we can track down where she went. Right now there are officers handling that. We do have the license and registration. Luckily we got her address because the car is still registered to her father. When officers called at her residence, no one answered the door. Shit, why does she have to be the governor's niece? This is a problem I didn't see coming down the pipe, dammit."

Double swearing in one sentence and for once it wasn't him. Metzger was right. Once the word got out, there would probably be national media coverage.

Jason frowned. "Maybe her roommate knows where she might go."

The chief looked interested. "MacIntosh said something about a roommate so we'll work that angle. Lauren Levine's parents live in a small town in between here and Madison. We are operating under the assumption she'll head that direction."

"Detective?" A nurse came into the waiting area.

Jason stood abruptly and winced at a twinge in his shoulder. He'd landed solidly on it when falling from the car. There were a few parts of his anatomy that were going to take time to get back to normal. "Yes?"

"We are getting ready to release her. Go on in."

Ellie was pale but lucid, her nice slacks cut away right at the knee because of her cast, and her arm was also in some sort of wrap. She looked irritated at the inconvenience of it all, and that was borne out by her first muttered words. "I hate this."

"Well, it's better than a trip to the boneyard." His tone was laconic, but that wasn't how he felt. She'd almost been killed trying to save his life. Second time. "I bet they give you some decent painkillers and if you don't use them all, we can sell them to Astin and make a decent profit, so buck up, sweetheart, and tough it out."

"Funny. What happened? Do we have Lauren Levine in custody?"

"Nope, but we have her car. Right now she's running." The sad thing was, Jason had to sit down, so he took the chair by the side of the bed. It felt like he'd been gone over with a baseball bat.

Metzger had followed him in. "Grasso and Rays can wrap this up. No worries. Just get some rest."

Ellie said succinctly, "Jefferson County."

There were circles under her eyes, but Jason thought she still looked beautiful, mostly because she was still breathing. "What about it?"

Metzger said slowly, "Her parents live in Jefferson County."

"There's a reason she dumped the third body there. I felt that at the time, and I am sure of it now. Young was killed somewhere else and she took him there. Why? The first two she left at the scene because she was new at it. That third one . . . she went to more trouble. Do you know how hard it must have been for her to drag him into her car, drag him out, and then use the sled to move him? She's about my size and dead weight is dead weight. If she used ropes and leverage, she could do it, but why bother? My answer is it meant something important to her."

"She did tell me she grew up in a small town." Jason added, "When we find her, I'd really like to talk to this roommate. I wonder if she has a clue as to what is going on."

"She might be in danger. We've two officers watching the condo already." Metzger was brisk but obviously concerned. "When she comes home, we'll bring her in for questioning, but the two of you don't need to concern yourselves with it, got it?"

"Our case," Jason objected, but it was halfhearted. He could maybe sleep for a year or two he was so tired.

"Not anymore." Metzger walked toward the door. "You know the drill. Once you're released for full duty, let me know. MacIntosh, I don't expect to see you for about two months. Keep in touch."

"This sucks." Jason slouched in the chair after the chief left the room.

"I rarely agree with you, but right now I do." Ellie sounded as tired as he felt. "Can you do me a favor and call my sister? Please tell her I'll be fine—she's pregnant and doesn't need to rush down here—and to not tell our mother who also doesn't need the anxiety. I never know what is going to make the news. My phone is in Grasso's car."

"You can't drive, Ellie." It took some effort on his part, but he did ask it anyway. "Should I call Grantham?"

"What's he going to do from New York? No."

"Rush back here. Hand you your crutches. Wait on you hand and foot."

"*This* is not why he should rush back here." She pointed at her injured leg. "If I asked him he would, but I'm not asking. In fact, I was thinking about moving out."

There was no question in Jason's mind that if she hadn't been a little out of it from whatever they'd given her for the pain she would never have confided that. Carefully, he said, "You could stay with me until you find a place. I sleep on the couch half the time anyway."

"Are you crazy?"

"There are those who think so, and half the time I don't disagree. Look at it this way, I know my apartment is not a luxury suite or anything, but I am going to drive you home one way or the other. You probably shouldn't be alone since we both know in the morning it will all be worse, and I have no desire to sleep at Grantham's house. Do me a favor and just take me up on my offer. Believe it or not, having had two stab wounds just stitched up, I am not in a romantic mood, so you're safe there, though I will say the cast is dead sexy."

For a moment she just looked at him, undecided, and then finally nodded. "Fine. Thanks."

Chapter 27

Georgia recognized the names and just about dropped her morning coffee on the polished table in her kitchen as she watched the morning news.

Detective Ellie MacIntosh. Detective Jason Santiago. One missing fugitive, two officers injured in a stabbing, a near abduction, and a vehicular accident that could be charged as attempted homicide.

Rachel had been absolutely right. Lea was going to hurt someone and she had.

Georgia set aside her coffee and called Ellie's cell phone. It was somewhat of a surprise when a man answered, but at least she recognized his voice. He said curtly, "What?"

"Jason? This is Georgia Lukens."

"Who? Oh hell. Fuck, it's on the news, isn't it?" He sounded a little groggy. "I should have expected that. What time is it?"

"Seven thirty."

He was silent for a moment. Then he said quietly, "El-lie's still asleep, and she probably needs it."

They were in the same place? It didn't surprise her actually. If his partner was injured, given his feelings, he would stay.

"From what I understand, you might need it too. Don't wake Ellie up, I can talk to you. It's about one of my patients. I've already talked to Ellie about this."

"I thought you didn't reveal—"

"I don't," she interrupted urgently. "It's about your suspect. I have a patient that I believe knows her. They live together."

That obviously rang a bell. "Okay . . . okay." It sounded like he came fully awake in an instant. "We've made that connection already. They live together. What else can you tell us?"

"Where Lea is from, what I believe to be the motivation for the crimes, details about her past. Confidentiality doesn't apply so much as she isn't a patient—"

"Lea? You can stop right there." His voice took on an edge. "We need to talk face-to-face. Meet us at your office? When can you be there?"

"Give me about half an hour."

"Thirty minutes. You got it. We're on our way."

They were waiting when she got there, Santiago looking a little worse for wear with a vivid scrape on his cheek and bruising around it, his blond hair unruly. She recognized the man with him as Lieutenant Grasso, intense, dark-haired.

No Ellie. Thank goodness. Two homicide detectives were more than enough.

Georgia let them in as her receptionist wasn't there, and unlocked her office. She sat down behind her desk, motioned at the chairs for them to do the same, and booted up her computer. "I want you both to know that I am violating confidentiality on a duty-to-warn basis, and did not do so before because there was no real perceived threat except in the mind of my patient. Since I could not substantiate it, I could not report it. It seems she was right, but I am not an officer of the law and had no knowledge of an actual crime, intended or committed. Are we clear?"

Santiago leaned slightly forward. "Dr. Lukens, the homicide division of the Milwaukee Police Department does not pick to death the ethical requirements of your particular branch of medical treatment. We just kind of want to take people who like to kill other people off the streets. Are we clear on *that*? Just tell us. We could use a break."

Fair enough. Georgia took in a breath. "I have a patient named Rachel who has been telling me for some time now she's uneasy about her roommate whose name is Lea. Nothing drastic: odd hours, some erratic behavior, she'd borrowed some clothing that has never been returned, and odd stains in her car. Rachel works at a hospital and is very responsible, but she seems to have a dysfunctional relationship with this young woman, and I have been concerned about it for some time. Lea takes advantage of her, and Rachel just goes along."

"Lea, huh?" Santiago looked dubious. "We think we have a pretty clean lead on our killer already, but go on."

Lieutenant Grasso asked, "Do you have any idea where we can find either one of them?"

"They live together and I can give you Rachel's address."

Neither of them reacted like she thought they would. Instead they exchanged glances.

As she'd had growing concerns for Rachel for weeks, Georgia said deliberately, "Keep in mind, I've really been troubled by this patient since her first session. She and Lea are very different, but rely on each other. If Lea is truly the person killing those men and Rachel knows about it, she could be a victim too."

"No offense, but you are kind of talking in circles here." Santiago was predictably blunt. "Let me get this straight. This Rachel was seeing you and gave the impression her roommate might be responsible for the murders? Tell me, what does she look like?"

"Lea? I've never met her. I'm sorry I can't help you there. She's attractive according to Rachel. Men like her, she dresses provocatively and is in general quite different from Rachel, which could be why they are drawn to each other."

He ran his hand across his jaw in a gesture of frustration. "Doc, please. We have a very strong lead—I can attest to that—on who probably killed those four men and tried to kill me. We'd love to talk to this Lea, whose name I suspect is something else, but we can't find her at this time. Do you have an address? I'd love to see if it matches the one we have for our suspect."

Georgia wrote it down and explained haltingly as she handed it over, "I don't want Rachel to know this comes from me. She's very vulnerable, and for that matter, so is Lea. From what I understand a traumatic experience in her past might have been a catalyst for everything that's happened."

"I had kind of a traumatic experience myself last night. I'll tell you all about it next week during our session." Santiago glanced at the slip of paper and something flickered in his eyes. "Okay, this rings a bell, Rachel might be a pretty valuable witness. Can you get ahold of her for us?"

Georgia thought about Rachel in general. "She's fragile. No confidence even though she's a pretty girl, diffident and withdrawn."

"You see a therapist?" Grasso said dryly to Santiago. "That's way past due."

Santiago ignored him. "If you can, explain we just want to talk to her about Lea for a few minutes. What we really need is insight into where she might have gone."

Georgia nodded but couldn't help but add, "I think Lea wants to right a wrong; she wants to punish someone, even if it isn't the right person. If it is her, like Rachel thinks, then she's done *something* when she commits the murders. She isn't powerless."

"What wrong?"

"I don't know exactly. Rachel didn't tell me. I don't push for confidences, I wait for the patient to offer them."

"I'll say." Santiago pointed at his forearm. "Four men are dead, I have ten stitches, and Ellie has a broken leg and fractured wrist. *Do* you know where either one of them might have gone?"

"They are both from a small town in Jefferson County called Olathe. They met in grade school. If Rachel has proof Lea is doing these things, I believe that's where Lea might have gone to escape it."

"Jefferson County." The two men looked at each other and then were on their feet. "Thanks."

"Find her." Georgia said it to Santiago, her voice firm. "I care about this."

"If you think I'm not going to do everything I can, I need to find a new therapist, because you don't understand me at all," he muttered as he stalked out the door.

"**We have our** warrant." Grasso slid his phone into his pocket. "I'm dropping you off at home."

"Like hell I'm not going with you," Jason said forcefully.

Grasso drove like he did everything else, competently, passing a delivery truck that spewed slush on his normally pristine car. "Last night you were hit with a stun gun, someone stole your weapon and your cell phone, you were stabbed, and a killer practically ran over your partner with a car. You need a day or two off, don't you think? Just a thought. Oh yeah, Metzger *ordered* you to take time off, if what your boss wants matters at all to you."

Jason glossed over that sarcastic observation. "Would we have gotten this last break if it wasn't for MacIntosh and me? The case is wide open. All we have to do is find Lauren. She doesn't have transportation that we are aware of, and I doubt she is exactly fugitive material."

"*All* we have to do is find her? Last I checked, this is a good-sized city. Rachel Summers might be able to help us, or she might not. As far as I can tell, she didn't realize her roommate was someone else entirely. Can we really count on her for answers?"

He had a point. Jason knew nothing about this person.

Rachel, quiet and shy. Lea, just the opposite, out there drugging men and killing them. The two of them living together despite their very different personalities . . .

Both of them very nice looking. Rachel had told Lukens Lea was attractive to men.

Oh shit.

"Oh shit." This time he said it out loud.

Grasso shot him a look as he braked for a light. "Oh shit what?"

"Call Ellie on your cell and hand the phone to me."

Grasso did it, though he said something under his breath, and to Jason's relief, she answered on the second ring. As usual, he forgot any greeting, but this was urgent. "Don't answer the door, okay? And I need Lukens's number again."

"My leg hurts, thanks for asking," she replied caustically. "And don't answer the door? Why? Talk to me, please."

"Lauren knows where I live."

That isn't new information . . . do you really think she'd come after you here? I've been trying to call you, by the way."

"Ellie, I don't have my phone. I probably dropped it in her car. If you've left messages, that means she knows exactly where you are. We're headed to Jefferson County right now, but don't open the door."

"I got that the first time around, believe it or not, and I have my Glock. Using it might be painful, but worth it if it got ugly." Her response was measured. "You have that tone. What's happened? Jefferson County? Fill me in."

"You aren't going to believe it. I need you to text a picture to Lukens. We just left her office."

"Why?."

"It could be stupid, so I'm going to let you text first and ask questions later."

"What picture?"

"Of Lauren. I took one of you and Lauren at the governor's dinner, remember? I used your phone."

If anyone would get it, she would. "So? What good would a picture of Lauren do us? I've talked to Dr. Lukens and she told me she'd never seen Rachel's roommate."

"Right. Rachel Summers is the patient. Only that is not the name on the lease. We checked that out this morning. Lauren's name is listed."

"I'm trying to follow this conversation and get your point. We know Lauren is responsible for the killings and Rachel thinks her name is Lea. I'm not surprised the lease is in Lauren's name by the way. Her family has a lot of money."

"But Rachel claims it is *her* apartment."

"Well, it is if she lives there."

"I don't think Rachel exists. At all. There's no Lea, and when you process that, admit there's a possibility there's no Rachel."

Grasso shot him a sharp look as they turned a corner. Jason went on, thinking furiously, talking it out. "Text the picture to Georgia Lukens and ask her if that is Rachel. I'm going to bet you she's a dead ringer for Lauren Levine."

"They're the same person?" She sounded doubtful, but not entirely. The hint of speculation in her tone encouraged him to keep thinking out loud. "You're crazy."

"Am I? It has struck me all along that Lauren seems to be a little different each time I meet her. There's quiet, shy Lauren, and friendly Lauren, and sexy Lauren who turned into a friggin' maniac and tried to kill me. Remember Hammet's comment that it could be two different killers. I think she might be right, but they are still the same person. Ellie, listen, Lauren found out where I lived without any problem. What are the odds the roommate of the person killing these men goes to the same therapist I do? If she accessed hospital records, by her own admission, she could probably find out I see Lukens just by following me, which is what Lea supposedly does. What if she was talking about herself?" Silence.

Finally she said, "I'll call and send the picture. Just keep me in the loop, okay? I now understand why you were such an ass while you were off on medical leave."

He grinned as he pressed the button. Grasso said, "What?"

"At last I've found a woman who I do think gets me."

Georgia saw the light come on, glanced at her appointment book, and set aside her pen. Only occasionally did she make notes by hand, but sometimes it was effective in a thinking-out-loud sort of venue. She wrote it down, examined the words, and then decided how valid the conclusions might be.

She didn't have an appointment scheduled.

As a matter of fact, her receptionist was off for the day. She stood and went to the door, opened it, and realized that she did have a visitor in the waiting room. Rachel stood there, her clothes a little disheveled. Under the circumstances, Georgia wasn't surprised to see her. Given what had happened, not at all.

But something was off.

In her office her phone chimed.

"Rachel?" She took a step forward and then stopped. There were dark stains on her patient's clothes and she seemed disoriented. "Are you okay? Did Lea hurt you?"

"No, she hurt someone else. Can we talk?"

Ellie had to use crutches to move around, but she was restless anyway. She'd even managed to get dressed. At least she'd cracked her left wrist, so she could comb her hair and brush her teeth right-handed.

Georgia Lukens wasn't answering her cell phone. She'd sent the text, but no response, so she'd called to make sure it came through but just ended up leaving a message. Maybe she was seeing a patient and would check her messages later.

Damn, Ellie hated delays, and she hated *this*.

Eight weeks off. It was a gloomy thought. With Bryce out of town, she wasn't sure she could take it.

It chafed to not be able to go along for the lead they had in Jefferson County.

She sat down and stared out the window, thinking about Santiago's off-the-wall theory. It sounded ridiculous but then again . . . he was correct about one thing. Rachel seeing the same therapist was a long shot.

It bothered her.

She tried again.

No answer from Georgia.

That bothered her even more and she really needed something to do. Santiago had just said Georgia was at her office.

Five minutes later she'd called a cab and was using her very underdeveloped skills with her crutches to go downstairs.

. . .

It was a rare morning when she had a third cup of coffee, and even though she'd made it and the fragrance of it filled the office, Georgia was extremely doubtful at the moment that she was ever going to get a chance to drink it.

Rachel looked unusual to the extent she was dressed very differently. There were dark splotches on the sleeve of her wool coat and she wore a short dress beneath it instead of the long flowing skirts she favored. She also had on stockings and short stylish boots, but her rumpled appearance suggested she might have slept in her clothes.

If she'd slept at all. Her eyes were rimmed with red and literally glittered when she took a gun from her coat pocket.

This was turning out to be a very unusual morning.

"Sit down." The gun indicated her usual chair.

Georgia took the not-so-subtle hint and sat behind her desk. It seemed like the prudent course. Her cell phone, which she had set on vibrate, hummed again. It was difficult to keep her voice even, but she was calm enough when she spoke even though her pulse was jumping in her throat. "All right. I'm sitting. There's no need to point that at me. I am not threatening you. Are you injured? Did Lea hurt you?"

"Lea? No. She tried to hurt someone else."

"Rachel, why don't you sit down too? Let's discuss what has happened."

"I'm in trouble."

"I think you must be or you would never do what you are doing now."

"You have no idea how much."

"I will if you tell me."

"I don't know if I want to."

Her phone vibrated yet again. Georgia ignored it because quite frankly the gun held all of her attention. She was pretty grateful when Rachel sank into her usual chair. Only her patient didn't tip her head forward in her usual manner, using her hair to hide her face, but stared at her directly.

Not Rachel.

It registered but in an abstract way, because multiple personality disorder was so rare there were experts who even discounted its existence. Even now, at this moment, Georgia wasn't sure that was the problem, but she certainly *was* sure the person sitting across from her was not the same young woman who'd been coming in for sessions. Everything about her screamed the difference, not just her posture. She asked quietly, "Am I talking to Lea?"

"Don't be stupid."

Reality was evidently *not* the problem. "What is your real name?"

"Lauren."

"I felt all along you were lying to me, but why conceal your name?"

She glanced away, but the gun was still in her hand. "I . . . I did not ask to be put in this position."

Georgia thought about her cell phone, ringing again just inches away on the polished desktop, but instinct told her it would be a bad idea to move a muscle. She said with credible poise, "Look, you came to me in the first place to talk. So let's talk. You have walked around your problems all along. This is your chance. Tell me what happened to the person you've portrayed as Lea but we both now know is you. I can't promise it will make you feel better, but I can promise I will listen to what you have to say."

When Lauren looked up, her eyes were empty. There was nothing there and Georgia experienced a chill that ran down her spine. *This* was the killer the MPD was looking for so frantically. It was there in her face.

And they were alone.

"I know you will. That's why I'm here." Lauren idly set the gun in her lap and briefly closed her eyes. "I'm going to tell you and then I want you to bring him here so I can kill him."

"Kill whom?"

Georgia had to admit her hands had gone cold so she massaged her fingers but in plain sight.

"There was a man. He had blond hair and very blue eyes. I remember the color perfectly."

That did fit Santiago's description and, according to what she'd been told, also the other victims. "He hurt you?"

"No. He lied to me."

"A lot of people lie, Lauren." It felt strange to call her that, but this was not the Rachel Georgia knew either.

"He said he was going to the hospital." It was a painful whisper.

That was confusing. "Who said that?"

"The man."

That narrowed it down.

The door to her office opened a little and she did her best not to react. *Not alone any longer*.

Lauren asked plaintively, "Why would he do that? Why lie to me?"

. . .

This was probably the worst situation ever. Ellie, only tenuously balanced on one crutch and she was hardly an expert after one morning with crutches in general, was riveted to the conversation, and had her hand on her weapon.

Very slowly she drew it out, remembering that horrific screaming from when Santiago was attacked. From the look on Dr. Lukens's face she also realized her danger, but was trying to talk her patient off a ledge.

Might work, might not.

As far as having the cavalry riding in, Ellie was not at all positive she currently fit the description with her two casts, but she was better than nothing and she knew Georgia had seen her crack the door.

She should have told Metzger where she was going. Or Santiago, or *someone,* but it was too late. She was there, and a woman with a gun that had probably committed a series of murders was right in front of her.

Lukens seemed relaxed but a sheen of sweat glistened on her forehead. She carefully kept her gaze on her patient. "This blond man represents something awful to you. Can you tell me what it is?"

"My brother was killed when I was eight." Lauren seemed to find the opposite wall interesting. "It was awful. I still remember the sound of the tires, the thud, the scrape of metal as his bicycle skidded along the street . . . I had nightmares for years."

Great time for a shot, but Ellie was still trying to find her balance between the door and her weapon, should she have to fire. At the same time she was trying not to give away she was even there. Not an easy process. Besides, she really needed more reason to shoot. You would think she wouldn't, but this disturbed woman was hardly an average criminal.

Georgia's voice was very gentle though her hand trembled where it rested on the blotter on her desk. "That's terrible. Why haven't we talked about this before?"

Lauren didn't seem to hear the question. "A man hit him with his truck."

"On purpose?"

Lauren shook her head, refocusing on her target, which unfortunately for Dr. Lukens, happened to be her. "I don't think so, but that doesn't matter. It was horrible enough, but afterward it was worse."

Georgia shot another swift glance at the doorway and she and Ellie made eye contact, but wisely she immediately looked back. "Forgive me if I don't understand. Can you explain to me why we are here now in this situation because of this incident in your past? No one is more willing to listen to the story than I am. Tell me. It will help."

Georgia Lukens should have been a prosecuting attorney. Her ability to draw out a witness was stunning. Just the cadence of her voice was calming.

Lauren whispered repetitively, "He hit him in the street. We were just riding our bikes and he came around the corner very fast. Then . . . I think he realized it, what he'd done, and he told me to go home and get my parents. He said we couldn't wait for an ambulance. That he was going to take my brother to the nearest hospital."

Lauren was rocking now in agitation, just a little, but her hands were still on the gun in her lap. Ellie wanted to edge in but she wasn't exactly able to do it at the moment, perched awkwardly on her crutch, so she just widened the gap in the door with one hand and said a silent prayer of gratitude it didn't make a sound.

"That seems like a reasonable request."

"I did what he told me." Lauren rose up, and then sank back down as if undecided whether to pace or not. "So I ran home and told my mother."

"What a very tragic responsibility for someone so young."

Lauren's voice was emotionless, which wasn't reassuring. "But when we got back there . . . he was gone. The man, the truck, the bicycle . . . and my brother." Her head came up again and so did the gun. "He took him away. I want you to call Detective Santiago and make him come here."

Georgia handled it pretty well. "Lauren, it *wasn't* him."

"How do you know that?"

Lukens evidently couldn't answer that question, especially with a gun pointed in her direction. Normally seeing the composed doctor rattled might be amusing, but not under the circumstances. Ellie made a decision to shove open the door fully.

The distraction worked anyway. Lukens was smart enough to duck down behind her desk, which left Ellie exposed but at least armed. Lauren swung around and fired, and Ellie went to the floor, her gun skidding.

Shit.

Ellie's adrenaline was running so high she couldn't do anything but crawl after her weapon, a few crucial feet away.

Having a broken ankle and cracked wrist was not much of a help when confronting a determined killer, she concluded at that moment. Luckily, even at this range, Lauren wasn't a great shot and the second bullet hit the floor by her head.

Ears ringing, Ellie lifted to her knees, her ankle protesting the entire procedure, and she gasped out ineffectually, "Police officer. Please put down your weapon."

A weak kitten was probably more of a threat.

Lauren Levine walked forward a few paces and pointed the gun at a much closer range. Just inches away, just like when she shot Gurst. Her expression was so cold Ellie could swear the temperature in the room dropped. "Detective MacIntosh. You already know I've done worse things than this."

That was when Ellie swung the crutch. The impact made a dull sound as it caught her target across the knees and Lauren staggered back. Then Ellie was on her feet, swaying, cursing like Santiago on a bad day, her ankle screaming at her . . .

The second shot was like adding ballast to an already sinking ship. She went down hard and the world disappeared.

Jason's phone beeped and he registered the number with misgivings and then punched a button. "What?"

"Detective, you are as charming as ever. Ellie is back in the hospital. I think she might qualify for a super-saver discount soon if she just comes in one more time."

An ice-cold hand clamped around his heart.

Dr. Lukens added, "I knew you'd want to know."

He turned to Grasso. "Head back. Now."

As they made a sudden turn, he caught the door handle and went back to the call. "What exactly happened?"

"A lot of shit hit the fan." Dr. Lukens sounded tired. "I can't even begin to describe it over the phone, and by the way, you are my one phone call. I'm at the police station. If you could help me out, I'd really appreciate it. I'm trying to explain, but given I am not even positive what was going on with Lauren and have no actual medical records with her name on them, *and* I shot her in my office, the police are naturally suspicious. I'm being held for questioning and not liking it very much."

Grasso could hear and gave a low whistle. Jason said, "The shit really did hit the fan. We're on our way."

Chapter 28

Metzger looked displeased, but then again, that wasn't new. The chief came up to her desk instead of ordering her to his office, which was nice of him, but she did have an in-the-line-of-duty injury. He pulled up a chair and took a seat. Ellie met his eyes and wondered what he was about to say because he had a very intent expression.

"Sir?"

"The governor is going to stop by and see you. He'd like a firsthand account of what happened from both you and Santiago. He's read the reports, but this is very personal for him, so he's naturally going to want to hear it directly and I told him no problem."

As if she didn't already have a residual headache from slamming her head on the floor. "Of course," she said reluctantly. There was no sin involved in dreading *that* conversation.

"I've already told Santiago to let you do the talking

unless he's asked a direct question and it is possible he will follow my orders for once, but I never know." Metzger's tone was cynical, but then again he had a point. "For someone with a good deal of passion for what he does, he seems willing to put his job on the line a little too often."

"I don't disagree."

Speak of the devil, she saw Santiago was headed their way, a sheaf of papers in his hand. As usual, he flaunted the dress code just enough to get by. His attire was probably not governor-worthy, but then again, it was easy enough to assume Santiago didn't care about it either.

He walked up and tossed the documents on the desk. "Notes, transcripts, and reports. I spent all morning on them."

Metzger picked them up. "Thanks. You seem resentful of that. Have a seat so we can chat. How's your arm by the way?"

"Itches like hell as the stitches tighten up. I have two more reports I know you want." Instantly Santiago was wary, and Ellie was a little uneasy herself. Metzger didn't chat. He lectured, gave orders, and his demeanor was usually brusque, but at the moment he seemed a little different.

"Santiago, sit down, dammit. I want to talk to you."

Her partner took a chair. There were requests you argued and the tone of this one was not indicative of any compromise. Metzger was not a subtle man.

"What?" Ellie asked it flat-out. "Please tell me that we are not going to be vilified for catching a killer, even if it proves to be the niece of the governor. I wish it were someone else—I wish it were *anyone* else—and to make it worse,

I understand to a certain extent how this all happened. She's a victim in so many ways."

Metzger nodded. "Agreed. I think the governor also agrees. Sometimes circumstances collide and there is just very little a person can do to predict the outcome."

Santiago, of course, couldn't keep his mouth shut. "Uh-oh. So, we're fine, right?"

"I don't want to talk to you about the governor, or even his niece. I just wanted to discuss the surveillance tape from the gas station."

Ellie had fought with taking that shot through the back window of a car, and she'd missed too, which was embarrassing, but knee-jerk had described the situation and that was, in short, part of their job. Stoutly she said, "I know I didn't hit her, but it was a tight call. I was also trying to not injure anyone else, and while in theory we are trained and ready for the worst, let's face it, there's no training for every situation. I reacted the way I thought I should."

Metzger didn't disagree. "You did fine. I am on board with how you handled it, though I have upon occasion wanted to shoot Santiago myself so your concern for him might not have come into play if I was the one in your shoes."

Ellie had to admit to a certain amount of confusion along with a stifled laugh. "So what are we talking about, sir?'

Metzger took out his phone. "This. Give me a moment . . . ah, here we go."

He turned it their way. The screen didn't display the footage of the actual altercation, but panned to a shot of Santiago carrying her through the doorway.

Okay, she was starting to get it. *Shit*. He slid to the floor, she was still in his arms, then he kissed her, not once but twice as they sat and waited for the ambulance. Her head was on his shoulder . . .

The chief cut off the video right before the medics came in, his thumb pressing a button. He said calmly, "Now, let's just review this situation, the three of us. If you were me, what would you think after seeing that?"

It was a reasonable question and she didn't want Santiago to answer it with one of his defensive smartass comments. So she said quickly, "Probably what you are thinking right now, sir, but—"

He just steamrolled right over her. "Are you sleeping together?"

"What? No!"

"Unfortunately, she's telling the truth," her partner said with a shrug.

Metzger believed Santiago but she had the impression maybe he wouldn't have taken her word for it. The chief leaned forward. "I am only going to say this one time. Normally I do not care what anyone does with their personal life, but in your case, I do. As partners you were kind of an experiment, and no one is more pleasantly surprised than I am that it worked out so well. Your job is to catch people who commit murder in our jurisdiction, and you know what? You are pretty good at it as a team. I'd really like for you to not screw this up with some romantic bullshit. Now nod if you get it, and I'll be on my way, because the governor is walking toward us and I know he wants a private conversation. I'm leaving. You two behave."

. . .

Jason could really live without this scenario. It just seemed like he was destined to teeter on the brink of disaster and it was one hell of a place to be, hovering there all the time. That little scene the chief had just played had been pretty much his fault, but then again, he hadn't even considered the security cameras because a lunatic had just tried to kill him and he'd fallen out of a moving vehicle.

So sue him for not being on his A game. He'd been worried as hell about Ellie.

"Detectives." The governor took the chief's abandoned chair. He gazed at Ellie's bandaged wrist. "I offer my apologies for what has happened. I understand you also suffered a broken leg."

He was tall and distinguished but had the hands of a workingman. Jason always noticed small details like that, and as much as he didn't want to give him credit for it, his father was responsible for that observation on the human condition. He'd read once that the governor enjoyed hunting and fishing, and he believed it. A man's hands said it all.

Ellie said neutrally, "It will heal. There is a certain amount of risk that just comes with the job."

The governor smiled ruefully. "A sound attitude." He turned to Jason. "You were stabbed multiple times."

"No big deal." He'd preferred that part to the stun gun actually. That damn thing had hurt. "Like Ellie just said, kind of comes with the territory every once in a while."

"My niece is a very disturbed young woman." The

governor said it heavily. "It seems impossible none of us knew how much, but I have talked to my sister and she had no idea either, though I have to say that we weren't as surprised as maybe we should have been given what happened all those years ago. I am not a mental health expert, but obviously those unresolved feelings were just below the surface, building up until something triggered them."

"I know the story and to a certain extent, I can't say I completely understand the way she tried to cope with it, but her rage is something I think anyone could empathize with."

Ellie, as usual, sounded reasonable and unruffled. Jason might have said something undiplomatic, but he'd been the one in the car. Though actually he wasn't unsympathetic either. He went for, "Sir, we all deal with anger and loss in different ways."

The governor didn't disagree. "This seems like a ludicrous request, given the circumstances, but I would like to ask the two of you for a favor."

Oh hell, he couldn't wait to hear this. Jason waited, following orders and not saying a word.

"Would you consider opening the cold case involving my missing nephew? I fully realize there are jurisdictional issues, but I think those can be negotiated with a phone call or two."

Of course they could. He was the damn governor, but on the other hand, they weren't miracle workers. "Sir—"

"It might help Lauren if she knew the man had been apprehended. Her trial is going to be a zoo and she is unstable enough as it is."

To Jason's dismay, Ellie agreed. "No promises made, but we'll be more than happy to try."

When the man left, Jason said with what he thought was incredible calm, "Are you fucking nuts? Twenty years is a long time."

"If I am nuts, it's because of working with you." She gazed at him with open cynicism. "Look, we are both on the edge of a reprimand as far as I can tell, both on desk duty, and I pretty much blame you for it. A chance to redeem ourselves is like a gold ticket, and besides, I like the idea of the challenge of a cold case. I say we do our best and see what happens."

He spread his hands. "Cold case? This one is buried under an iceberg, Ellie. The only witness is a kid that turned into a murderous lunatic."

"I'd like to think we can do it. Please don't tell me you don't."

After that interview with Metzger, he'd better cut his losses. Jason said, "Okay, I'll roll with that."

Chapter 29

The house was simple, with small gothic touches on the front porch and a single tan sedan parked in the driveway.

The crutches really did not work well on the snow-covered drive, but Ellie was mastering the art of it little by little, like learning to walk again. Besides, the sun was shining, which was a nice change and the arc of blue above did not hold a single cloud.

Next to her as they went up the walk, Georgia Lukens said, "At the risk of sounding like a coward on an emotional level, I'm not sure I can deal with this."

"You wanted to come along."

"I failed their daughter."

Ellie sent her an exasperated look. "If I operated like you, I'd feel like a failure all the time. I don't catch every single criminal. I don't save every victim, and just so that we're clear, I don't expect that of myself. I do the best I can."

"Are you giving me advice on coping with this?" Her

hands in the pockets of her long coat, Dr. Lukens's mouth twitched into a smile. "Is this a 'physician, heal thyself' kind of moment? And just so that we're clear, you come along after the damage is done. My role is to prevent the damage in the first place."

Mrs. Levine was waiting for them. The door opened before they came up the steps. She was slender, middle-aged, and the resemblance to her daughter was striking. She looked tired and drawn, which stood to reason since her daughter was currently the most infamous woman in the state of Wisconsin. She said, "Please come in. Having the sun shining is deceptive, isn't it? It's cold out there."

The living room was tidy, the furniture a little worn but comfortable, and there was a woodstove with a fire in one corner, the flames licking the glass. Lauren's mother had been doing a crossword puzzle, the paper and a pencil left carelessly on the coffee table. The woman eyed Ellie's cast. "Perhaps you'd like to sit down."

She would. The problem with crutches, she'd discovered, was that if she had to use them very much, her arm started to hurt worse than her leg. She chose a plaid armchair and sank down. "Thank you. We won't stay long, I promise. I just have a few questions."

Georgia didn't have much choice but to sit beside Mrs. Levine on the couch, a sympathetic expression on her face. "We've spoken on the phone. I'm Dr. Lukens. When Detective MacIntosh told me she was coming to see you, I asked to come along. Lauren was one of my favorite patients."

And she'd had to shoot her. No wonder Georgia was uncomfortable. Ellie would be too.

"They didn't even offer her bail," Mrs. Levine said with very little inflection, but her eyes were glassy with unshed tears.

"I am sure your lawyer explained to you that a search of her residence turned up the identification of all three victims, and the gun used to kill the drug dealer who sold her the rufilin used in the murders was in her possession and she used it to threaten Dr. Lukens." Ellie sounded reasonable and non-judgmental. "We also have the murder weapon for the knife killings and she assaulted two police officers in front of witnesses. More than that, she confessed."

The discovery of the IDs had given them the identity of the second victim. He'd been a part-time janitor at the same hospital where Lauren worked who had stopped coming for his shifts and administration assumed he had simply quit without notice. He'd been studying for his real estate license, which indicated that was how he'd found out about the empty house in foreclosure. Grasso and Rays were still trying to locate any family but not having much luck.

There was a box of tissues on the floor and Mrs. Levine took one out and clutched it in her hand. "It feels like a nightmare that won't end. I can't say I don't know why it happened, I just can't believe it did. My daughter never dealt with her grief after her brother was gone. I suppose it didn't help I was trying to understand why God had forsaken us myself and maybe didn't give her what she needed."

Ellie thought of the sharpened crucifix and the postmortem wounds on the victims. "Did the two of you discuss it in those terms? That God had forsaken your family?"

"Detective, my son was hit and killed in front of a church."

That matter-of-fact statement explained quite a lot.

Mrs. Levine went on, her voice hushed and broken. "After it happened, Lauren would go there and lie in the grass, looking up at the steeple. When she would disappear, or not come home right away from school, I always knew where to find her. Eventually, she seemed to get past it, or at least she didn't talk about the 'lion man' any longer. I was relieved."

Evidently she hadn't gotten over it, but that explained the wounds in the shape of a cross anyway. Ellie asked, puzzled but intrigued, "I've read the police reports on the accident. No lion reference is mentioned in their notes. What did she mean? She gave a very clear description of the accident and the man driving for a child her age. Obviously she remembered what he looked like to a certain extent."

"I don't know." Mrs. Levine looked over to where a set of stairs led upward to the second story. "Right after it happened she'd have nightmares about someone she called the lion man. Then they stopped and she never mentioned it again."

Georgia said quietly, "I am sure he was a monster to her. Someone who had taken her brother away. Her young psyche gave him an identity that she found frightening. Lions are scary, so maybe that's where the reference comes from."

Ellie wasn't as sure. She respected Georgia's professional opinion, but then again . . .

When they were back in the car, Ellie stowed her crutch carefully in the backseat, still thinking, but out loud. "This lion thing . . . It's pertinent. Lauren was a child . . . it means *something*. Santiago is as bored as I am right now. We can't do anything about Lauren's case, but we can look into this cold one as asked, and so far, this is our first clue."

Georgia lifted a brow as she started the car. "I am starting to see the passion for law enforcement that gives you and Jason Santiago something in common that not everyone shares. By the way, want to talk to me about him? Not as a patient-to-doctor consultation, but as a friend."

"Why?" Ellie gave her a swift glance. "I talk to you about him enough. How he annoys me half to death, and—"

"And?" Lukens began to back the car out.

Ellie asked carefully, "What's the actual question? I feel a little like I'm in high school or something."

"Is there a romantic element to your relationship that has nothing to do with being partners in the homicide division of the Milwaukee Police Department?"

"Seriously? Have I said something to indicate there is? Did Metzger call you?"

"It's what you are *not* saying that makes me wonder." She pulled out onto the street. "You just indicated that you wouldn't mind spending time with him voluntarily when not on duty. He's appealing and your relationship with Bryce is less than ideal right now. And let's face it, as women, we usually know when someone is attracted to us."

There was no way she was going to discuss that unsettling kiss. "I can't get involved with Jason Santiago. I have Bryce."

"I think you do. That does not mean you are necessarily right for each other."

"Is this your professional assessment of our relationship?"

"Just an observation. I assume you want to drive by the church where the accident happened."

The change in subject was welcome. Ellie adjusted her foot to a more comfortable position. "You just read my mind."

Georgia said serenely, "If only I could."

You want me to what?" Jason picked up the remote and flicked off the television. They were just recapping the play-offs anyway.

"Pick me up. I still can't drive." Ellie sounded impatient. "I want to go to a little town north of Olathe. You're coming with me."

He was already on his feet, picking up his keys from where he'd tossed them on the table near the door. "What's this about?"

"The last piece of the puzzle. I just talked to your good friend Lauren. Or maybe it was Rachel or Lea, I have no idea which one, but I have a lead . . . or maybe it isn't one, but I can't not go after it. Are you in or not?"

"Relax. I'm already walking to my truck. Where exactly are we going?"

"Lexington. Home of the Lions."

"Home of the Lions? What the hell does that mean?" He passed one of his neighbors on the stairs and nodded, aware that since he'd been on the news again, most of the people in the building knew what he did for a living. Since he'd also had his car blown up once in the parking lot, it was a dubious celebrity status he didn't really appreciate.

"High school. The truck that hit Lauren Levine's brother

had a bumper sticker on it, and guess what? There was also a class date that matches the year of the accident. I have to give Dr. Lukens the credit. Lauren trusts her and she was able to walk her back in time and somehow cajole the memory out of her."

He pressed the button for the automatic starter. "No shit?"

"Now all we need is to go through the yearbook and see if anyone in that graduating class kind of looks like you."

"Yeah, lucky me."

Georgia sat in the chair on the opposite side of the desk and smiled. "I'm usually where you are. Behind the desk."

Grant smiled back. "If we were in your office, I'd let you sit here. In fact, if you'd like to switch places—"

"No, we're fine. I just needed to talk and it seems like when that happens, you are the one I think of, so I took a chance you might have the time."

"I'm flattered." He was as distinguished as ever in tailored slacks and a sweater over a crisp blue shirt, like a benign college professor, the kind that inspired a girlish freshman crush.

"My patient murdered four people."

"I can honestly say I wondered if that wasn't her just on the basis of our previous conversations."

"Clever deduction." She was no longer smiling.

"Georgia, you told me enough that it really was not all that clever. I assume you are now wondering what you could have done differently."

"Of course."

"Nothing." He spread his hands on the desk. "As clinicians we need to face that there will always be patients who successfully deceive us and don't respond to treatment. You cannot shoulder the burden for those four lives."

"Five," Georgia argued softly. "Let's not forget hers. I shot her."

"I stand corrected. Five. But she'll recover."

"Physically. She was trying to obliterate the memory by slashing their faces until she could no longer find a hint of the man who killed her brother."

"By your account, she is a bright young woman. Isn't it fascinating how our minds work when rational thought is at war with emotion?"

"I think I can still help her."

Grant looked interested. "Oh? How?"

"In this life, one thing that holds true is that it is who you know. I might not have been able to help Lauren Levine, but I think I know someone else who will."

Ellie limped up the sidewalk, but it was Santiago who knocked on the front door. The man who answered was too old to be the one they were looking for, but maybe he could provide an answer.

"Mr. Upton?" Santiago identified himself by flashing his badge. "Can we have a word about your son, Terry? We'd like to locate him and this is his last known address."

Tall and spare, his weathered face perplexed, the older man said, "Well, he lives here. He's taking over the farm little by little . . . what's this about?"

"Can we talk to him?"

"I suppose so. Mind telling me why?"

"Dad? I've got a question about—" A man, mid-to-late thirties, blond, leanly built, and blue-eyed came into view. "Oh, sorry. I didn't realize you were talking to someone."

A perfect match in many ways, but it was hardly conclusive. Ellie was torn over whether or not this was even the right thing to do, but she had confidence that Georgia would tell her everyone needed closure, not just Lauren. To a certain extent, given the emotional impact of this case, she needed some herself. The family of the missing boy at least deserved being able to properly mourn.

"They're police detectives. They want to talk to you."

Terry Upton went utterly pale, but he wasn't shocked, and that said something. When he spoke his voice was somber. "I think I might know why. I've been waiting for this visit for twenty years. You might not believe this, officers, but in a way, I'm glad you are here."